YOUNG
SHERLOCK

STONE COLD

Books by Andrew Lane

The Young Sherlock Holmes series

Death Cloud
Red Leech
Black Ice
Fire Storm
Snake Bite
Knife Edge
Stone Cold
Night Break

www.youngsherlock.com

The Lost Worlds series

Lost Worlds
Lost Worlds: Shadow Creatures

www.thelostworlds.co.uk

YOUNG
SHERLOCK
STONE COLD

ANDREW LANE

MACMILLAN CHILDREN'S BOOKS

First published 2014 by Macmillan Children's Books

This edition published 2015 by Macmillan Children's Books
an imprint of Pan Macmillan
20 New Wharf Road, London N1 9RR
Associated companies throughout the world
www.panmacmillan.com

ISBN 978-1-4472-2801-1

11

A CIP catalogue record for this book is available from
the British Library.

Printed and bound by CPI Group (UK) Ltd, Croydon CR0 4YY

Dedicated to: my expert and friendly UK and US editors (Gaby Morgan and Wes Adams), for being incredibly supportive while still taking me to task for errors and overwriting, plus all the editors and translators in the overseas territories who have worked on these books. Thanks are also due to Talya Baker, who copy-edited this manuscript so perfectly. Thanks also to my wonderful and patient publicist, Beatrice Cross. Thank you all – I owe you.

Dedicated also to Peter Darvill-Evans, Rebecca Levene, Andy Bodle and Simon Winstone, for being there at the beginning and giving me a chance to prove myself. I owe you as well.

CHAPTER ONE

Sherlock Holmes leaned forward in his seat, entranced, as the young man on the stage brought his violin up to his shoulder, nestled his chin into the chin-guard and raised his bow until it hovered above the strings. The flickering light from the gas lamps along the edge of the stage illuminated the violinist with dancing shadows, making it seem as if a hundred different expressions were playing across his face within a few moments.

The audience seemed to tense. For a long moment you could have heard a handkerchief flutter to the ground, it was that quiet in the theatre, and then he started playing.

The first note swelled up out of nowhere until it filled the auditorium. It was pure and exquisite, and the sort of note that Sherlock would have given a year of his life to be able to play. It seemed to him almost impossible that something made out of wood and catgut, played by someone human and fallible, could be that close to perfection.

'He's playing a Stradivarius,' Rufus Stone whispered from beside Sherlock, but Sherlock's attention was fixed upon the young man onstage, and he barely registered his friend and tutor's words. He concentrated on the music, on the succession of notes and chords that were emanating from the small stage as if they were something absolutely real and it was the theatre and the audience who were insubstantial. Sherlock had never imagined that it was possible to play the violin that beautifully.

For the next forty-five minutes Sherlock listened, oblivious to anything around him, barely even breathing, as the violinist played a succession of pieces. One or two Sherlock recognized from his own exercises – some Spanish dances, and a few well-known tunes from operas – but many were new to him. He suspected that the man had written them himself, he appeared to be that comfortable playing them. Some of them were fiendishly complicated as well as beautiful, requiring the violinist's left hand to move along the fingerboard so fast that it was a blur.

After a while he became aware that his brother, Mycroft, seated on the other side of him to Rufus Stone, was shifting in his plushly upholstered seat. It was too small for him in the first place, and his elbows were pushing against Sherlock's arm and the arm of the man on the other side of him. Sherlock could hear him huff every now and then, as if he was unconsciously trying to send a signal out to everyone around him that he was unhappy and wanted to be somewhere else. Or perhaps it wasn't unconscious. Perhaps Mycroft knew exactly what signal he was sending to the increasingly irritated people around him, and just didn't care.

After a particularly difficult volley of notes which the

violinist threw away as if they were nothing, the first half of the concert ended. The musician bowed to enthusiastic applause, and the curtain came down.

'Thank the Lord,' Mycroft muttered. 'I was beginning to think that I had died and gone to hell. Who did you say this young fiddler was?'

Sherlock glanced sideways at Rufus Stone. The expression on Stone's face was somewhere in the ambiguous territory between amusement and outrage. 'His name is Pablo Sarasate,' Stone said in a carefully controlled voice. 'He is Spanish, he is twenty-six years old, and he is probably the most accomplished violinist since Niccolò Paganini.'

'Humph!' Mycroft said. 'I would have preferred a brass band in the park. The music would be more tuneful to my ears.'

'And the deckchairs would be more accommodating to your . . .' Stone hesitated. Sherlock sympathized – Mycroft was technically Stone's employer. '. . . To your natural sitting position,' Stone finished smoothly.

'I feel the need for a large dry sherry,' Mycroft said as if Stone hadn't spoken. 'Do you think we might have time to visit the bar during this welcome break from the caterwauling onstage?'

Stone winced, and opened his mouth to say something cutting, but Sherlock got in first. 'I think that would be a good idea,' he said.

Stone caught Sherlock's elbow as they manoeuvred

their way along the row of seats to the aisle. 'Your brother will be the death of me,' he hissed, 'and if it's not because of the dangerous undercover tasks that he assigns me then it will be because I will punch him in the face if he goes on about how much he hates this music for much longer.'

'I don't even know why he wanted to come along,' Sherlock said. 'This is not the kind of thing he normally enjoys.'

'He told me he wanted to talk to the both of us in a comfortable and informal setting.'

'Even so . . .' Sherlock looked around the auditorium. 'There must have been something more to his taste than this.'

Stone grimaced. 'I may have told him that I was taking you to the theatre without being specific about what we were going to see. Looking back, your brother might have got the idea that we were going to a play rather than a concert recital.'

'He does like a good melodrama,' Sherlock conceded. 'He once told me that Shakespeare's *Hamlet* taught him everything he needed to know about Scandinavian politics.'

They were in the aisle by now, heading up towards the bar. 'What do you think about the concert?' Stone asked.

'Incredible.' Sherlock paused for a moment, recalling the feelings that had poured through his mind as the violinist had played. 'His technique is flawless.'

'He is going to be famous,' Stone confirmed. 'Just be glad you got to see him early in his career.'

They got to the bar. Mycroft pushed through the crowd like a galleon pushing through rough seas. Within a few minutes they were all settled in a bow-front window and sipping their drinks.

Mycroft took a sip of his sherry, and grimaced. 'If this is dry,' he said, 'then the Thames must be an arid, dusty wasteland by comparison.' He shook his head ponderously. 'This is what happens when one leaves the comfortable environs of one's office, one's club and one's rooms. The world becomes unpredictable.' He glanced up at Sherlock and Stone. 'I believe I will not return for the second half of the recital. I cannot imagine that the music will become any more listenable or my seat any more comfortable. I do, however, wish to say something before I leave.' Turning his attention to Sherlock, he went on: 'You have been staying in London now for a month since we returned from Ireland, and we need to make a decision about your future. The cost of your hotel room and your food is small, in the scheme of things, but not negligible. Sadly, with the death of our Uncle Sherrinford, I see no way that you could return to Farnham.'

'What about . . . home?' Sherlock asked quietly.

'The situation there has not changed.' Mycroft's face was grave. 'Our father is still abroad, in India, with the British Army, and our mother is still confined to bed, too weak to move. The only things that pass her lips are the occasional slice of toast and sips of weak tea. I fear for her future.'

'And . . . our sister?'

Mycroft shook his head. 'In the absence of any parental guidance, she has, I am informed, fallen under the spell of a most unsuitable admirer. I have tried to speak to her about it, but she will not listen to reason. No, I fear that the family manor house is not a suitable place for you either.'

'Then what else is there?' Rufus Stone asked.

'You could find me rooms in London,' Sherlock pointed out. 'I have got used to living here now. I love this city.'

'You are fifteen,' Mycroft pointed out. 'I am not going to let you live by yourself in a metropolis this sordid.'

'I'm actually sixteen,' Sherlock pointed out, 'and I have got quite used to surviving and even thriving by myself. I don't need anyone to look after me.'

'Indeed?' Mycroft gave Sherlock a lingering glance, rising from the tips of Sherlock's shoes to the crown of his head. 'I see that you have been consorting with that disreputable canal-dwelling friend of yours – Matthew Arnatt – who has apparently relocated his water-borne dwelling place to Camden Locks. I see also that you have together visited many markets in London, as well as travelling on the Thames several times. During those escapades you have got into –' he paused for a moment, looking at Sherlock's hands – 'five separate fights, and you have escaped from trouble over rooftops on three occasions. You have also been stopped and questioned by the police eight times. Is this what you mean by "thriving"?'

Sherlock opened his mouth to say something in his own defence, but Stone spoke first. 'You can tell all that just by looking at your brother's clothes, shoes, face and hands?' he asked. 'Mr Holmes, I have been impressed by your deductions before, but this is just amazing.'

Mycroft preened, like a large cat being stroked. Sherlock couldn't help himself, and said, 'He knows all that because he's been having me followed and his agents have been giving him daily reports.'

Mycroft's lips pursed in annoyance.

'Is this true?' Stone asked, disappointed.

'Young Sherlock has a habit of getting into trouble,' Mycroft grunted, 'and in our father's absence it is my responsibility to make sure that he gets to his twenty-first birthday intact in body and mind.'

'I thought it was me that was supposed to be looking after him,' Stone murmured, looking away, out of the bay window into the crowds outside the theatre.

'You have had other things to do for me,' Mycroft pointed out in a tone of voice that had no apology in it, 'and besides, Sherlock would have recognized you. His ability to see through disguises has improved markedly over the past two years.' He glanced at Sherlock and raised an eyebrow. 'I am, I confess, somewhere between amused, pleased and irritated that you spotted your followers.'

Sherlock smiled at his brother. 'Not only that, I found a bellboy at the hotel who was my general size and build, gave him a shilling and my coat and got him to walk around London in my place. Your people never noticed.'

'You are mistaken,' Mycroft said levelly. 'They followed you and him both. He went to a music hall; you went to the British Museum.'

'Oh.' Sherlock was crestfallen.

'There is also the question of your continuing education to consider,' Mycroft said, as if the previous discussion had never occurred. 'You were removed from the Deepdene School for Boys before your exams, and your experiences since, while they may have taught you a great deal about the way the world works and how to survive in street fights and climb across roofs, have left you woefully under-equipped in the fields of Latin, Greek, the natural sciences and the great body of English literature.'

'I see no need to know about dead languages or old books,' Sherlock murmured.

'You may not,' Mycroft countered, 'but the rest of the world disagrees – at least, the bits of it that count. In order to secure a lucrative job in the Civil Service or one of the major banks you will need to learn a great many things that you may not think are important. It is my job to make sure that you do so.'

'You are sending me back to school,' Sherlock said, feeling his heart grow heavy. He had dreaded this moment. His life for the past two years had been interesting, exciting and even dangerous. He had travelled to foreign countries and seen things that he would never have believed had he not experienced them himself. He had been thrown on to his own resources, and he had survived. He couldn't go back to school and meekly do what he was told to do by the teachers. Not now. He was a different person to the one who had left Deepdene School at the end of the summer term two years before, in uniform and with his cases packed.

'No,' Mycroft said, surprising Sherlock, 'that would be looking backwards, not forward, and to do so would be a capital mistake. No, I believe that your future lies at one of the great universities, so I propose that you live either in Cambridge or in Oxford for now, having one-to-one sessions in the important subjects with an experienced tutor, with a view to your entering either of those universities two years hence.'

'Cambridge is nearer to the family manor house, for when father returns home,' Sherlock said, feeling his heart lighten just a little bit. This could actually be fun.

'I have acquaintances in Oxford,' Mycroft continued, 'so I propose to send you there. You will recall that I studied at Oxford a few years ago. It was not a happy time in my life, but I value the education I received there and the friends I made. In particular, I knew a man named Charles Lutwidge Dodgson, who is now a lecturer in mathematics at Oxford, specializing in the field of logic. I will find you rooms in the town, and he will teach you for an hour a day, when he is not engaged on lecturing duties or one of his odd hobbies. There was also a police officer named Weston with whom I shared several very interesting conversations.'

Quickly going over Mycroft's proposal – well, more of a fait accompli than a proposal, Sherlock thought – he found there were several things that caught his attention. A lecturer in logic sounded fascinating. Sherlock's mind had always worked in a logical manner, and he found the trust that other people appeared to put in luck, faith or superstition quite odd. His former tutor and friend, Amyus Crowe, had done a lot to make him think in a rational manner. He thought he might enjoy studying logic.

'What does this Charles Lutwidge Dodgson do that is so odd?' he asked.

'For a start, he is interested in this new-fangled thing called photography. You are familiar with it?'

Sherlock frowned, trying to remember things that he had read, or overheard. 'It's a way of capturing the details of a scene not in a painting or a drawing, but by letting the light from that scene fall upon a chemically treated glass plate and recording the image directly, is it not?' he said.

'Indeed. The chemicals involve a nitrate of silver that changes colour when light touches it, or so I understand. I find myself in two minds about photography. On the one hand, the final result is much less pretty than a painting, and is only represented in shades of grey. On the other hand, it does represent what is actually there, rather than what the artist thinks is there, or hopes is there, or wants you to believe is there. It is either a fad or it will supplant portraiture and landscape painting and also help considerably in the investigation of crime – I do not yet know which. I used to talk with my police acquaintance about that.'

'You said, "On the one hand . . .",' Sherlock pointed out. 'What are his other hobbies?'

'He is apparently, in his spare time, a writer of children's books under the pen name "Lewis Carroll". In particular, one with the title *Alice's Adventures in Wonderland* has caught the public imagination and sold rather well. It is published by Macmillan and Co, who are themselves a reputable publisher. It is even said that Her Majesty Queen Victoria has read it and let her approval be known.'

'A children's book?' Sherlock said, rather sniffily.

'Indeed, and a rather odd one. On the face of it the book is a tale about a girl who falls down a rabbit hole and finds a fantasy world inhabited by talking animals, or who may just have fallen asleep and dreamed the whole thing, but it is possible that there is a deeper meaning and

11

that the entire thing is a satire on various mathematical and logical concepts.'

'You've read it?' Rufus Stone asked.

'Certainly not,' Mycroft huffed, but he wouldn't meet Sherlock's or Stone's gaze, and Sherlock wondered if he was telling the truth. 'But we are moving away from the point, which is that I have already written to Mr Dodgson at his rooms in Christ Church College, and he has agreed to take you on as an extraordinary – in all senses of the word, Sherlock – student. I am currently seeking accommodation for you in Oxford, probably at some boarding establishment close to Christ Church and beyond reproach.'

'And will you have anyone following me around Oxford the way you have in London?' Sherlock asked.

'Will I need to?' Mycroft countered.

Before Sherlock could say anything, Rufus Stone said, 'Almost certainly.'

A bell rang, indicating the end of the intermission.

'I shall leave now,' Mycroft said, but he made no move away from the bay window. 'Or perhaps I will stay for one more dry sherry. You two head back in and listen to the rest of that infernal racket. Sherlock – I will send you a note within the next few days outlining where you will be living, when you will be moving and when your tutorials will start.'

Sherlock opened his mouth to argue, but one look at his brother's face made him shut it again. Once

Mycroft made his mind up about something, there was no changing it.

As a second bell rang out, Sherlock and Stone headed back into the auditorium. Sherlock glanced back briefly over his shoulder. Mycroft was still there, sitting in the alcove – filling the alcove, to be more precise – and sipping at his sherry. As Sherlock watched, a man in a faded jacket and trousers that were too short for him approached the bay window and hesitated, holding back. Mycroft looked up and nodded to him. The man took an envelope from his pocket and handed it over. Mycroft took a small knife from his pocket and slit the envelope open. Taking out the letter inside, he read it briefly, then sighed. Sherlock was too far away to hear any words, but he could distinctly see Mycroft's lips forming the words 'The Mortimer Maberley problem again – I don't know what he thinks I can do!'

Even when he was supposed to be at an evening's entertainment, Sherlock reflected, his brother still appeared to be working. Sherlock turned away, shaking his head. He loved his brother, but he was increasingly becoming annoyed by him. Sherlock was growing up, but Mycroft still treated him like a child.

The second half of the concert was, if anything, more technically and artistically amazing than the first, but Sherlock didn't enjoy it as much. His thoughts kept turning to what his brother had said, and to his own particular future. He had no great love for Farnham – it was a pleasant town, with pleasant people, but he had never considered it as anything more than a temporary waypoint in his life, a stopping station, like those places horse-drawn carriages used to break their journeys across country so that the passengers could eat a meal and sleep before continuing their travels. London, on the other hand, had captivated him during his short time there. The city was almost like a person – it had its own character, its own moods, and it could change in a moment. He loved it, and he wanted to live the rest of his life there, if he could.

But first, Oxford. There seemed to be no way to avoid it. The trouble was that it was all built up like a row of dominos in Mycroft's mind – two years living in Oxford, being tutored by this Charles Dodgson, leading to entrance into the University and full-time studies, leading to a degree in some useless subject, leading to a dull job in government or in a bank, leading to . . . what? Retirement somewhere by the sea? That was not the kind of life he had planned out for himself.

Of course, he didn't actually have a plan for his life. At the moment he was just drifting, testing the waters, seeing where the currents would take him. Somewhere in the back of his mind was the vague thought that he might turn his logical thoughts and his ability to see through complex problems to the simple truths that lay within them into a full-time career – but as what? Some kind of policeman? A secret agent, maybe, like the ones that obviously reported to his brother?

He sighed. Life appeared to get more and more complicated the older he got.

That thought led on naturally to thoughts of Virginia Crowe. He had, in the past, assumed that she and he would have some kind of life together, although he had never dared wonder at the nature of that life. It had just seemed that she would always be there for him, and him for her. But she was in America now, engaged to be married to someone else, and her father – the man who had taught Sherlock more in two years than he had learned in his entire life up to that point – was probably teaching someone else's son. Life, it would appear, had other plans for Sherlock.

It would be nice, he reflected bitterly, if life could actually let him know what those plans were.

The concert came to an end. The violinist took several curtain calls as the applause kept on coming. Stone was on his feet, clapping wildly. Sherlock joined in, but his heart wasn't in it. Thoughts of Oxford, and degrees, and banks, kept intruding.

The two of them made their way out of the theatre, along with the rest of the audience. On the pavement, Stone turned to Sherlock and extended a hand. 'Good night, Sherlock,' he said, and then added, 'Don't let your brother's words discourage you. He may have his plans, but it's your life to live. Go with your heart.'

'Thanks,' Sherlock replied, shaking Stone's hand. 'But

wherever I end up, I hope you will seek me out there. I haven't made many friends in my life, but I count you as one of them.'

Stone nodded. 'And I you.' He smiled. 'I have friends in the Oxford area – well, to be completely honest, I have friends pretty much everywhere. Farnham was always just somewhere to live while I carried out a job – a job that became something much more, I should point out. I could just as well live in Oxford as in Farnham – and, I have to say, the chance to listen to, and play, good music is much better there. Do not be surprised if you bump into me sometime soon.' He raised a hand to his head in a sketchy salute. 'I will see you again, Sherlock. Until then, be careful, and take care of yourself.'

Stone vanished into the crowd, Sherlock turned away. He had only taken two steps when a voice beside him said, 'What was all that about then?'

It was Matty – Matthew Arnatt. Sherlock knew the voice without having to look.

'It looked pretty serious,' he went on. 'It looked like a "goodbye and fare thee well". You're not off to China again, are you?' Matty's tone was casual, but Sherlock could detect an undercurrent of unease in his friend's voice. Matty had once told Sherlock that he had spent his life watching friends and family leave him. He had resigned himself to being lonely all his days.

'It's Mycroft,' Sherlock admitted without turning. 'He's got plans for me. He wants me to go to Oxford.'

There was a moment's silence. Sherlock didn't dare look at Matty's face. He and the boy had spent a lot of time together over the past few years, but that had been broken by his unplanned visit to China. Although the two of them had grown close again since they had met up in Ireland, the more so after a few weeks in London, he wasn't sure that Matty would want to be uprooted again.

He was surprised.

'Oxford's nice,' Matty said. 'You can get there by boat, all the way up the Thames, pretty much. Been there before, I have, an' it's very pleasant. Lots of toffs leaving half-eaten food lying around on the grass by the river after they've 'ad a picnic, an' lots of absent-minded lecturers doin' the same. Rich pickings, for someone like me. Even the swans there eat better than some of the people 'ere in London.'

'You would come with me?' Sherlock asked, finally turning to look into Matty's face.

The boy was smiling. 'Why not?' he said. 'This city's too big for me, an' the market stallholders are too fly. It's difficult to get a decent meal without them chasin' after me twice a day. When are we off?'

'Soon, I think,' Sherlock said.

'Fair enough. I've got everything I need on the barge, an' Harold's been itching for a move. 'E's not like my old 'orse, Albert. 'E just wanted to stand in one spot an' eat grass an' 'ay forever. 'Arold likes to move around.'

'Can you get the barge along the Thames?' Sherlock

asked. 'After all, it's a river, rather than a canal.'

Matty nodded. 'It's possible, but the width makes it tricky – not so much when you're movin' along the river, but more when you need to come off it on to the Oxford Canal. Thinkin' 'bout it, might be better if we went straight up the Grand Junction Canal, then came off on to the Oxford Canal at the top rather than the bottom an' get to Oxford from the north, rather than the south.'

'Sounds good to me.' Sherlock caught the boy's eye. 'Look, are you sure you want to come? Don't do it just because you think I need looking after.'

Matty nodded. 'Yeah.' He seemed as if he was about to go on, then he looked away, suddenly embarrassed. 'That is, if you want me to. I mean, if you'd rather be on your own . . .'

'No,' Sherlock said firmly. 'There might be times when I like being alone, but there are definitely times I need to be with friends – and I haven't got that many of them.'

'Suppose I'll 'ave to do then,' Matty said with a lopsided smile.

'Suppose you will,' Sherlock echoed.

'Besides . . .' Matty said, and trailed off.

'Besides what?'

'Well, I don't like to say. It's not very nice.'

'Force yourself.'

'Well, I s'pose we'll be seeing less of your brother in Oxford.'

Sherlock thought for a moment. It was getting harder and harder to get Mycroft out of London. In fact, it was getting harder and harder to get Mycroft out of the Diogenes Club. There was a distinct correlation between his reluctance to travel and his size. 'I doubt,' Sherlock replied, 'that Mycroft would spend as much time with us as he does here, in London.'

'That's good.' Matty glanced sideways at Sherlock. 'It's not that I don't like 'im – it's that he don't like me. An' besides, he keeps tryin' to teach me stuff, like readin' an' writin'. I don't need that stuff.'

Sherlock thought back to his argument with his brother only an hour or so before, when he had told Mycroft that he didn't need to learn about dead languages or old books. Wasn't that more or less a refined version of what Matty had just said? Perhaps he should be less picky about the facts he allowed into his brain.

He shook himself to get rid of the uncomfortable thought.

'Now, let's get some food,' he said, changing the subject. 'Where do you recommend?'

'Borough Market'll be closin' down now. There'll be plenty of pies an' apples goin' spare.'

'Spare?' Sherlock questioned.

'Well, if the stall-owner's back is turned. The way I see it, we're doin' them a favour. If we didn't take the food then, they'd only 'ave to carry it 'ome again, then back to the market next day, an' the chances are that it might

19

have gone off overnight an' someone'll get stomach ache from eatin' it.'

'You're right,' Sherlock said. 'We're actually providing a public service.' He clapped Matty on the shoulder. 'Let's go, and on the way you can tell me more about Oxford.'

CHAPTER TWO

They left five days later, after Mycroft had written to, and received a reply from, his friend Charles Lutwidge Dodgson. He showed the reply to Sherlock over lunch one day. It said:

My dear Mycroft,

Thank you for your letter, which finds me in a state of extraordinary good health and good fortune. I trust that the same can be said of you. Although I never see your name in the newspapers, I am sure that you have made yourself into a success in whatever field it is that you have chosen to enter. I have nothing but fond memories of our time together here at Oxford, although you at least made it out into the wider world. I, as you may have heard, travel to other worlds, but only in my imagination. Some of these worlds are mathematical, and some fantastical, but all of them I find preferable to the dull solidity of supposedly 'real' life.

I would, of course, be more than happy to tutor your brother Sherlock in the logical arts. I recall how I used to envy you for having just the one sibling, considering that I have ten, all of whose birthdays I have to remember. I also remember how you used to speak of Sherlock when you were here. It was usually with some mixture of pride and exasperation, most notably when he hid a live toad in your trunk just before you left home to travel here for the summer term, and when he redrafted an essay you had written over the holidays in a perfect copy of your handwriting but with conclusions that would make sense only to a lunatic. How well I recall your reading that essay aloud in one of my tutorials, and with increasing panic as you realized that it was diverging further and further from what you remembered having written! How we laughed! I cannot, of course, guarantee Sherlock's acceptance into Christ Church, or any other of the colleges here – that will depend upon his abilities and demeanour – but with the Holmes family name behind him and a character recommendation from me he should be in with a good chance.

I have taken the liberty of securing him lodgings with a local landlady of good character – a Mrs McCrery of 36 Edmonton Crescent, just around the corner from this college. He will be on terms of room and full board – that is, breakfast and dinner – for the sum of one shilling a week. I trust this will be acceptable. I have lodged with her myself in the past, and found her standards of cleanliness to be unimpeachable, her peach cobbler to be a clean winner in the pudding stakes and her steak pudding to be perfection itself.

I look forward to young Sherlock presenting himself at

my rooms in college at some time in the near future. I also
look forward to you visiting him regularly so that we may
renew our acquaintance.

    Yours, ever,

    Charles

Mycroft's only response as he took the letter back from Sherlock was, 'I had forgotten about the toad.'

'What happened to it?' Sherlock asked innocently.

'It became something of a college mascot,' his brother replied, 'that is, until an unfortunate incident with a senior master's dog.'

'It was eaten?' Sherlock was aghast. He hadn't intended any harm to come to the creature.

'No – the dog tried to eat it, but choked. The master pulled it out of the dog's throat and threw it into the river in a fit of rage. Misplaced rage, of course, as the toad was perfectly happy in the water – happier, I suspect, than it had ever been at college. Certainly happier than the dog, who would never eat anything after that without carefully inspecting it and turning it over several times first.'

Mycroft had offered to pay for Sherlock to take the train to Oxford, but, remembering his conversation with Matty, Sherlock had declined. He had rather taken to the idea of a slow journey by barge, experiencing the landscape as they went – two friends, together. When he explained this, Mycroft had made a 'harrumph' noise, and muttered, 'How uncivilized. How uncomfortable.'

Sherlock spent the last day before they left London revisiting his favourite places – the bridges over the Thames, the bookshops of the Charing Cross Road, the London Zoo and the hustle and bustle of Paddington Station. He would miss London. He would miss it terribly, and he vowed, as he walked up Baker Street away from the station, to come back and live there one day.

On the appointed day, Sherlock took what few possessions he had – some clothes, his violin and a few books – and joined Matty on his barge in Camden Lock. They set off in silence, with Matty very aware of his friend's mixed feelings about leaving. Matty, by contrast, was happier than Sherlock had seen him in a while. Matty was, in so many ways, the exact opposite of Mycroft Holmes. He was thin where Mycroft was fat, intuitive where Mycroft was logical and, critically, restless and active where Mycroft was settled and lazy. The only point of similarity they had was their fondness for food.

Harold, Matty's horse, walked steadily along the towpath, pulling the barge slowly and sedately along the Grand Junction Canal. Matty stood at the back, steering with the rudder to ensure that they neither ploughed bow-first into the bank nor drifted out into the centre of the canal, pulling Harold into the shallow water. Sherlock sat cross-legged at the front, watching out for obstacles and tunnels, and letting his mind drift. They passed fields and forests, roads and rivers. Whenever they passed a barge travelling in the opposite direction, usually laden with coal or wood or metal pipes, Sherlock would raise a finger to his forehead, and the man on the other barge would do likewise. Whenever they came to a lock – one of the gated enclosures that allowed the water level of the canal to rise and fall in line with the landscape – Sherlock would leap out and guide Harold to a stop, throw his weight into closing the first set of massive wooden gates behind the barge while Matty carefully steered, then he would open the water sluices set into the equally massive second set of gates to let the water on the other side pour into the enclosure, raising the level of the water inside and therefore the barge until the second set of gates could be opened. Even as he was rushing around, opening and closing gates and winding metal pump handles, Sherlock marvelled at the inventiveness of the mechanisms. How incredible that human ingenuity had come up with something so complicated, so useful and so clever!

The two of them ate when they were hungry – buying food from farms or taverns that they passed – and slept when it was too dark to keep moving safely. Rather than measuring their journey by the towns and villages they encountered, as he would have done if travelling by road or rail, Sherlock found himself tracking their progress by the names of the various locks they travelled through and the rivers that either passed under them or joined with them. The ones that stuck in his memory were Black Jack's Lock, Iron Bridge Lock and Lady Chapel Lock, the River Musbourne, the River Bulbourne and the River Chess. About the only major population centre that he was aware of was the market town of Aylesbury, where the two of them stopped for a day to look around and to buy cheese and pies.

They came off the Grand Junction Canal eventually, on to the Oxford Canal.

'It runs between Oxford an' Cambridge,' Matty yelled from the rear of the barge as they made their laboured turn into the offshoot, 'prob'ly for all them students that get thrown out of the one an' fancy their chances at the other. You might need to know that one day!'

'I'll bear it in mind,' Sherlock said laconically.

As they got closer to Oxford, Sherlock began to see signs of increasing wealth – bigger houses, set in their own grounds, and buildings made of cut stone transported from distant quarries rather than rough stones cut locally. The clothes that people were wearing were better quality as well, with straw boaters increasingly replacing flat caps.

One house, which they passed at dusk one day, particularly caught his attention. It was illuminated by the setting sun, making it shine with a macabre crimson light. The various sharp decorations along the edge of the roof looked like teeth raking at the darkening sky. There was something about the structure of the building – the way the wings joined on to the main body, and the way the lines of differently coloured stone that marked the divisions between the floors ran across the frontage, that made him feel uneasy, even faintly nauseous. No two lines seemed to be exactly parallel, and no angles summed to exactly ninety degrees, giving the house a strange, lopsided feel. It didn't appear to be falling down however. It seemed more as if it had been deliberately built that way – constructed using a geometry that wasn't based on the rules that Sherlock had been taught at school. There was something about the way the windows gaped, black and empty, which made him think of many eyes all staring down at him pitilessly, measuring him up and finding him wanting.

He shook himself. He'd been travelling for too long without any distractions, and he was hungry. His imagination – usually the quietest part of his mind – was running wild.

'Can you see that place?' Matty called.

'Yes,' Sherlock said, more quietly than he had intended. It was as if he didn't want the house to hear them.

'Weird, ain't it?'

'Yes.' He felt as if he needed to keep his answers as short and direct as possible, to avoid attracting attention. 'It's just a badly designed house,' he said sharply. 'Nothing to get panicked about.'

"Arold don't like it,' Matty pointed out, and indeed the horse did appear to be shying away from the building, as far as the rope that connected him to the barge would allow. Matty was having to steer the boat further out into the canal just to stop them from being pulled into the bank.

Sherlock glanced back towards the house as the inexorable progress of the barge carried them past its baleful gaze. The building almost seemed to shift with them as they moved, keeping its frontage facing them and its black windows fixed on them. Just as he was about to look away, the light from the setting sun illuminated a shape on the roof that was distinct from the chimneys and the carved decorations. It looked for all the world like a gargoyle, a stone demon poised up there, overlooking the house's grounds, but who would decorate their house with just one gargoyle – and why put one on a house anyway? Gargoyles were generally found on churches or cathedrals, and usually came in groups rather than individually. Weren't they meant to be water spouts for when it rained? Who would put just one water spout on a roof?

Even as the thoughts crossed Sherlock's mind, the massive figure shifted. It moved to one side, and its right arm reached up to catch the edge of a chimney, stabilizing it against a sudden gust of wind that ruffled the waters of the canal and briefly caught the side of the barge. The figure looked to Sherlock as if it was about seven feet tall, with a chest like a barrel and a head that was bald and strangely lumpy, rather than smooth like a man's scalp should have been. Its arms appeared overly long too. He shuddered, feeling an inexplicable fear. Then he blinked, and suddenly the figure was gone. The roofline was once again just chimneys and spiky decorations.

A trick of light and shadow – it must have been. He took a deep breath, suddenly aware that he had stopped breathing for a few moments.

'Did you . . . ?' he called, then bit down on the words he had been going to say.

'Did I what?' Matty asked.

'Nothing.'

'Do you want to stop for the night? It's getting dark. We've got some sausage left, an' some cheese.'

'Let's keep going for half an hour more.' Sherlock glanced again at the house. 'I want to get some more distance under our belt before we stop.'

'You're the boss,' Matty said cheerfully, then added, more quietly, 'even though it's my barge an' my 'orse.'

They kept going until the house was out of sight and Harold had calmed down, then they stopped and tied the barge up for the night. The sky was cloudless, speckled with stars, and the two of them lay back on the barge's deck and ate their provisions as Harold noisily munched grass from the bank. They talked about everything and nothing, important things and trivial things, all mixed together. Sherlock hesitantly put forward his plans of moving back to London once he had finished at Oxford and working for, or with, the police, and Matty for the first time talked about his dreams of finding a girl, getting married and having a large family. They slept there, on the deck of the barge, and if Sherlock dreamed then he didn't remember the dreams.

The next day they arrived in Oxford.

They tethered the barge on the outskirts of the town and walked in. By the time they got to the centre, Sherlock had fallen in love with the place. The various colleges – Christ Church, of course, but also Balliol, Jesus, Merton and many others, were scattered through the town like plums in a plum duff. The town itself was the usual mixture of shops, taverns, houses, official buildings and storehouses, but the college buildings were magnificent ancient stone edifices, like walled medieval mini-towns in their own right. Students in black robes and flat black caps were everywhere: walking, riding bicycles or standing around in groups and conversing. Sherlock noticed that the students appeared to stay in their own groups, and the townspeople just talked to each other. There was little mixing between the two. He filed that away for later consideration.

Remembering the address that had been in Charles Dodgson's letter, Sherlock found the house where he would be living just around the corner from Christ Church College. Number 36 was a three-storey stone house set in a terrace of similar houses. There was nothing special about it, but the stone steps outside were scrubbed clean and the windows gleamed. Mrs McCrery was obviously very house-proud.

'What d'ya want to do?' Matty asked.

Sherlock thought for a minute. 'I want some lunch,' he said, and then I want to go back to the barge and get my stuff. I'll need a carriage, I guess, to get it all here. I can't carry it all the way, even with your help, but that's going to be expensive.'

'Don't worry about a carriage,' Matty said mysteriously. 'I'll sort that out. You see about getting us some lunch.'

They ate sitting on the banks of the River Isis – a tributary of the Thames, Sherlock remembered. Rather than steal something off a stall or from the counter of a shop, he had spent some of the money that his brother had given him on a couple of bread rolls filled with roast pork and bottles of lemonade. They watched the boats, barges and punts float past them as the clouds sailed past overhead.

When they got back to the barge Sherlock moved his stuff out on to the bank while Matty vanished off on some mysterious errand. When he returned, he was leading Harold, his horse, who was now attached to a cart. There was straw on the cart. He had obviously borrowed it from some nearby farmer or workman.

Sherlock just hoped that the owner knew that it had been borrowed.

'Load 'er up,' Matty called cheerfully.

'I doubt this is the way that most students arrive in Oxford,' Sherlock said dubiously. 'Even the ones who are here to prepare for the University, rather than actually attend it.'

'Well, that's okay then,' Matty said. 'You ain't like any other student.'

'A fair point, well made,' Sherlock conceded, and so they spent the next hour or so riding sedately through the town, both perched on the driver's bench at the front of the cart while Sherlock's possessions teetered precariously on the back. Several times he had to dive backwards to prevent a bag or a trunk from sliding into the road.

When they got back to Edmonton Crescent Matty helped Sherlock unload his stuff. 'Well,' he said brightly, 'that's it then. I'll see you around.'

'Perhaps you could come in,' Sherlock said. 'Check the place out.'

Matty looked down at his scruffy clothes and dirty hands. 'I dunno. People around 'ere are very particular about who they invite into their houses. I ain't sure I'll fit properly.'

Sherlock was about to argue with him when a voice interrupted them. 'You'll be young Master Holmes then?'

He turned to see a large lady dressed in black crinoline. She was standing on the steps of number 36, staring down at them. Her hair was grey, her eyes were a faded blue, but her fierce demeanour was offset by the way her eyes crinkled in a smile of welcome.

'I am,' he said. 'My friend here was just—'

'Get yourselves inside, into the parlour, both of you. I'll make a pot of tea. There's scones, jam and cream, if you're hungry.'

'Actually—'

'We're starvin',' Matty interrupted.

'Well then, come ye in and relax. I can't have starving children on the street. What would the neighbours think?'

Sherlock indicated his bags and trunks. 'What about—'

'I'll get one of my boys to fetch them in,' she said. 'That's "my boys", as in the boys who fetch the coal and shine the shoes in the house. There are also "my boys" who are staying here, as you will be, and "my boys", as in the five strapping lads that my late husband left me with, but they're scattered around the south of England now.'

'I'm sorry to hear about your husband,' Sherlock said. That would explain the black clothes – she was in mourning. 'When did he die?'

'Thirty-five years ago next month,' she said. 'Now, come on in. You're making the street look untidy, and if there's one thing I can't stand, it's untidiness.' She thought for a moment. 'And gypsies. And dogs.'

Sherlock glanced at Matty and raised an eyebrow. Matty looked back at him with an unreadable expression on his face. 'I think you'll fit in here just fine,' he said quietly.

They climbed the steps to the doorway and passed through into the house. It was possibly the neatest place Sherlock had ever seen on land. He was used to life on ships, where everything had to be stowed away where it couldn't fall over and break in case of rough seas, but this was the first time he had seen the principle applied on terra firma.

'Your husband was a sailor,' he ventured.

'Bless you, that's right.' Mrs McCrery was right behind them as they entered the sitting room. 'How can you tell? Is it the drawing?' She indicated a framed sketch on the wall of a bearded man in uniform, arms folded and staring out at the observer from beneath heavy eyebrows.

'Er, yes,' he replied.

'You two make yourselves comfortable. I'll go and get the tea.'

'And the scones,' Matty said, settling into a comfortable chair as Mrs McCrery left. 'I like this place.' He leaned back, and the frilly lace material that ran along the top fell across his face. He struggled free. 'What *is* this thing?' he said, holding the lace up and examining it.

'It's an antimacassar,' Sherlock explained patiently.

'What's that when it's at 'ome?'

'It prevents macassar oil from gentlemen's heads from staining the material of the sofa.'

'Oh.' A pause. 'What's "macassar oil" then? Is it like oil for oil lamps?'

'No, it's for the hair. It conditions it, and makes it

easier to comb. It's made from coconut oil and ylang-ylang oil.'

Matty ran his hand through his own unruly hair. 'Oh. Should I be usin' it?'

'I don't think so. I really don't think so. The grease from the hot pies you keep eating seems to do a good enough job.'

Matty sniffed. 'Reckon you're right.'

Sherlock looked around. There wasn't that much to see – apart from the portraits on the walls and a ginger cat dozing by the glowing fireplace the room was remarkably bare – no knick-knacks or odd little possessions that might have helped Sherlock get a handle on Mrs McCrery's personality, although he had already begun to develop an opinion.

He walked over to the fire and bent down to stroke the cat. Best to start making friends straight away, he thought. He ran his hand over the cat's back, brushing it from head to tail. It didn't seem to mind. In fact, it didn't even seem to notice. Possibly it was fast asleep, but it didn't seem to be breathing: its sides were stationary, rather than going in or out. Listening closely, he couldn't hear any purring either, and he noticed that it was cold.

Maybe the cat was dead. That would be a terrible way to start his time here – having to tell Mrs McCrery that her cat was dead.

He rested his hand cautiously on its back again. No reaction. He pressed harder. The cat was curiously stiff.

Maybe rigor mortis had set in – that stiffening of the muscles that apparently occurred within a few hours of death.

He pressed harder still, but there was no give at all in the cat's flesh. It was as hard and as cold as stone.

'It's stuffed,' he said in surprise, leaning back on his heels.

'What is?'

'The cat – I think it's stuffed.'

'Well –' Matty started to say, but before he could get the words out Mrs McCrery reappeared in the doorway with a tray. She set it down on a low table next to Matty, turned her head to look at Sherlock, and said: 'Ah, you've met Macallistair then?'

'Macallistair?' He glanced at the cat. 'Yes – we've made our introductions.'

'The poor thing, he died last winter. It was fearfully cold, and I found him on the front step one morning, frozen solid.'

Sherlock glanced at the cat again. Surely it wasn't still frozen? Not in front of that coal fire.

'So you had him stuffed,' he said casually.

'So he could always be here with me, curled up in his favourite place.' She straightened and gestured towards the contents of the tray. Tea and scones and jam and cream. 'Just help yourselves, and don't stand on ceremony. I'll come and show you to your room later, Mr Holmes.'

She turned and sailed out of the room.

There was silence for a few moments.

'I wonder what she did with her husband,' Matty said eventually. 'If I were you, I wouldn't go down into the cellar, especially at night.'

'Maybe all of her previous lodgers are somewhere still in the house,' Sherlock observed darkly, 'all curled up comfortably in their favourite places.'

Matty looked dubiously at the tea tray, then at Sherlock. 'Do you want to try the tea and the scones first?'

Sherlock laughed suddenly. This was just too stupid. 'She's not a mass murderer,' he said, 'she's just a lady who loved her husband and her cat. There's no law against that. The tea isn't poisoned, and neither are the scones. Come on – let's eat.'

They did, and the scones were lovely – crumbly and still warm. After he'd finished two of them, and had a cup of tea, Matty decided it was time to go. He left, and Sherlock sat there for a while in the sitting room, letting his thoughts wander.

'I'll show you to your room now,' Mrs McCrery said, reappearing quietly in the doorway. 'Och, you and your young friend certainly enjoyed the scones.'

'They were perfect,' he said, following her out of the room and up the stairs.

'I made the jam myself,' she announced. 'You'll never guess what fruit I used.'

'Holly berries?' he asked innocently.

'Oh, no,' she said, shocked, 'those are poisonous! I used redcurrants.'

Sherlock's room was on the third floor. It was small but very tidy, with a comfortable-looking bed and a desk where he could work. There was also a stuffed chair where he could relax and maybe read, and a wardrobe. A porcelain basin on a stand completed the room's furnishings. His cases and trunk were set against the wall beneath the window.

'The bathroom is down one flight of stairs,' Mrs McCrery said. 'You need to know that there can be a bit of a queue in the mornings when the students have lectures to get to. I understand from Mr Dodgson that you will be attending his rooms for lessons, rather than the college, so you might want to wait until everyone has finished.'

'I'll do that,' he said. 'Unless I'm up really early and get in there before anyone else.'

'Don't leave a dirt ring around the bath if you use it,' she continued, 'and don't leave whiskers in the sink if you shave. Apart from that, I don't really have any rules, except for general ones about tolerance, quietness, sobriety and no women in the house under any circumstances.'

A sudden and bittersweet memory of Virginia Crowe flashed across Sherlock's mind. 'I don't think,' he said, 'that will be a problem.'

'Dinner tonight, and every night, will be at seven

o'clock. Breakfast every morning will be at seven o'clock as well. Apart from that, you are free to make your own arrangements.' She paused, thinking. 'Although I don't allow food in the bedrooms.'

'Of course.'

'Neither do I allow food in the bathroom. I only mention that because one undergraduate, a few years ago, used to smuggle pies in and eat them in the bath, knowing that they weren't allowed in his bedroom. That's undergraduates for you – always trying to find a way around the rules – bending them without actually breaking them.'

Sherlock thought back to all the times he had obeyed the letter of a rule while disobeying its spirit. That was the curse of a logical mind – you could usually see a way around something.

'No food in the bathroom,' he promised.

Mrs McCrery nodded. 'Haddock tonight,' she said brightly, 'and I made some special sauce myself!'

'Lovely!'

As she left the room, Sherlock crossed to the window and looked out. His room was at the back of the house, and he could see the gardens of this and the neighbouring houses below. Further away were the gardens of the houses in the next road, and then the houses themselves: their backs looking less well maintained than their fronts that he remembered passing earlier. It was, he thought, human nature to clean those things that everyone could see and ignore those things that were usually unobserved.

Beyond the roofs of the houses in the next road he could see the needle-like spires of one of the college chapels, thrusting up against the blue sky. He thought, from the position relative to the house, that it was Christ Church College chapel. Tomorrow he would head to the college and introduce himself to Charles Dodgson. He wondered what the man would be like. Based on the fact that he wrote children's books, and based also on the way he had written the letter to Mycroft, Sherlock pictured him as a free spirit, a man who always wanted to be – or perhaps always *had* to be – amusing and unusual, whatever the circumstances, but how did that square with the fact that he was a lecturer in logic at one of the world's greatest universities?

Tomorrow, he thought, was going to be interesting.

Thoughts of his brother reminded him that he ought to write to Mycroft, reassuring his brother that he had arrived safely in Oxford. He did so, then sealed the letter up and left it, intending to post it on the morrow. Checking his watch he found that he still had several hours before dinner. He didn't feel like going out again, so he got on to the bed and closed his eyes, intending to rest. He drifted for a while on the edge of sleep, kept from falling deeper by the noises from outside, but eventually he did sleep, and found himself dreaming of a dinner table where all the other guests – boys of his own age – were stuffed and varnished. He awoke with a start to find that it was dark outside. Shaking off the last vestiges of the dream, he got up, unpacked his possessions, washed in the cold water in the bowl and changed his clothes before heading down the stairs to dinner.

CHAPTER THREE

Dinner was a surprisingly entertaining affair. There were five of them around the table – apart from Sherlock they were all students at Christ Church College. Initially he felt out of place, younger and less experienced than the others, but soon he realized that the various things he had done in his life made him into something of a celebrity in their eyes – not just travelling to Russia, America and China, but even something as simple as living in London, which they regarded as the centre of sophistication. As dinner went on he found that they were asking more and more questions of him, and he was finding it more and more difficult to answer those questions without getting into dangerous territory regarding Mycroft's sensitive job in the British Government and the schemes of the Paradol Chamber. He had to resort to various stratagems to turn the conversation back to his co-diners and find out more about them.

Thomas Millard was a rather plump youth with thick glasses and thinning hair. He was studying theology, with a view to becoming a vicar like his father and his grandfather. He had a way of speaking that made it sound like he was giving a sermon, even when he was asking Sherlock to pass the gravy boat. Mathukumal

Vijayaraghavan was a slight Indian boy with black hair and dark eyes, who said little but listened to everything – he was, rather oddly, considering his first name, actually studying mathematics. Reginald Musgrave was a tall chemist who spent most of the meal discussing cricket with the person sitting beside him – Paul Chippenham, who was studying natural science. None of them seemed to mind that Sherlock wasn't yet a student at the University itself.

As promised, the main course was haddock, with potatoes and beans, but it was preceded by mulligatawny soup, the spicy flavour of which made Vijayaraghavan raise his eyebrows in surprise.

'Remind you of India?' Musgrave asked.

'Not in the slightest,' the boy replied. Sherlock wondered whether he was the only one who could detect the ironical tone in his voice.

When Sherlock tried to turn the conversation to the subject of Charles Dodgson, in an attempt to prepare himself for the meeting the next day, all four of them raised their eyebrows and shared amused glances. Vijayaraghavan was the only one to say anything, and all he would murmur was 'An interesting man. Very, very clever. Very, very strange.'

'I say, did you hear,' Musgrave said excitedly, 'that he was questioned by the police last week?'

The others shook their heads.

'What was that about?' Chippenham asked.

'Some thefts that had occurred, but here's the thing – the things that were stolen were *body parts*, and they were taken from the mortuary!'

'What is a "mortuary"?' Vijayaraghavan asked in his quiet, precise voice. 'I do not recognize the word.'

'It's the place where people's bodies are taken after they die,' Musgrave explained.

Chippenham added, 'But only if they died in some unusual way – either murder, or due to some kind of disease or an accident that might need to be investigated. A pathologist will cut the body up and examine the organs in order to ascertain the cause of death so that it can be recorded properly. Otherwise, when the cause of death is obvious, the bodies just get prepared, put into a coffin and then left for a while in the front room so that people can sit with them and say goodbye. Then they are buried.' He nodded towards Millard. 'In anticipation, that is, of the resurrection of the dead and the achievement of life everlasting at some undefined time in the future.'

'I thought,' Sherlock said, remembering the endless sermons that his Uncle Sherrinford had written for sending to ministries all over England and abroad, 'that people went straight to heaven or hell when they died. I didn't realize they had to wait around until the Resurrection. And how do they get out of their coffins, which have been buried six feet underground? It's all going to be a bit messy, isn't it?'

A look of panic crossed Millard's face. His gaze

skittered around the dining room as he tried to think of some theological response, and failed.

Sherlock's mind – at least the part of it that wasn't still thinking about the moment of resurrection, when literally millions and millions of dead people would be climbing out of their buried coffins – was still fixed on Charles Dodgson and his connection to these bizarre thefts. 'Why was Dodgson questioned?' he asked. 'I mean, he's a mathematician and a lecturer, not a pathologist or a doctor. What possible connection could he have?'

'Ah, there's the interesting part,' Musgrave explained. 'Dodgson is well known around Oxford for this photography lark that he does – capturing a picture of a scene or a person using light and chemical stuff and glass. Apparently, as well as taking photographs of the river, the college buildings and of his friends, he also takes them of dead bodies.'

'Why?' Sherlock asked, noticing that Vijayaraghavan beside him was shuddering again.

'What he told the police is that he's fascinated with the way that the body works, and he wants to make a record of all the bits for posterity, and to help with the teaching of anatomy here at Oxford.'

'As if anyone needs to,' Chippenham sniffed. 'Leonardo da Vinci drew all the aspects of the functioning human body three hundred and fifty years ago. There is no more to be said on the matter.'

And that was the end of the discussion about Charles Dodgson.

They repaired to the sitting room after dessert, which was sherry trifle. Coffee was served, and Paul Chippenham fetched a bottle of port from his room, which they drank out of small glasses.

Musgrave pointed at the stuffed cat, curled up – as it always would be – by the fire. 'You've met Macallistair, I take it?' he asked Sherlock.

'I have. What's the story there?'

'It was before my time, but apparently Mrs McCrery was completely in love with that cat. She used to heat up its dinner every night, and it's said that the cat ate better than any of the students who were here. When it died – as all pets do, in the end – Mrs McCrery was devastated. She stopped cooking, stopped cleaning the house and just retreated into herself. One of the students in the house at the time was studying anatomy, and was a bit of an amateur taxidermist. In desperation, he offered to stuff the beast for her, so she could always have it around. She agreed, it's been here ever since, and the house has been happy all that time.'

'There's a parrot in the visitor's room,' Vijayaraghavan said quietly. 'I am told that it is much the same story. She loved the parrot, the parrot died, and one of her lodgers offered to stuff it for her – although whoever did it was not as talented as the person who stuffed the cat. It looks decidedly dowdy.'

'I did hear,' Chippenham added, 'that the student who stuffed the parrot kept all the meat on ice, and then had a friend of his who was a butcher sell it back to Mrs McCrery as fresh grouse. The entire household dined on parrot that night, without anyone apart from the student in question knowing.' He paused. 'Apparently it was delicious.'

Sherlock remembered his talk with Matty earlier. 'Has anyone seen any of the students who used to be here since they left?' he asked casually.

There was a long silence as the other four thought for a while and glanced at each other.

'I'm sure we've seen them around – somewhere,' Millard said with a trace of concern in his voice.

After that, the conversation turned to other, more pleasant matters. When Millard brought out a silver case of small cigars and offered them around, Sherlock decided it was time to leave.

He slept heavily, with no more dreams of stuffed and varnished dinner companions, and awoke to a bright blue sky.

The other four had already risen, dressed, eaten breakfast and left by the time he got downstairs. Despite Mrs McCrery's insistence about breakfast at seven o'clock on the dot, she managed to rustle up some bacon, sausages and egg for him, along with a pot of tea. He left the boarding house in a good mood, whistling one of the tunes that he had heard Pablo Sarasate play at the recital.

Christ Church College was only a short walk away. The entrance was a huge arch that was almost entirely closed off by a wooden gate. A doorway in the gate allowed students and lecturers in and out.

As Sherlock made to go through the doorway, a gruff voice from inside said, 'Can I help you, sir?'

Off to the left, through the doorway, was a small window in a stone wall. Behind the window a man in a dark uniform was making notes on a piece of paper. He had a flourishing moustache and luxuriant sideburns. He hadn't looked up when Sherlock was going through the doorway, and didn't look up when Sherlock stood in front of the window.

'I have an appointment to see Mr Charles Dodgson,' Sherlock said.

'At what time, sir?'

Sherlock frowned. 'I'm not sure. It was left ambiguous.'

'That doesn't sound like Mr Dodgson. Very precise, he is. Very particular about times and places and suchlike.'

He reached out to take a clipboard off a shelf to his left, and Sherlock noticed a tattoo on his forearm as the cuff of his shirtsleeve pulled back. It was a fish, entwined with an anchor, but the colours were subtle, more like watercolours than the bright tattoos that sailors normally got at ports like London or Southampton, and the lines were so fine and so precise that they could have been drawn on with a single hair. 'South China Seas?' Sherlock ventured.

The man smiled, making the ends of his moustache curl up. 'Indeed, sir. Very clever of you to spot that.'

'I would say . . . Shanghai.'

'Correct again, sir.' He cocked his head to one side, eyes twinkling. 'Care to narrow it down further, sir?'

'Down on the quayside,' Sherlock said, suddenly thrust back in his mind to the heat and the smell of the Shanghai docks, and a small shack in which an ancient Chinese man sat making the most marvellous pictures on the skins of sailors who would never appreciate the artistry. 'Chen-shu's shop.'

'Well, bless my soul!' The man leaned back in his chair, amazed. 'I never thought I'd meet someone who could tell where in the world a tattoo had been done.'

'Sheer luck,' Sherlock said. 'I just happen to know Chen-shu's shop. I took tea with him, a few times, while I was waiting for my ship to leave.'

'An artist,' the man said. 'A true artist.'

'But he made a terrible cup of tea,' Sherlock remembered.

The man straightened, brushing down his jacket self-consciously. 'I spent five years before the mast, all over the Asiatic. Then I came here, because the wife wanted me to settle down. My name is Mutchinson, that's *Mr* Mutchinson, and I'm the Porter here at Christ College. It's my duty and my privilege to check everyone in and out, to lock the gates at ten o'clock at night and not to open them until six o'clock next morning, and to patrol the walls of the college to spot any young gentleman who comes back late after an evening in the taverns and tries to climb over.'

'And I'm sure you do a wonderful job of it.'

'Mr Dodgson, you said.' He consulted the clipboard. 'Would you, by any chance, be a Mister Sherlock Holmes?'

'I would.'

'Mr Dodgson notified me that you might be visiting. I am to escort you straight up to his rooms when you arrive.' He glanced over his shoulder, into the shadows. 'Stevens, look after the lodge for a minute – I'm escorting a visitor.'

Within a few seconds he was out of the lodge and leading Sherlock into the quadrangle – a large area of grass, bordered with a paved path, that lay just inside the main gates. He headed around the path, avoiding the pristine green grass, and through an archway. All the while as he led Sherlock along several zigzag paths, across tiny open areas and then finally up a set of narrow and twisted stairs, he engaged the boy in conversation about China and sailing. It was obvious he missed the old days, and by the time they arrived at Charles Dodgson's door the two of them were best friends. Sherlock had a strong feeling that, if ever Mr Mutchinson found him climbing over the walls of Christ Church after the gates were locked, then the Porter would turn his head and look the other way.

Mutchinson rapped on the door, which was tiny and warped. 'Mr Dodgson – a visitor for you, sir!' He turned his head to look at Sherlock. 'Mr Dodgson hasn't got any tutorials this morning, otherwise I'd have asked you to wait,' he said more quietly.

'Thank you, Mutchinson. I will attend to him m-m-momentarily,' a thin, reedy voice called from inside.

'Will you be dining in college tonight, sir?'

'I will, Mutchinson. Is there any of that rather excellent claret left?'

'I dare say, sir. I dare say there will be.'

'And giraffe? Will there be giraffe?'

'No sir.' Mutchinson turned to Sherlock and raised an eyebrow. 'We appear to be completely out of giraffe. It will be mutton, sir.'

A sigh came from inside the room. 'There's never any giraffe, and precious little hippopotamus on the menu these days. I sometimes fear for this college.'

'Good luck, sir.' Mutchinson nodded at Sherlock, then turned around smartly and marched off down the stairs.

Sherlock stood there for a few moments. Nothing happened. He could feel his heart beating fast within his chest. This meeting was going to be important, and he wanted to make a good initial impression. He wondered whether to knock on the door himself and remind Mr Dodgson that he was there, but he didn't know how the man might react. Could he take offence at being reminded?

Eventually, just as he was about to screw up enough courage to knock on the door, it abruptly opened.

The man standing inside was tall and thin – taller and thinner than anyone Sherlock had ever seen. His hair was a glossy brown: straight on top but curled at the ends, which were further down his cheeks and neck than fashion normally dictated. His suit was slightly too small for him, and his wrists projected from the ends of his sleeves. He wore white cotton gloves on his hands – inappropriate both for indoors and the weather, Sherlock thought. He wondered briefly what it was about his hands that Dodgson was trying to hide. He put the thought to one side. Looking down, he could see Dodgson's socks in the gap between the bottom of his trousers and his shoes, which were scratched and had traces of mud on them. A walker then, and one with little money to spend on either clothes that fit or shoe repairs. Or one who cared little about his appearance. Or perhaps both.

'Yes?'

'Mr Dodgson? My name is Sherlock Holmes. I was told to report to you here by—'

'By your brother M-M-Mycroft, of course.' Dodgson's voice was as thin and reedy in person as it had sounded from outside the room, and he had a slight stammer on certain letters. 'Come in, come in. I can offer you tea or sherry, or tea *and* sherry, although I do not recommend the m-m-mixture. I can also offer you biscuits in the plural, as I have three left and I only require one myself.'

'Thank you.' Sherlock entered the room, which was larger than the cramped stairway outside had suggested. It was furnished as a sitting room, with comfortable chairs, a table and bookcases. Other doors led off to other rooms – presumably a bedroom and perhaps a dining room, although Sherlock was fairly sure, from what his brother had told him, that the students and lecturers all ate together in some large refectory on the college site.

Dodgson gestured to a chair. 'Please, sit down.'

Sherlock noticed a book open and upside down on a side table. 'My apologies, sir.' He said politely. 'I am disturbing you.'

'I was merely reading a b-b-book,' Dodgson replied. 'It is an activity which can be easily interrupted and then be restarted, unlike the activity of b-b-beading a rook, of course. Once you have started beading a rook you have to keep on going to the end, if only because rooks are such impatient c-c-creatures. Once they start shaking their wings the beads go everywhere, and you have no option but to start again.'

Sherlock stared at him. Giraffes and hippopotamuses for dinner, and rooks covered with beads? What was going on in this man's mind?

Dodgson folded himself up into a chair that was far too small for him and gazed at Sherlock.

'Where have you been living?' he asked, normally

but seemingly randomly. 'Not at the family home, I suspect. Your brother has told me a little about your circumstances.'

'Recently I have been living in London, and before that China. Before *that* I was with my aunt and uncle in Farnham.'

'Ah, Farnham. Yes, I have recently purchased a house in Guildford for my own family.' He glanced sideways, out of the window. 'My father died a few months ago. Your father is in India, is he not?'

'Yes, he is.'

Dodgson considered for a moment. 'China? What took you there, might I ask.'

Sherlock couldn't help himself. 'A three-masted schooner,' he said.

He had judged Dodgson's attitude perfectly. The mathematician let out a sudden sharp laugh. 'Oh, very good!' he said. 'Very quick.' He stared at Sherlock for a moment, seemingly re-evaluating him. 'So you've been to China. Where else in the world have you travelled?'

'France, America and Russia,' Sherlock replied, remembering briefly his various adventures in those countries.

'Ah, Russia. I too have been there. A fascinating country, but the local population seems to have so little imagination. All of their books are t-t-turgidly long t-t-tomes about what people do and say from day to day.' He shrugged. 'It is interesting to compare their literature with their folklore. Look at the legend of Baba Yaga, for instance. An old witch who lives in a hut that stands on chicken legs! What whimsy! Why do we not have anything like that in British folklore?'

'I don't know.' Sherlock thought for a moment. 'Perhaps there is a correlation between the harshness of people's lives and the stories they tell each other at night. In Britain our lives are generally pretty pleasant, but in Russia the winters can be harsh and the food scarce.' He had said all that off the top of his head, without thinking it through, but he made a mental note to come back to that thought. Perhaps he could write an essay about it, or something similar.

'An interesting point, and possibly a valid one,' Dodgson said. 'But we digress from the point of your visit. You wish to study m-m-mathematics here at Cambridge.' It was more of a statement than a question.

'Ye-es,' Sherlock said, hoping that Dodgson had not noticed the hesitation.

'And you have missed some schooling recently, for reasons that your brother is hesitant to describe.'

'That is so.'

'And, given those two postulates, the conclusion is that your brother wishes me to prepare you for the rigours of university life by tutoring you privately for a period of time, until I feel you are ready.'

'That,' Sherlock said carefully, 'is, I believe, my brother's intent.'

'Very well. Can I presume that you have studied at least a *little* m-m-mathematics during your incomplete schooling?'

'I did.'

'What can you remember? Did you, for instance, study Euclid's *Elements*? Can you tell me what Euclid's five basic n-n-notions are?'

Sherlock thought for a moment. 'Firstly, that things which are equal to the same thing are also equal to one another.'

'Correct.'

'Secondly, that if equals are added to equals, then the wholes are equal.'

'Also correct.'

'Thirdly, if equals are subtracted from equals, then the remainders are equal.'

'Without doubt.'

'Fourthly, that things which coincide with one another are equal to one another.'

'Spot on!'

'And fifthly, that the whole is greater than the part.'

Dodgson clapped his hands together. 'Ideal. You have them in a n-n-nutshell. From Euclid's basic propositions and notions, of course, the whole of m-m-mathematics can be constructed, theorem by painstaking theorem.' He threw his head back and stared at the ceiling. 'It is a fine subject, m-m-mathematics. God's universe is described in the language of numbers, just as Rembrandt's universe is described by the colours of the oil paints on his palette and Mozart's by the vibrations of air that we call musical notes.' He paused, thin fingers steepled beneath his chin. 'Let us see how far your mathematical knowledge extends. Tell me, young Sherlock, what is the next n-n-number in this sequence: 1, 2, 4, 8, 16 . . . ?'

'32,' Sherlock said immediately. 'Each number is double the one before it.'

'Of course. Elementary, in fact. What, then, is the next number in *this* sequence: 1, 1, 2, 3, 5, 8, 13 . . . ?'

Sherlock thought for a moment.

'There is p-p-paper and a pen on the table beside you, should you require them.'

'No need.' Sherlock considered the numbers, both in relation to the ones before them and the ones after them. The numbers increased each time, suggesting some kind of additive process, and –

'Each number is the sum of the two numbers that precede it,' he said triumphantly, the words coming out of his mouth a split second after the answer had arrived in his brain.

'Just so. That is a very interesting set of numbers known as the Fibonacci sequence. It was first described by the mathematician Leonardo of Pisa, also known as Fibonacci, over five hundred and fifty years ago, although an Indian student of mine here at Christ College tells me that the sequence has been known in Indian mathematics for a great deal longer.' He appeared to be talking to himself now, more than to Sherlock, and his stammer had disappeared. 'I must try and find out as much as I can about the Indian poets and philosophers Pingala, Virahanka and Gopala. I suspect I may have to learn Sanskrit, although this college is probably as good a place to do that as anywhere else.'

'That Indian student – is his name Mathukumal Vijayaraghavan, by any chance?'

'You k-k-know him?'

'We are boarding at the same establishment.'

'Ah.' Dodgson thought for a moment. 'What about the following sequence: 1, 5, 12, 22, 35, 51, 70, 92, 117, 145 . . . ?'

Sherlock mulled the numbers over in his head for a few moments. There was no obvious link – the numbers weren't squares, or cubes, or multiples, or anything simple. Eventually, and with a looming sense of impending defeat, he took the paper and pencil from the table and scrawled the numbers down, then scribbled various possibilities around. Eventually, however, he had to admit defeat.

'I'm afraid I can't work it out.'

'No shame in that. What if I t-t-told you that the fact the second number is a 5 is important?'

Sherlock considered for a moment, then shook his head. 'Still no.'

'Very well. I will see you . . .' he considered for a moment, 'every Monday, Wednesday and Friday between the hours of ten o'clock and twelve o'clock. Tea and b-b-biscuits to be provided by you.'

'That would be . . . fine.' Sherlock stared at Dodgson for a moment. 'What *is* the next number in the sequence?'

'I will let you tell me. It will give you something to think about between now and the next time we meet.'

Sherlock sensed that the discussion was at an end. He was about to get up and make his farewell when Dodgson said, 'Your brother – I haven't seen him for a good few years now. Well, they have been a good few years for me. I trust they have been good for him as well. How is his *character* nowadays? Does he still take offence easily? Does he hate to be teased?'

'He can be rather . . . prickly,' Sherlock conceded.

'Yes, I was afraid of that.' He frowned.

Sherlock wondered what exactly Dodgson's question was about. It seemed to be bothering the mathematician quite a bit. Suddenly he remembered what his brother had told him, about Dodgson writing children's books under the pen name Lewis Carroll. 'Are you proposing to put my brother in one of your books as a character?' he said, feeling a sudden elation. 'What a marvellous idea!'

Dodgson looked guilty. 'I have been thinking about it,' he confessed. 'Obviously your brother told you about my first book – *Alice's Adventures Under Ground*. It has done tolerably well, and I am considering a sequel, of sorts. Alice's c-c-continuing adventures, as it were. I have been telling the story piecemeal to the daughters of some friends, and the character of Humpty Dumpty has appeared in it – from where I do not know. You are familiar with the nursery rhyme?'

'Indeed.'

'It was only when I received your brother's letter asking me to take you under my wing that I suddenly realized, to my eternal shame and horror, that I appeared to have put M-M-Mycroft into my story as Humpty Dumpty!'

Sherlock had to stifle a laugh. 'Based on his . . . size?' he asked.

Dodgson nodded. 'Is he still . . . ?'

'More than ever,' Sherlock confirmed.

'That is not the whole of it,' Dodgson admitted. 'The character of Humpty Dumpty – haughty, rather argumentative, a pedant – that is how I remember your brother being.' He smiled. 'Not that it was a problem when he was here. I had, and always will have, the greatest respect for Mycroft. I am not, however, blind to his foibles.' A pause. 'Do you think he will mind?' he asked plaintively.

Sherlock thought for a moment. 'As long as the character is not *obviously* him,' he said eventually, 'I think he would be flattered. He would not, however, wish to be *recognized*, especially by those who do not know him very well.'

'Then I will plough on with the telling, and the writing, and send him a copy when it is finished, inscribed to the man who inspired the most majestic character in the whole book.'

'I think he would like that.'

'Then I think our business here is done, young man,' Dodgson said, clapping his hands together and springing to his feet. 'Now, if you will forgive me, I have a rook to bead, and you must be going. I will see you in two days at the appointed time. Don't forget the tea and biscuits.'

Sherlock stared at him for a few moments. Was Dodgson serious or not? 'If I bring the tea as *leaves*,' he asked, as if this was the most ordinary conversation in the world, 'and the biscuits in a bag, would you be able to work with them? It's just I'm not sure I can carry a tray with a pot and a plate all the way here, and the tea would probably get cold.'

'By all means bring the elements,' Dodgson replied, 'and we shall construct the final proposition together.'

'Thank you,' Sherlock said, baffled but also intrigued about what lay in store during his course in mathematics. He had a feeling that, at the very least, he wasn't going to be bored.

CHAPTER FOUR

Sherlock spent the rest of the day walking around Oxford and its environs, familiarizing himself with the town. The sun was shining, making the light-coloured stone from which the various colleges were constructed seem to glow in the ruddy afternoon light.

Sherlock never liked being in a place where he didn't know what was down the street or around the corner. Wherever he went, he had to know the local geography. He even bought a street map from a shop in the town and checked it as he walked, so that he learned the names of the areas through which he was passing.

While he wandered, he turned over and over in his mind the conversation he had engaged in with Charles Dodgson. The man had a very eccentric mind – that much was clear – but he had to be an able mathematician and logician, otherwise the University authorities would not let him lecture. They obviously turned a blind eye to the odder side of his personality. Sherlock wondered how much of that odder side was deliberate affectation.

It occurred to him that there were other things that he wanted to talk to Dodgson about, but that he had forgotten to mention. There was the question of how Dodgson could balance his serious mathematical work with his writing of books for children, for a start. There were a lot of things Sherlock wanted to know about his brother's early life too, when he was at Oxford. There was also the question of the thefts of body parts that had come up over dinner the previous night. Sherlock remembered Reginald Musgrave saying that Dodgson had been questioned about the matter, and he desperately wanted to get more facts from the man. Why body parts? How had they been stolen? Where had they gone? Sherlock found that, as he walked, his brain was turning more and more to these unanswered questions.

He knew what he was doing, of course. He was looking for a mystery. Over the past two years he had been confronted by several of them, seemingly insoluble ones, and he was getting a taste for thinking his way through a maze of conflicting evidence and impossibilities to find the truth within. Maybe this was another one.

Acting on the thought, Sherlock asked a couple of passing locals where the mortuary was. He wasn't sure why – he had no actual plans of going there – but he was interested to know. The first two people he asked – ladies doing their shopping – looked at him strangely and just carried on walking. Perhaps they thought it strange that a boy was asking about something as macabre as a place where bodies were stored. The third person – a burly, whiskered man in a waistcoat that was too small for him, muttered, 'Students!' and walked away. Fortunately the fourth person – a businessman in bowler hat and suit –

told him. It wasn't far away – part of the local hospital. He filed the location in his brain in case he ever needed it and continued on with his explorations of the town.

At one point he passed by a building that, according to the sign outside, was the place where the local newspaper was compiled, printed and distributed. He had discovered before that local newspapers were valuable resources of information, and equally valuable ways of getting messages out quickly to a large number of people. He had no intention of ever having to do that again, but then, he had never had any intention of doing it before, but that hadn't stopped it from being necessary in the past.

He grabbed lunch from a stall outside a tavern and kept on going, hitching lifts on hay-wains and carts so that he could get farther out into the surrounding countryside. By dinnertime he had seen outlying villages such as Jericho and Sunnymede, Wolvercote and Cowley, and in his head he had a more or less complete map of the whole area.

Towards dusk, as he was thinking of getting back to Mrs McCrery's lodging house to be ready for dinner, he found himself walking past a long brick wall. He was somewhere near the canal: he could smell the water and hear the voices of the bargemen as they called to one another. The wall was about ten feet high, and halfway along it was a set of gates. He was walking at this point, waiting for a passing cart that could take him back to the centre of Oxford, and he slowed down momentarily to look through the gates.

He saw something that he had seen before, but from a different direction.

It was the house that he and Matty had seen when they were on Matty's barge, heading into Oxford. He could only see a corner of it from the gate, but he knew instantly, instinctively, that it was the same place. His heart felt as if it lurched inside his chest as he looked at it, and he had the oddest urge to put his head on one side and squint in order to make sense of the construction of the house.

Even though he could only see a fraction of the place, it still appeared as if the various lines and angles that made it up didn't make any sense. He was reminded of the conversation he'd had with Charles Dodgson about the elements of Euclid. According to Euclidian geometry the interior angles of a triangle always added up to 180 degrees, but looking at the house Sherlock wondered if there was another kind of geometry entirely, one in which the angles of a triangle added up to less than, or more than, that, and in which parallel lines could actually meet at some distant point. The house gave the impression of being *skewed*, as if a giant hand had taken it and twisted it slightly, so that everything was out of true.

Despite the warmth of the day, he suddenly felt cold. He shivered. This was not logical. This was not *right*. Buildings couldn't inspire *feelings* like this, surely. They were just stone and brick and plaster and lathe. They couldn't inspire *dread* in the way that this building did. He was obviously hungry, and this was making him dizzy. Either that or the sun had caused a slight case of sunstroke.

A clattering behind him made him turn expectantly. If this was a cart heading for Oxford then he could ask for a ride. He could lie back and rest, and hopefully be more like himself when he got back to Mrs McCrery's. Once he had some food inside him, he would be fine.

It wasn't a cart; it was a carriage, constructed from black-painted wood and pulled by two entirely black horses. The driver was dressed in black as well: not just his clothes, but his broad-brimmed hat and the kerchief which was tied over the lower part of his face. Only his eyes could be seen, and in the late-afternoon sun they looked black too.

The carriage slowed as it approached the gates. Sherlock stepped out of the way, on to the grass verge. The gates opened, apparently by themselves, as Sherlock couldn't see any evidence of anyone pulling them. The horses turned into the gateway, and the carriage began to follow. Sherlock looked up into the window, and froze.

All he could see inside the carriage was a hand, resting on the lower part of the window frame. The hand was large and pale, and a crimson scar ran around its wrist. Other scars, also a livid red, ran around the bases of the fingers, where they joined the palm. A further scar ran up the arm, away from the wrist and into the darkness inside the carriage. All of the scars bore evidence of having been stitched at some time in the past.

And somehow Sherlock knew that he was being watched from inside the carriage by eyes that regarded him with interest but no emotion. Cold, empty eyes.

The whole incident took just a moment to play out, and then the carriage had passed him by and the gates were closing again. Sherlock stared after it, trying to work out what had just happened. The house might cause strange feelings of panic within him, and whoever lived there seemed to have the same effect. The owner and the property were perfectly matched.

He half walked and half ran along the wall to the corner, where the road went one way and the wall went off at a right angle – or maybe something that was close to a right angle but not exact. Sherlock headed away from the house, along the road, and felt a weight gradually lift from his mind.

What *was* that place?

Twenty minutes later a cart came along, and he hitched a lift back to Oxford with the farmer who was driving. Several times along the way Sherlock tried to ask the man about the house that he must have passed, but each time the words caught in his throat. He just didn't want to raise the subject.

After twenty minutes of silence, it was the driver himself who spoke first. 'You ought to be careful, wandering around them woods.'

'Why is that?' Sherlock asked, thinking that the man was going to raise the subject of the strange house himself. Instead he said, 'Folks are saying there's some kind of creature wandering around. I don't give it much credence myself, but other people say they've seen it – some godless thing that's been made out of bits of dead bodies, all sewn together. They even wrote to the local newspaper about it, but nothing happened. Like I say, I've never seen anything, but I still wouldn't wander around them woods by myself. You never know.'

'I'll be careful,' Sherlock said. He remembered the man he'd seen in the carriage that had driven into the strange house. His wrists had been marked with scars. Had someone glimpsed him in the shadows and drawn the wrong conclusion? 'Thanks for the warning.'

Back at his lodgings, Sherlock had time for a quick wash and a change of clothes before dinner. Three of the other lodgers were absent – probably eating in college – and Sherlock shared a quiet meal with the theologian, Thomas Millard, and the mathematician, Mathukumal Vijayaraghavan. Nobody had very much to say, and Sherlock went straight to bed afterwards.

Coming out of his bedroom the next morning, he bumped into the lanky Paul Chippenham coming down the stairs.

'Got anything on today?' Chippenham asked, pulling on his jacket as he passed Sherlock.

'Nothing,' Sherlock admitted. 'I thought about taking a look around Oxford – maybe going out on the river. What about you?'

'Lectures,' Chippenham called over his shoulder. 'We're doing gross anatomy – the structure of the skeleton and the arrangement of the internal organs.'

'I thought you were studying natural science?'

'Biology is part of that, and anatomy is part of biology. We're running a book on which of the students gets sick first and has to leave.'

Sherlock's brain spun for a few moments. Lectures in anatomy? That sounded fascinating.

'Could I come along?' he called after the student. The sound of the words coming out of his mouth surprised him, but a moment's thought confirmed his split-second decision. Why limit his subjects just to logic and mathematics, and why limit his teachers just to Charles Dodgson? Why not take advantage of all the teaching that Oxford had to offer?

Chippenham looked back up the stairs, frowning. 'I don't see why not,' he said finally. 'There's usually spaces at the back. Just don't draw attention to yourself, don't ask any questions and don't, really don't, be sick.'

'I promise,' Sherlock replied.

'We need to get a move on though. I'm late as it is.'

Sherlock followed Chippenham down the stairs and out of the house. The older student ran down the street, round the corner and towards the imposing facade of the college, with Sherlock doing his best to keep up. He waved at the Head Porter, Mutchinson, as he passed, and the man saluted smartly back. Chippenham ran around the edge of the lawn and ducked through a side-arch, with Sherlock on his heels. They were both panting by this time. Sherlock glanced up to where he remembered Dodgson's rooms as being, but there was no sign of the man at his window. Another two archways, and diagonally across a paved quadrangle, and then Chippenham was rushing into a narrow doorway and up some stairs.

At the top of the stairway, a door opened on to a lecture theatre. Sherlock had been expecting something like one of the classrooms back at Deepdene School for Boys, where he had initially been educated – desks lined up in rows with a teacher in front at a blackboard – but the room he found himself in was more like the theatre where he had seen the violinist, Pablo Sarasate, a few weeks before. The stage was smaller, and the slope downward from the top row of the audience to the bottom was much steeper, but the general feeling was similar. Except, he noticed, that there were no seats. Instead, the students were lined up – in some places crowded up – against a series of railings that ran around the edge of their balconies.

The noise was very much the same as in the theatre, with all of the students apparently talking at once to their neighbours, or yelling across from one side of the lecture theatre to the other.

Sherlock and Chippenham had come out on the top balcony. Chippenham quickly wriggled through the crowd, moving down the nearest set of steps to where a group of his friends were based. Sherlock stayed on the top row and found himself a gap in the crowd where he could stand against the railing and look downward.

They were just in time. The lecture hadn't started yet, but the lecturer himself was in position. Beside him was a table, covered with a white cloth. On the table, covered by the cloth, was a lumpy object that Sherlock, with a slight chill, realized was probably a dead body.

The lecturer was a tall man with bushy eyebrows and a bald spot on top of his head that shone in the glare of the flickering gaslights that were placed around the lecture theatre. Sherlock could smell the press of all of the students' bodies, as well as their various shaving lotions and hair tonics. Beneath that smell was the smell of the burning gas, and beneath that was a sharp smell, like disinfectant.

The lecturer stepped forward. Immediate silence fell. He was obviously highly respected, or a strict disciplinarian, or both.

'A word before we start, gentlemen,' he said in a deep voice that carried to every nook and cranny of the tall room. 'Shortly you will watch me as I take a body apart, piece by piece, demonstrating to you at every stage what the various bits do and how they are connected to the rest. Next year you will, if you are allowed to return

71

to this college, take a body apart yourselves. These are important – even vital – parts of your education. If we go back in history, people have believed all kinds of odd things about the human body that have turned out not to be true, and that have only been proved false by direct observation of the *insides*.' He paused, gazing around with his penetrating eyes. 'Please remember two things, however. Firstly, bear in mind that students in your situation are fortunate enough to be living in an enlightened time, when students who wish to become doctors or surgeons are able to see how the human body works by examining an actual human body. There have been times, not that many years ago, when such things were forbidden, for religious or for ethical reasons. Secondly, these bodies, which we so casually dismember, were once living people, and that they have donated their body voluntarily for your education. Treat them with the respect they deserve.' He placed his hand on the sheeted body beside him. 'This is Mr Adam Bagshawe, lately of this parish. We are indebted to Mrs Rachel Bagshawe for donating her husband's body for the purposes of medical research, as per the wishes expressed in his will. I may inadvertently refer to Mr Bagshawe's body as "it" later, as if I was referring to a piece of machinery, or a block of wood, but try to keep in mind, as I will try, that there was once a man's soul inhabiting this machine, this block, and that he had loves and hates and desires similar to yours.'

72

The students were mesmerized by this introduction. Glancing around, Sherlock could see that the lecturer's words had hit home. A few of the students were swallowing nervously, presumably imagining that one day it might be them lying on a table in a lecture theatre, rather than the unfortunate Mr Bagshawe.

The lecturer plucked at the sheet covering Mr Bagshawe's body, bunching the material up, and then paused. He glanced around the lecture theatre again, frowning.

'You may have heard talk around the town,' he added, 'or perhaps seen reports in the local newspapers, that parts of human bodies have been stolen from the local mortuary in recent months. It may have occurred to you that these thefts have been, in some way, connected to this course of lectures – either to obtain fresh specimens for us to use here in front of you or, perhaps, by more mature students undertaking some form of grotesque homework. I can assure you that the former is not true – every body that we dissect here has been provided whole, by the family of the unfortunate deceased. I can also assure you that if any students were found to be obtaining body parts illegally, by theft or other means, so that they can conduct their own research after hours, they would be immediately dismissed from the college, and prosecuted to the full extent that the law allows. We do not – I repeat, do not – countenance that sort of activity. Do I make myself clear?'

He was silent then, staring around and meeting every set of eyes that was fixed on him, until a murmur of assent rippled around the room.

'Very well,' he continued eventually. 'Now, let us meet Mr Adam Bagshawe.'

He pulled the sheet off the body. A hushed silence fell around the room. Sherlock found himself thinking, bizarrely, of the deaths he had witnessed. He had probably seen more death than anybody else in that room, save the lecturer, but he still leaned forward, hushed in reverence, as the lecture continued.

After the body of the late, unfortunate Mr Bagshawe had been comprehensively sliced up and his various internal organs displayed for public appreciation, and after no less than five of the students in the audience had been suddenly taken ill and had to run for the door, the lecture finished. As the remaining students clapped politely the lecturer covered the remains of Mr Bagshawe with a sheet – which immediately began to stain with the seepage of blood from the corpse – and two assistants wheeled it away. Sherlock stood there for a while, as the students filed past him, thinking about what he had seen. Thinking about the fact that the miracles of the human body could be treated in much the same way as the cogs, wheels and springs within a clock – disassembled and laid out on a table for inspection. The difference being, of course, that the various components of the body couldn't be reassembled, whereas a clock could. Life, once gone, could not be regained. So what, he thought to himself, did that make life? Was it the same as the soul? Was it the same as consciousness? What exactly was it?

Big questions. Perhaps that was what University was for, in the end. Not answering the big questions, necessarily, but asking them.

Eventually he left the auditorium. The sun was shining outside, and Matty was waiting for him.

''Avin' fun?' Matty asked.

'I've been looking at a dead body,' Sherlock confided.

Matty thought for a moment. 'Is that a yes or a no?' He looked at Sherlock, then shook his head. 'Never mind. I'm assumin' it's a "yes" in your case. You love all that kind of stuff.'

Sherlock was about to reply, pointing out that he also liked all kinds of things that people might consider normal, when he saw Chippenham across the other side of the paved area, talking to some friends. He was about to suggest to Matty that they head across to join Chippenham when he saw two men in blue serge uniforms and helmets walking over as well. He held back, watching.

One of the men took hold of Chippenham's elbow. 'Mr Paul Chippenham?' he asked.

The student look puzzled, and concerned. 'Yes. Who are you?'

'I am Sergeant Clitherow, of the Oxford Constabulary.

This is my colleague, Constable Harries. We'd like to ask you a few questions.'

'Oh. All right then – what do you want to know?'

'Not here, sir. Down at the police station, if you'd be so kind.'

'I've got a tutorial!' Chippenham protested.

'Don't worry, sir – this won't take long, and there'll be other tutorials, I'm sure.'

One of Chippenham's friends stepped forward. 'I'm studying law,' he said, trying to sound officious but just sounding pretentious. 'I demand that you tell us why you want to talk to Mr Chippenham.'

'Inquiries in connection with a series of recent thefts,' the sergeant replied.

'Thefts of bodies,' the constable confided. 'Well, bits of bodies.'

The sergeant stared at him, frowning, and the constable subsided.

'Is Mr Chippenham a suspect?' the law student asked.

The sergeant shrugged. 'Let's say he's helping us with our inquiries,' he said. He turned to Chippenham. 'Aren't you, sir? Might look suspicious if you refused. Might look like you had something to hide, like.'

'I'll come along and answer any questions you've got,' Chippenham said firmly, but Sherlock could detect a slight tremor in his voice. Chippenham turned to his friends. 'Tell my tutor,' he said. 'Let him know what's happened. He might be able to . . . intercede with the police, or something.'

The policemen guided Chippenham away by the elbow. He cast a last, despairing glance over his shoulder before they vanished around a corner.

'I'm glad I'm not 'im,' Matty said darkly. 'The Oxford police have a reputation. They don't like cheek, or anyone talking back to them. 'E'd better cooperate, otherwise 'e'll find 'imself trippin' up every time 'e walks down a flight of stairs. Man could do 'imself some nasty injuries that way.'

'I can't see him being guilty,' Sherlock said.

'Why's that then?'

'He seems too normal, too ordinary. And when he talked about the thefts, the other night at Mrs McCrery's, he was completely open.' Sherlock shrugged. 'I suppose you can't tell what's in people's minds, but I'd like to know if there's any evidence against him. I'm not convinced that the police actually care that much about evidence, just as long as they have someone in the cells.'

'Surely,' Matty reasoned, 'if there keep on bein' thefts, then they'll have to let him go.'

'Not necessarily,' Sherlock said bleakly. 'The thief might stop for other reasons. Or, if I were them and someone had been arrested for the crimes I was committing, I might move to a different area, a different mortuary, and start again.'

'You've got a cunnin' mind,' Matty pointed out. 'Ever

thought of becomin' a criminal yourself?'

It was much later in the evening, after dinner, that Paul Chippenham returned to Mrs McCrery's boarding house. He was pale, and his hands shook as he sipped at the sherry that Reginald Musgrave poured him. There was a fresh bruise on his forehead.

'What happened?' Sherlock asked.

'They asked me a lot of questions about the Oxford hospital mortuary, and why I had been visiting it. I tried to persuade them that it was nothing suspicious, but they were fixated on the idea that I was the one who had stolen those body parts that have been in the newspaper, and that the lecturer mentioned this morning.' He raised a hand to the bruise on his forehead. 'Things got a bit . . . physical . . . and the constable belted me across the head when he thought I was being cheeky.'

'What did you tell them?' Thomas Millard wanted to know.

'The truth.' He looked embarrassed. 'It was going to be a jape – a joke. A small group of us were going to steal a body from the mortuary, dress it up like a student and prop it up in the lecture theatre for the anatomy lecture. We thought it would be funny, knowing that there was a dead body in the audience as well as on the table.'

'Sacrilege, treating God's creation like that,' Millard murmured, shaking his head sadly, but he didn't sound surprised. Presumably it was the kind of thing that students regularly got up to.

'I'm guessing that you didn't manage to get hold of a body,' Sherlock said.

Chippenham shook his head. 'The pathologist – Doctor Lukather by name – was too fly. He wouldn't give me the time of day, let alone a look at a body. I told the police that. They said they'd check with Lukather, but they seemed to believe me. I won't say they were satisfied, but they let me go.'

The conversation moved on to famous jokes and japes that had been played by students on each other, and on the lecturers, over the years. Sherlock slipped out after a while and went up to his room. He had a lot to think about.

The next morning he rose early, had breakfast and went straight out into the town. Something had occurred to him overnight, and he wanted to try it out.

He went straight to the offices of the *Oxford Post*. At the reception, he asked to see whichever reporter was on desk duty that day. He knew that most reporters would be out researching stories, but there was always one left behind just in case anyone wandered in with something.

The one left behind today was Ainsley Dunbard, a man not that much older than Sherlock with a sparse moustache and beard and an expression that suggested he'd seen too much of life and didn't like what he had seen.

'What can I do for ya?' he asked when Sherlock was shown to his 'office' – actually a room barely larger than a broom cupboard with a desk, a typewriter and no window.

'Sorry to bother you,' Sherlock started, 'but I'm interested in becoming a reporter myself when I leave school. I wondered if there are any tips you can give me?'

'Just what I need,' the man muttered; 'competition.' He stared at his desk, then at the wall. 'There's only a couple of things you need to know,' he said eventually, sighing. 'First is, always check your facts. Make sure that if you print something, at least two people have told you about it, and check that the first person didn't tell the second one.'

Sherlock dutifully wrote this down in a notebook he had bought from a stationer's just a few minutes before.

'Second thing is, people don't talk in a way that makes good newspaper reporting, so you got to tidy it up. Take out the "um"s an' the "ah"s an' the "oh, I say"s, an' put the events in the right order, cos people tend to remember things out of order an' keep correctin' themselves. When it all gets printed they'll remember it the way you wrote it, not the way they said it. Third –' and he glanced sideways at Sherlock through eyes that were bloodshot and tired – 'remember that if a dog bites a man then it ain't news, but if a man bites a dog then it is. People want stories that are out of the ordinary, maybe a bit grotesque.' He thought for a moment. 'Take this story I worked on last year,' he continued. 'Some people wrote to me from one of the local villages. It was like a petition – they all signed the letter. They told me that there's this creature that lives in the woods near them who's not actually a real man, with a mother an' all that, but 'e's been *made* by sewing bits of dead bodies together. Now *that's* macabre. Would've made a great story, except that it sounds just like that book *Frankenstein* by the poet's wife – Mary Shelley. I reckon someone'd read the book, or seen the play, an' 'ad a nightmare about it. Too much cheese for supper, I 'spect.' He sighed. 'I did do a bit of digging around, just in case, but I couldn't find any corroboration. There was nothing to the story.'

This story sounded like the one he'd heard from the farmer who had given him a lift back to Oxford – about the strange creature living in the woods near that strange house. It suddenly gave Sherlock an opportunity that he had thought he might have to manufacture himself. 'Talking of bits of bodies,' he said, deliberately roughening his tone a bit to match the journalist's, 'what 'appened at the mortuary then? I hear there was some thefts there. Nothin' to do with this creature then?'

Dunbard nodded. ''S right. Strangest thing I ever heard of. Couldn't make it up, if you know what I mean. 'Parently it's been 'appening for a while – someone dies, their body is brought into the mortuary for an autopsy, an' then they're sent off for burial, but it turns out that there's less of the bodies bein' buried than there was at the autopsy. Always different bits missin' – eyes, ears, hands, feet, anythin'. I did wonder if it was connected to that monster story, but I reckon it's just students muckin' around.'

'Bodysnatchers?' Sherlock ventured, remembering the lecturer at Christ College.'

'Nah – they'd've taken the whole body. That's where the money is. Bits of bodies aren't worth anything.'

'How did it get discovered?'

He laughed – a bitter sound, like a barking dog. 'Gent buried 'is wife, then realized she'd been interred along with 'er weddin' ring, some earrings an' a pearl necklace, so he 'ad her disinterred. Trouble is, the ears was missin'. Cue big rumpus an' lots of runnin' around.'

'And nobody knows where these body parts have gone, or who took them?'

Dunbard shook his head. 'Not a clue. The police're stumped. We've run out of different ways of reportin' the case, so we've stopped runnin' the story.'

'Didn't I read that the police questioned a lecturer from Christ Church College?'

'That's right,' Dunbard confirmed. 'We never actually named 'im, because it turned out 'e had an alibi for all the dates on which things went missin'.'

'And did you ever talk to the pathologist in the mortuary?' Sherlock asked. It was an important question, as the answer would dictate what he did next, but he tried to make his tone as innocent as possible.

'Nah. Tried to, but 'e wouldn't see me.' He shrugged.

'Okay, is that it? Cos I've got an important story about silt in the canal to type up.'

'Yes. Thanks.' Sherlock started to move away, then turned back. 'Sorry, but do you have a business card, or a visiting card or something? Just in case I have any more questions?'

Dunbard reached into his shirt pocket and took out a slip of cardboard. ''Ere's me details, but you can find me in this place most days.' As Sherlock was walking away he heard the man saying, more to himself than to Sherlock, 'an' to think I left the *London Gazette* for this. Supposed to be more responsibility, but the office cat gets out more than I do!'

Sherlock tucked the business card into a pocket of his jacket. He had plans for it, and didn't want it to get lost.

CHAPTER FIVE

Sherlock left the newspaper building and headed in the direction of the mortuary. Oxford Hospital was an impressive red-brick building set in the middle of a small lawn. The mortuary was in its own single-storey building, set discreetly off to one side. Walking through the hospital grounds towards it, Sherlock took a deep breath and ran over in his mind the story he was going to tell. Of course, it all depended on how well-known the reporter Ainsley Dunbard was. If the doctor who carried out the post-mortems on the bodies of the dead knew Dunbard by sight, then Sherlock's entire ruse was doomed from the start, but Sherlock had specifically asked Dunbard if he had interviewed the pathologist, and the answer had been in the negative. Surely the reporter would have mentioned if he had known the pathologist from before?

The door to the mortuary was white-painted, with panes of frosted glass set into the top. Sherlock knocked smartly on the glass. A voice from inside called: 'Enter!'

Sherlock walked in and shut the door behind him. He wasn't sure what to expect – dead bodies stacked up on shelves perhaps? – and he was a bit nervous as a result, but in fact he found himself standing in a long corridor that ended with the mortuary's back door, which appeared to be bolted from the inside. The only indication that he was somewhere medical was the strong smell of disinfectant that assailed his nostrils.

'Yes – who are you?' a man said, stepping out of one of the side doors. He wore a white coat and gloves, both stained in ways that Sherlock didn't want to think about. The man himself was elderly, with a thick white moustache and white hair that was brushed straight back from his forehead. His face was lined and also tanned. In a part of his mind, Sherlock wondered if he had been abroad in the recent past.

'My name is Ainsley Dunbard,' Sherlock said, holding out the business card he had taken from the *real* Ainsley Dunbard and holding his breath. This was the point where his bluff might be called. 'I'm a reporter for the *Oxford Post*.'

'You're a bit young for a reporter, surely?' the man said, raising bushy eyebrows in surprise. He took off his gloves, reached for the business card and examined it suspiciously.

Sherlock took a relieved breath. The man clearly didn't know who Dunbard was. 'I'm actually an apprentice,' he said apologetically. 'The paper has taken me on so I can get some work experience. I want to be a full reporter one day.'

'Good for you,' the man said. 'I admire someone with a touch of ambition. M'name's Lukather – Doctor

Wilberforce Lukather. What can I do for you?'

'I was hoping that the newspaper could do a feature on you,' Sherlock said. He wanted, of course, to ask about the theft of body parts, but that would raise Lukather's suspicions straight away, and he would probably be refused an interview. On the other hand, if he started off by asking about the job of a pathologist, and then gradually got around to the thefts – or, even better, Lukather volunteered the information himself – then he would get what he needed and the pathologist would be none the wiser.

'A feature?' Lukather said, suspicious but intrigued at the same time. 'Why on earth would anyone want to know about me?'

'Well, it's the final mystery, isn't it?' Sherlock asked, remembering his thoughts after the lecture: 'What happens when we die? How does a vital, alive person suddenly become a block of flesh and bone and tissue? What happens to the soul? What happens to the personality? These questions are the kind of thing that would fascinate our readers, and you are right at the sharp end, dealing with a person's final moments every day of your life! People will be fascinated!'

'Never really thought about it that way,' Lukather said, brushing his moustache. 'Autopsy work has always been the un-regarded cousin of the medical profession.'

'Not any more,' Sherlock promised. 'I want to open the whole thing out – get your opinions on the whole business of life and death. Would that be all right?'

'I suppose it would.' He took a watch from the pocket of his waistcoat. 'I can spare half an hour, I suppose. I was about to make a pot of tea. Can I interest you in a cup?'

Lukather led the way into a small room with several chairs – somewhere that grieving relatives could be comforted, Sherlock assumed. Light was provided by a large skylight in the roof. They spent the next hour – far longer than the thirty minutes that Lukather had promised – with Sherlock asking questions about the process of death and autopsy, and Lukather answering them carefully and with due gravity. Despite the fact that he desperately wanted to get on to the subject of the theft of body parts, Sherlock was fascinated. This man was, in his own quiet way, a genius! His job – in fact, as it turned out, his passion – was taking the evidence that was set out on the metal tables in his laboratory – the bodies of people who had died unusually or suspiciously – and painstakingly searching inside them for evidence as to how and why they had died. It was very much what Sherlock had started thinking that he might do with his own life, with the exception that it was confined to a laboratory rather than taking place out in the real world. In a strange way it was the kind of thing that Mycroft might have ended up doing, if he could have conducted autopsies from the comfort of an armchair.

Sherlock was particularly interested in how Lukather could tell the difference between an accidental death and a murder. Flattered by the attention, Lukather was very informative on the subject.

'Let us assume,' he said, taking a sip of his tea, 'that you are called in to a place where a man's body has been discovered. Let us say that it is his bedroom. He is lying beside his bed, face down. There are no obvious marks of violence – no blows to the face, no blood, no stab wounds or suchlike. The body is just lying peacefully on the floor. Now, the average constable might think the man died from a heart attack or a stroke, and perhaps ask the man's family whether he has been feeling out of sorts recently, but you as a medical man are not so easily convinced. Rather than making a decision and then seeking evidence to back it up, you look for the evidence first and then see where it leads you. So, you have the body brought back to the mortuary here, and you examine it from head to foot. Perhaps you notice that the corpse's face is unnaturally pink, which may indicate that he has suffocated after breathing in a poisonous gas such as carbon monoxide. Now, having found that, you ask the constable to investigate the man's bedroom carefully. Is there a stove there that might have produced carbon monoxide that filled the room so that he breathed it in? Are the windows closed, despite the fact that it is summer, meaning that perhaps someone deliberately closed them so that the carbon monoxide has no way to escape? Maybe there is no stove, but is there perhaps evidence that a pipe has been introduced into the room through a wall or the floor through which carbon monoxide might have been pumped from a stove outside? You see the kinds of questions you might start to ask, just based on the fact that the corpse has an unnaturally pink face?'

'I see,' Sherlock replied, fascinated.

'Alternatively, the corpse might *not* have a pink face, but you might notice a small pinprick wound on a shoulder or on the neck. Perhaps the man was accidentally stung by a wasp and died of a severe reaction, but if so you might expect to find some swelling around the wound. Or if there is no swelling, then perhaps the man was injected deliberately with some poisonous substance from a hypodermic syringe while he was asleep, in which case you are back to deliberate action again.'

Sherlock nodded.

'Or you might not find any pinprick wounds, but inside the man's mouth there is evidence of blistering, suggesting that he drank or ate something toxic. You ask the constable again to look in the man's bedroom for evidence of food or drink, and if it is found then you test it on a rat, perhaps. If there is nothing there, or if the things that are there are innocuous when fed to a rat, then you might suspect that the man was given something poisonous, which killed him, but then the evidence was removed by his killer. Do you see?'

'Absolutely.'

'But let us say that there is no blistering inside the mouth either. You then have to investigate *inside* the body, by cutting it open. You may find a blood clot inside the heart, in which case you might report a heart attack as the cause of death. You might find that the liver is enlarged and scarred, in which case you might diagnose liver failure due to excessive alcoholism as the cause of death. You might find some aneurism in the brain which has resulted from a defect in the blood vessels. You might find that there is something caught in the gullet which has caused the man to choke. All of these would indicate death from natural causes. However, if the man has been suffocated, perhaps by having a pillow held over his face, then in my experience there would likely be broken blood vessels in the eyes, caused by the struggle for breath, and perhaps evidence of bruising around the mouth. If alternatively the man has been strangled then there might be marks either on the surface of the neck or beneath the skin, and there are certain small bones that might well have been broken by the pressure. All of these indications, taken together, might point towards deliberate or accidental death.' He paused for a moment. 'Perhaps, when you examine the body, you find that despite the initial apparent absence of any wounds there is actually a depression of the skull, hidden beneath the hairline. Did the man accidentally fall as he was getting out of bed, getting his legs caught in the bed sheets perhaps, and knock his head against the wall, or the head of the bed? If so, you might find hairs the same colour as his, or marks from his hair oil, on the plaster of the wall or the wood of the bed. If those hairs or marks are not there, then you might conclude that you are back to deliberate action, and you would suggest to the constable that he looks around the house for a stick or a club that *does* have these traces.'

'This is fascinating!' Sherlock said.

'The problem is,' Lukather sighed, 'that most of the time I end up with a body on my table where the cause of death is sadly all too obvious. The poor fellow might have been hit over the head by a bottle during a fight in a tavern, or caught himself with the sharp point of a scythe when cutting corn, or he might have tripped over in the street and had his neck run over by a cart. It's all too rare that I get something interesting to exercise my brain properly.'

Sherlock thought quickly. He wanted to get Lukather around to talking about the theft of body parts from the mortuary that he had heard about, but that was likely to be a sensitive subject, and Lukather might get angry about being questioned directly. Sherlock already had the impression that he was a bit of a prickly customer. He would have to lead around gradually to the subject.

He remembered again the anatomy lecture that he had attended in Christ Church College. That might give him a lead-in.

'I presume,' he said carefully, 'that in order to detect all of these various signs of natural or unnatural death that you must have trained on lots of bodies which had died in different ways?'

'Oh, of course,' Lukather said. 'You can't spot the signs of carbon-monoxide poisoning unless you have seen several bodies that you know died of the same thing. You can't recognize the signs of a heart attack unless you have cut open many, many hearts and seen what they look like under all conditions.'

'Isn't there a bit of a problem with the process of anatomy?' Sherlock went on. 'I mean, I presume that a lot of people are very religious, and object to the bodies of their relatives being cut open and examined by a group of students. Partly I suppose they want their relatives buried intact, but partly they don't want them being gawped at and perhaps laughed at. And you do hear about some students playing practical jokes with the bodies – leaving them in chairs in people's rooms and suchlike.'

'It is true,' Lukather sighed, 'that the supply of bodies for anatomy lessons is . . . problematic. Fortunately, there are enlightened people who make it a condition of their will that their body be left to science for medical investigation. There are also those poor unfortunates who die with no family or friends, and therefore there is nobody to have any say in what happens.'

'I presume,' Sherlock said carefully, 'that there might be a tendency, perhaps in other, less moral institutions, to accept bodies from . . . dubious sources?'

'You mean bodysnatchers?' Lukather's mouth twisted into an angry line. 'Yes, there have been times in the past when some unprincipled researchers have accepted, as you say, "bodies from dubious sources".' He stared at Sherlock from beneath his shaggy eyebrows. 'I hope you are not suggesting that I have *ever* taken advantage of such a grotesque opportunity? I treat the bodies in this mortuary with the utmost care, and I have never accepted a body where I have not been completely sure where it came from!'

'Of course!' Sherlock said, raising his hands. 'I did not mean to imply anything else. I just wondered whether you have ever heard of anything like that happening to anyone else?' He held his breath for a long moment.

Lukather frowned and looked away. 'I presume,' he said stiffly, 'that you are referring to the thefts that have recently occurred here.'

Sherlock tried to look as reassuring as possible. 'I realize it is a sensitive subject, and I also realize how much you must be professionally offended by it, but I was wondering whether you had any theories as to why the thefts had occurred?'

'I am at a loss.' Lukather frowned. 'If it had been entire *bodies* that had been stolen, then I might think they had been taken as a prank, by students, or so that a hospital or medical university that was short of bodies for training might obtain some in an underhand manner, but *parts* of bodies? It makes no sense!'

'Can you tell me what exactly happened?' Sherlock asked.

'It is, on the face of it, very simple, and yet very puzzling. On perhaps ten or twelve occasions I have left a body here in one state, and when I came back the next morning I found it . . .' he paused, apparently distressed, '*diminished.*'

'And what parts were taken?'

'Various ones. On several occasions a hand has been removed at the wrist. On one occasion an entire arm was taken. Several ears have been cut away from the head. Two feet – one left and one right – were taken at different times.'

'And . . . forgive me for asking . . . this wasn't scavenging animals, like wild dogs or foxes?'

'Absolutely not. The missing parts were removed with a knife or a hacksaw, not chewed or bitten off. This was not wild creatures scavenging for food. And besides, hands and feet and ears are not the obvious targets for hungry animals. They have precious little meat.'

'Which raises another interesting question,' Sherlock said. 'No . . . internal organs.'

Lukather frowned. 'What are you getting at?'

'It just seems an odd selection,' Sherlock went on. 'Hands, arms, ears, feet . . . they are all, if you like, obvious body parts – the things you can see in a person when they are walking along. From what you have said, no *hidden* bits have been taken. No bits beneath clothing, or beneath the skin.'

'That is a good point,' Lukather acknowledged.

'Which does suggest that it has nothing to do with a student prank – as they would probably much rather take the whole body and leave it somewhere amusing. It also suggests that it has nothing to do with medical teaching, as they would be more interested in the internal organs – the heart, the lungs and so on.'

'Also a good point.'

'Which leaves us still with a puzzle.' Sherlock considered. 'Why would anybody take just those things?'

'I don't know.'

'Is there any security here?'

Lukather looked embarrassed. 'It never occurred to me that it was necessary. There was nothing valuable here, nothing we thought was worth stealing. The front door was locked and the back door was bolted when I left, of course. There is a skylight but that is sealed shut. The only possible way in is a small window that we leave open for ventilation, but it is far too small for a man to climb through. The hospital gates are locked at night too, of course,' Lukather added, 'but that's of little use. There are plenty of trees that overhang the wall which a thief could use to get into the grounds, and I know that there is at least one place where the wall is crumbling and someone could get through, if they were small enough.

Once I knew that the thefts were occurring I made sure that the door was double-locked and the skylight sealed, but somehow the thief still managed to find a way in. I did ask the police to mount a guard, but they told me they were too busy doing *important* work.'

'Who had the key to the door?'

'There is only one copy, and I have it myself.' Lukather delved into one of his pockets and brought out a bunch of keys on a chain. He selected the largest one. 'This is it. Stays with me all the time. Never leaves my person.'

Sherlock thought for a moment. Maybe the thefts of the body parts were covering up something else?

'Were any valuables kept here – from the bodies? Things like watches, or jewellery, or even wallets?'

Lukather shook his head firmly. 'All that kind of thing would have been removed by the constables before the bodies were brought to me. They would have been kept at the police station as evidence.'

'The bodies were brought straight here from the places they were discovered?'

'They were.'

'And they go from here to . . . ?'

'To the undertakers, to be prepared for burial.'

Sherlock shook his head, confused. 'I can't see why anybody would want to steal parts of bodies. It just seems so . . . bizarre.'

'I know. It has me puzzled too.'

'Do the police have any suspects?' Sherlock asked

the question innocently, but he already knew what the answer was likely to be.

'There's some chappie who keeps asking me if he can take one of these newfangled photograph thingies of the bodies. I think he's a lecturer at Christ Church College. He says he wants to record them for posterity. I can see the point, of course – it would be valuable for teaching purposes – but there's something about his manner that I find a bit strange, so I keep saying no. He's very insistent. I told the police about him, and I think they have taken him in for questioning, but there is no direct evidence that he might be involved. Oh, and there's a student as well – a Mr Chippenham. He's an odd one too. Studying natural science, but he's tried to get in here a couple of times. Claimed that he wanted to do some extracurricular research, if you please! I told the police, of course, and I think they've questioned him as well.'

'Yes, they have,' Sherlock murmured. He looked up to find Lukather staring at him penetratingly. 'I heard one of the other reporters talking about it,' he said quickly.

'I see.'

Sherlock glanced down at his tea cup. It was, fortunately, empty. 'Could I possibly have another cup?' he asked. 'I'm fascinated by everything you've been saying, and I'd like to stay for a little longer, if you would let me.'

Lukather nodded. 'Nice to have someone here who isn't spooked by the whole idea of dead bodies on the premises,' he said. He got up and started to head out to the little kitchen area, then stopped and stared at a picture on the wall. 'I never married,' he said. 'There was a girl once, but when she discovered what I did every day, she ended it. Said she couldn't stand the idea of me touching dead bodies all day long then coming home and kissing her. Never met anyone after that. Never saw the point.' He shook himself, then walked out into the kitchen. Sherlock glanced at the picture on the wall. It was a drawing of a woman in her twenties, striking rather than beautiful, but with large, soulful eyes. Then he looked at the door through which Lukather had vanished, and sighed. It was sad, he thought, how a man could choose a career that cut him off from ever having a happy home life.

He pulled himself together. He had work to do, and quickly. He stood up and reached out for the bunch of keys, which Lukather had left on the table next to his own cup. He picked them up. They were surprisingly heavy. He quickly flicked through them until he found the largest one – the key to the door of the mortuary. He held it up to his eyes, wishing momentarily that he had something that would allow him to see the detail of the key clearer – a magnifying glass, or something like that. He was looking for traces of material caught in one or two of the metal corners between the tines of the key – little flecks of something like clay, or putty. That might indicate that someone had taken the key from Lukather's key ring while he wasn't paying attention – while he was asleep perhaps – and pressed it into a block of clay, leaving an impression. Once they had taken the impression, they could have returned the original key immediately. They could have then used the impression to mould a new key out of some metal with a low melting point. They might even have carved a copy out of some hard wood. All it would have taken was time, and a little skill. The copy – whether it was metal or wood – wouldn't have to last for very long: just enough for them to get in and out of the mortuary late at night several times.

The problem was, there were no traces of anything. The key was pristine. That didn't mean that it hadn't been copied, of course – just that if it had then the evidence had been removed.

He put the key back on the table just as Lukather returned.

'Did the thefts of the body parts occur on a regular basis?' he asked. 'I mean, every week, or every month?'

Lukather thought for a moment. His brow creased in a frown. 'I don't recall the exact dates,' he said eventually. 'Let me check my diary.' He reached across to a table and retrieved a leather-bound volume. He pulled up his half-moon spectacles, which were hanging from a chain around his neck, and perched them on his nose. He flicked through the diary, sometimes going backwards or forwards a few pages to check something and then returning to where he had been. 'I have the dates here,' he said eventually. 'I made sure I recorded them all. The problem is that there is no obvious correlation between them. They never happened on the same day of the week, or the same day of the month.' He shook his head in irritation. 'There's no obvious pattern. If there was, I would have spotted it. I even wondered whether the thefts might have occurred every full moon, perhaps, but that was not the case.'

'Because the full moon would have provided the most amount of light for the thief?' Sherlock guessed.

'Partly that, but partly also because there is a known correlation between insanity and the night of the full moon.' Lukather took his glasses off and polished them with a small cloth from his pocket. 'Nobody is quite sure why,' he went on, 'but lunatics do appear to be influenced by moonlight. The fact has been known for years. Indeed the very word "lunatic" derives from "*luna*", the Latin word for "moon".'

'Could I have a look at the diary?' Sherlock asked. 'I realize it's your own private information, but I think there might be some pattern there, if only I can spot it.'

'It's not as if I have an active social life,' Lukather said heavily. 'There is nothing there I would be ashamed for my mother to see, if she were still alive, and if she had ever cared about what I do for a living.'

'And there's no confidential police information in there – reports of the autopsies themselves, or something like that?'

He shook his head. 'That's all put into special reports on printed forms, and collected by hand by the police.' He handed the diary across. 'The dates where the thefts occurred are marked by a large exclamation mark in the top right-hand corner,' he said. 'While you take a look I'll go and check on that kettle.'

Sherlock went backwards through the dates, starting that day. The entries were in neat, precise handwriting. They mainly covered meetings with the police or with the medical authorities in the hospital, dates for inquests or court appearances, dates blocked out for autopsies to take place, with the names of the deceased carefully recorded, with the occasional note for 'reception' or 'dinner'. Whenever Sherlock came across an exclamation mark in the top right-hand corner of a day he made a note in his own notebook of the date, the day of the week, the phase of the moon (which was conveniently noted by the diary's printers by means of a small illustration showing what the moon would have looked like on each day) and what Lukather had been doing on that day and on the day before, just in case that was relevant. There was, as Lukather had said, no obvious relationship between the dates. Sherlock looked in particular at the numbers of days between the incidents, but they varied – sometimes thirty days, sometimes forty, sometimes only eight.

Except . . .

Except that something was bothering Sherlock. There was a pattern there, somewhere – he just couldn't see it. He needed time to concentrate.

Lukather came back then with another tray of tea and biscuits. Sherlock opened his mouth to say, 'I'm really sorry, but I need to go . . .' but then he saw from the pathologist's eager expression how much he was enjoying having the unexpected company. If Sherlock left now, then, he suspected, Lukather would just sit there for a long time, alone, drinking the tea and eating the biscuits, maybe staring at the portrait of the woman hanging on the wall. 'Are you sure I'm not imposing on your time too much?' he asked instead.

'Not in the slightest,' the pathologist replied. 'I have a foreign student from the University, a Mr Daniel Hussein, on my table at the moment. He arrived but recently from the Middle East, and then dropped dead at a market at Rokeby, nearby. I suspect a pre-existing disease, which is why I have taken precautions to isolate the body and wash it with carbolic acid. I will sterilize my tools afterwards, twice, just to make sure. But yes, Mr Hussein can wait while we finish our tea and biscuits. He isn't going anywhere.'

A thought came to Sherlock that really should have occurred before. He frowned, considering it. 'If the thefts happen at night,' he said, 'then that means the bodies are actually stored here. I mean, they aren't taken away as soon as the post-mortem examination has taken place.'

'That's correct,' Lukather confirmed. 'Sometimes, if there have been a lot of deaths, then I have a queue waiting for my attention, so they have to be stored in a separate room. The room is cooled with ice, to prevent . . .' he hesitated, '. . . to prevent the natural processes of decomposition from taking place. Also, I sometimes finish a post-mortem examination late in the day, after the funeral directors have closed, and the body has to wait to be collected the next day. On rare occasions, if I cannot determine a cause of death, then another pathologist has to be called in to examine it, and that also takes time. So, for all these reasons, there are always bodies in the mortuary. It is no stretch for the thief to know that.'

They sat there for the next forty-five minutes, with Sherlock asking as many questions as he could about death, the various ways it might happen and the evidence that would be left behind in each case. In particular he found that the pathologist was very experienced in poisons that mimicked symptoms of disease, so that a woman who had died from drinking a tea made with belladonna leaves could well be diagnosed as having died of a heart attack if the pathologist wasn't paying particular attention to his job. Again Sherlock found himself thinking back to something that he had been involved in, but in this case it was the death of the philanthropist Sir Benedict Ventham in Edinburgh, who had been killed in a very similar way to the one Lukather had described.

They did circle back to talking about the thefts, briefly.

Sherlock asked a question that perhaps he should have asked before. 'Is there any blame attached to you? Do your superiors think that you should be doing more to protect the mortuary, or do they even think you might be involved?'

'I've spoken to the Board of Directors at the hospital several times,' Lukather confided. 'I have told them everything I know, and the police have also reassured them that I am not and never have been a suspect.' He laughed, but there was little humour in the sound. 'And they must be asking themselves – Where else could they get someone to do this work? I don't see a queue forming.'

Eventually, however, despite the conversation, the temptation to analyse the dates became too much. 'I really will have to go,' Sherlock said, 'but I'd like to thank you for a very interesting conversation.'

'I have really enjoyed myself as well,' the pathologist replied, rising and shaking Sherlock's hand. 'Do let me know if the newspaper piece ever comes out, but please also feel free to come back for tea and biscuits any time you wish.' He paused for a moment, thinking. 'I could always bend the rules and allow you to watch an autopsy being performed,' he said tentatively. 'It really is a most instructive experience.'

'That really would be amazing,' Sherlock said, touched by the pathologist's suggestion. 'I certainly will be back to see you, and I may well take you up on that offer.'

Lukather smiled. 'That would be capital,' he said. 'I don't get the opportunity that often to talk with a like mind. There was a man, some time ago – Ferny Weston, his name was. Big fellow. Very big. Policeman, he was. He stopped coming.' His face fell, and he looked away. 'I think I must have bored him.'

'You won't bore me,' Sherlock promised.

CHAPTER SIX

Leaving the mortuary and the hospital grounds, Sherlock took the shortest route back to where he knew the river was to be found. He located a bench looking over an attractive spot and settled down, getting his notebook out to check the dates of the thefts. Perhaps it was the talk he'd had with Charles Dodgson about mathematic sequences of numbers, but he knew there was a pattern in this one, if only he could see it. He sat there for a long time, while the sun gradually went down and the shadows of the trees on the other side of the river lengthened across its rippling surface. At one point he became aware that Matty was sitting patiently beside him, but he didn't remember noticing that his friend had even arrived.

Eventually he looked up. His mouth was dry and tasted funny, and he had a slight headache, but he thought he had it.

'There is no pattern,' he said to Matty – the first words he had spoken for several hours. 'That's the pattern.'

'What does that mean?' Matty asked.

'Things have been going missing from the local mortuary – parts of bodies. My new tutor, Charles Dodgson, is a potential suspect, and so is one of the students I'm rooming with – Paul Chippenham. You remember, we saw him being taken away yesterday by the police for questioning. I've talked to the pathologist, and I've got a list of the dates when the body parts went missing. I thought I could find a pattern, so I could predict when the next theft will occur, but I can't.'

'So that's it then? You need to find another line of investigation.'

Sherlock shook his head. 'No – the lack of a pattern is actually a pattern. The thief, whoever it is, has deliberately avoided a theft on the same day of the month, or when the moon is in the same phase, or with the same number of days between thefts. They've done thefts on the same day of the week – they could hardly avoid it, because there are only seven days of the week, but they won't do the same day on consecutive thefts. There are no Mondays together, no Tuesdays together—'

'I get the idea.'

'They also vary the weather conditions. There's only one rainy Monday, only one sunny Monday, only one cloudy Monday. In their attempts to avoid setting any kind of pattern, they've set a different pattern.'

Matty scratched his head. 'What do you mean?'

'Put it this way: it's been twenty-two days since the last theft. The thief has already put a twenty-two day space between thefts, so they won't conduct a theft tonight. Tomorrow is a possibility, according to the gaps, but not according to the weather. It's a Thursday tomorrow and there's bright sunshine forecast, which rules it out because the very first theft was on a sunny Thursday. If I can figure out all of the variables, I can go through the calendar and work out which days are left.'

Matty nodded slowly. 'That,' he said, 'is real clever thinkin'.' He paused. 'Does thinkin' actually take energy, the same way that runnin' or carryin' boxes does?'

Sherlock considered. 'I'm starving now, if that means anything.'

'Let's go an' get some food then. I reckon you're goin' to need it.'

They ate, and then went their separate ways.

It took Sherlock most of the next day to work out the cycle. He ended up having to buy a large roll of wallpaper and borrow the dining table at Mrs McCrery's boarding house – with her permission, of course. He unrolled the wallpaper so that it covered the table, and then with a ruler and a pen he painstakingly set up a calendar for the next three months, with each day marked separately, and space marked on each day for listing the weather, the phase of the moon and all the other variables that he thought the thief was using, including whether or not they were public holidays or market days. He then painstakingly annotated the calendar as far as he could. Weather was the problem – the local newspapers only predicted it up to a few days ahead, which at least told him that the thief was not planning any further ahead than that anyway. It would have been pointless to arrange a robbery for a sunny Monday with a new moon only to find out that, on the day, it was snowing and he'd already conducted a robbery on a snowy Monday with a new moon. Sherlock would have to do what he assumed the thief was doing, and plan only a few days ahead, checking the weather and predicting it as far as he could. What he did do, however, was to cross through the days that could be ruled out because their set of characteristics had already been used. That at least told him which days the next robbery *wouldn't* occur on. Unsurprisingly, a lot of the combinations had already been used up, and there weren't that many days left when a robbery *could* occur.

The next one was three days away, but it depended totally on the weather.

At various times as he worked Mrs McCrery, or her scullery maid, or one of the boys who stoked fires for her, or one of the other students in the house, would pass by the doorway, glance in and either frown or smile, but there must have been something about the expression on Sherlock's face that stopped them from coming in and questioning him. Twice a tray of tea and scones appeared on a side table, although he had no idea how they had got there.

The next two days passed with agonizing slowness. Sherlock went to one more tutorial session with Charles Dodgson, at which they went through Euclidian geometry, attempting to derive it all from first principles. Sherlock felt stretched and exhausted by the session, but also exhilarated. Dodgson, he felt, was training his mind the way that a sports coach would train an athlete's body.

At the end of the tutorial, Dodgson suddenly said, 'Oh, I nearly forgot – would you wish to see some photographic images of your brother? I found them just the other day, and thought you might like sight of them.'

'That would be – fascinating,' Sherlock said, meaning it.

Dodgson went across his room to a bureau, from which he took a cardboard box. He placed the box on a table and took the lid off. Sherlock joined him, and saw that inside the box was a pile of pieces of stiff paper. On the top piece was an image in black and white of Sherlock's brother, Mycroft, sitting at a table beneath a large, overhanging plant. He was staring pensively off to one side – probably wondering what his next meal would be, Sherlock thought uncharitably. Judging by the relative thinness of his face, the length of his hair and the way his waistcoat buttons were not straining against the cotton, the picture might have been five or six years old.

Sherlock smiled, despite himself. This was like a window on to the past. This *was* his brother – not an artist's interpretation, prettied up to please the subject, but the way Mycroft had actually been on a particular day at a particular time. Even the fact that it was just black and white didn't worry Sherlock – Mycroft only ever dressed in black or pinstripe material, his hair was black and his face was pale, so the image looked exactly like him.

'That,' he said softly, 'is quite amazing.'

'He is looking at a plate of biscuits,' Dodgson said. 'I told him that he had to sit there for fifteen minutes without moving while I took the portrait. In fact the process only took eight minutes, but I was so enjoying seeing him pining for the biscuits that I just left him there to suffer.' He pulled the paper image out and placed it to one side. Beneath it was another image. This one had been taken outside, in a garden. It showed Mycroft standing with a group of other people – a large man with broad shoulders and a bowler hat, a pretty woman in a frilled dress, a boy who looked to have been about nine years old, and an older man with white hair brushed straight back off his forehead.

'This is your brother again, with some friends,' Dodgson said. 'I forget now who they were.'

'Mycroft had friends?' Sherlock said, amazed.

'Yes,' Dodgson replied quietly. 'I was one of them.'

Sherlock left Dodgson's rooms still amazed by this newfangled process of photography, and fascinated by what effects it might have on society.

He read the local newspaper every day, hoping desperately that there would be no reports of any more robberies at the mortuary. If there were, it meant that his entire theory was wrong. He also kept his ears open as he was going around the town, but nobody mentioned anything to do with robberies. Lots of discussion of other matters of interest, but nothing about bizarre or macabre thefts.

On the morning of the third day, Sherlock awoke and glanced immediately out of the window. It was cloudy, which was what he wanted, but it didn't look like rain, which was also what he wanted. So far, so good.

He went through the day in an agony of expectation. Eventually, as night was approaching, he met up with Matty just outside the hospital gates. Matty was wearing dark clothes as instructed. Sherlock himself had dressed in the darkest trousers and jacket he had. He only had white shirts, so he had a dark scarf wound around his neck and tucked inside the jacket, hiding the whiteness. He even had gloves.

'Ready?' Matty asked in a hushed voice.

'As I'll ever be. I hope I'm right.'

'You're right,' Matty said. 'You always are.' He glanced around. 'So what's the plan. If we see somethin', do we interfere, or do we run off an' call the peelers?'

'Neither of those things,' Sherlock said firmly. 'If we see anything, then we just observe from a distance, and follow. I want to know where the thief goes and what he does with these body parts. If he's arrested here, then he might clam up and I'll never know.'

'So this is basically a huge exercise to satisfy your curiosity then.'

Sherlock considered for a moment. 'I suppose it is,' he

admitted. 'Do you think I ought to call the police?'

Matty shrugged. 'I dunno. I'm just followin' you.'

The gates to the hospital were locked, and there were only a few scattered gas lamps shining from inside the big building. Sherlock and Matty headed around the outside wall, which was set apart from the trees and bushes surrounding the estate by a ten-foot gap. The wall was ten feet high – and if that wasn't difficult enough to climb under normal circumstances, the top was set with broken glass bottles to deter intruders. Sherlock assumed that the hospital had been someone's home until it was converted, which would explain the security measures. People didn't usually break into hospitals: they were usually more keen to get out.

Every now and then they passed a particularly old and large tree whose branches overhung the wall. Matty looked at Sherlock each time, but Sherlock shook his head. He wanted to get closer to where the mortuary was located in the grounds, and he was also looking for something special.

Up ahead, Matty seemed to be listening for something. Sherlock listened as well, but apart from the sound of night birds waking up, and the occasional screaming of a fox, there was nothing.

'What are you listening for?' he asked eventually.

'Guard dogs,' Matty said over his shoulder. 'Can't hear any barkin', but I thought I might hear 'em breathin' as they paced us along the inside of the wall.'

113

'There aren't any guard dogs.'

'You sure?'

'It's a hospital, not a bank. Why would there be guard dogs? And besides, there's always the possibility that someone confused on painkilling drugs might get out of bed late one night and go wandering around outside. The last thing the hospital directors would want was for a patient to get ripped to pieces by a guard dog.'

'All right then,' Matty said dubiously, but he still appeared to be listening as they walked.

In the end, Sherlock found the thing he was looking for just as the sun was dipping beneath the horizon. Not too far away from where he estimated the mortuary was, there was a place where the roots of an unusually large tree had undermined the wall, buckling the bricks upward. Some of the bricks had fallen out, leaving a hole, and the roots themselves had spaces between them, washed out by rain perhaps, which would allow a person to crawl through. Based on the fact that there were clear marks of spadework, Sherlock assumed that the thief had come through this way as well.

He glanced around nervously. He had planned their expedition so that they would get to the mortuary before the thief, but that was based on an assumption that the thief would operate late at night. If he was going to conduct this theft at sunset, then he might already be there. That meant he might be watching Sherlock and Matty at that very moment.

Sherlock shivered.

'Cold?' Matty asked.

'No.'

'Cold feet?'

'Definitely not.'

'Let's go then.'

Matty dropped to his knees and then squirmed his way through the gap. His booted feet waved for a moment in the dark space, and then he was gone. Sherlock counted to ten, looked around again, and followed.

The short tunnel under the wall was damp and smelt of mould, earth and some animal that Sherlock assumed was either a fox or a badger. The thought triggered another one in his mind – what if Matty, crawling ahead of him, suddenly came across a badger coming the other way? Badgers were notoriously fierce, with sharp teeth and even sharper claws. Matty wouldn't stand a chance!

Sherlock speeded up, knowing that it wouldn't affect Matty's speed but unable to help himself.

In the end he felt a clean breeze on his face moments before he emerged from the earth inside the hospital grounds. Matty was standing a few feet away, brushing himself off. 'That was fun,' he said, smiling. 'We should do it again sometime.'

Sherlock decided not to mention badgers. Best not to worry his friend too much.

Together they sprinted across the hospital grounds, going from bush to bush, tree to tree, until the red-brick mortuary was ahead of them. Sherlock caught Matty's shoulder, holding him back.

'We goin' to watch from 'ere?' Matty hissed.

'No. If the thief comes through the same place in the wall we did, then he's going to come right past here. We need to move around so that we can see the approach and the building as well.'

Sherlock circled the mortuary, Matty in tow, until he found a large holly bush that the two of them could lie beneath. From there they had a clear line of sight straight ahead to the door of the mortuary and left to the direction Sherlock thought the thief would come from. If the thief came from a different direction, such as behind them, then the bush would still provide cover.

The sun was gone by now, and the stars were beginning to twinkle in the sky. Faint wisps of cloud drifted across the darkness. There was, fortunately, still no sign of rain. The conditions were perfect.

And that's where they stayed for the next three hours. Time passed slowly, like treacle trickling from a tin. Sherlock felt himself begin to doze a couple of times, and had to jerk himself awake. Once he heard Matty snoring, and nudged the boy in the ribs with his elbow to wake him up. He didn't mind if Matty caught some sleep, but making a noise like a pig eating its swill was too much. It might alert the thief.

Sherlock had taken some scones from Mrs McCrery's kitchen before coming out and hidden them inside his jacket. When he got hungry enough he pulled them out and passed a couple to Matty. Unfortunately he didn't have any water. He should have got a hip flask from somewhere, he realized, and filled it up before setting off. Next time he was in this situation, he would prepare better.

After that realization, he couldn't stop thinking about how dry his mouth was.

At some time during their vigil, a fox trotted across the lawn around the mortuary. It paused, head held high, and sniffed the air, then it moved on. Later a family of badgers – two adults and five cubs – crossed the area in a line. They didn't react to any smells or sounds – they just kept on moving, fearless.

The moon appeared from above the trees. It was three-quarters full – just the right size for the theft to take place on that day of the week, on that day of the month, in those weather conditions.

Matty's hand closed over Sherlock's and squeezed. Sherlock glanced sideways to see that his friend was staring off to one side. He followed the boy's gaze and noticed a black-clad shape moving through the bushes. Whoever it was, they were crouching down and moving slowly, checking in all directions to see if they were observed.

Sherlock felt a warm flush of triumph run through him. He had been right! He had successfully predicted the theft!

The figure emerged into the clear area around the mortuary and looked around one final time, pausing and sniffing the air a bit like the fox had done. It was a man, and he was wearing a long poacher's coat – the kind with large pockets for hiding rabbits and grouse. He went up to the door. His body shielded what he was doing, but Sherlock thought that he was reaching into an inside pocket of his coat. The pocket seemed to be full of something – something that squirmed as the man's hand closed on it. He brought his hand out, and both Matty and Sherlock gasped. There was a small figure, like a doll, crouched on his palm – and it moved!

'That's sorcery!' Matty breathed.

'No,' Sherlock said, 'that's a monkey.'

'I knew that,' Matty said.

It had, to be fair, taken Sherlock a couple of seconds to recognize that the thing was a monkey. He had seen creatures like it before, at fairgrounds, at circuses and in zoos. This one was small enough to be hidden in a man's pocket, obviously, but intelligent enough that it could be trained. As the two of them watched, the monkey's handler whispered something in its ear. Quick as a flash it jumped from his hand to a drainpipe that ran up the side of the building to the roof. Sherlock saw it silhouetted against the sky for a moment, then it was gone.

The man looked around, checking to see if there was anyone there, and then slipped around the side of the building. Matty and Sherlock followed, keeping in the shadows and behind shrubbery as much as they could.

They found the man by the back door. He was leaning against it, listening. After a few seconds, Sherlock heard a sliding sound as the bolts were pulled open by his little companion. He pushed against the door, and it opened. Within a second the man had slipped inside and vanished into the darkness.

Sherlock considered for a few moments. Using a monkey to open the door was very clever, but Sherlock still wanted to know what was going on inside. Should the two of them wait, or should they move closer?

The decision was obvious – he had to see. He had to know.

He pulled Matty with him, out of the shelter of the holly bush and towards the mortuary. For a few moments he debated whether to go in through the back door, as the thief had done, but he decided that would be a mistake. He might meet the man as he was coming out, which would be a disaster. When they got to the wall, he gestured to Matty to stand with his back against the bricks and his hands clasped in front of him. Matty realized immediately what was going on and gave his friend a leg-up. Sherlock virtually flew on to the roof, and had to extend his hands to catch his weight as he fell forward. The air whooshed out of his lungs as he hit the stonework. He stayed still for a few moments, desperately hoping that the thief somewhere below hadn't heard him. There was no sound; no movement. Eventually, when he thought it was safe, he moved on.

The roof was sloped, and there were several skylights in it. Sherlock quickly crawled across to one of them and looked down. Fortunately the moon had risen higher in the night sky, and its silvery light shone down through the glass and into the room. It took a few moments for Sherlock to recognize it, but it was the room where he and Lukather had talked a few days before. The room was empty.

Sherlock crawled across to the next skylight. The room below him now had two metal-topped tables, the size of beds, in its centre. They were set side by side. The edges of the tables were raised, and each one had a drain set towards one corner so that it could be washed down. Presumably this was where Lukather actually conducted his post-mortems. Again the room was empty, but there was an open door over to one side. Sherlock crawled in that direction, and found himself staring through a third skylight into a room that was empty apart from a series of large drawers set into one wall, stacked five across and four up. The drawers were large enough that there could be a body inside each one. On the outward face of each drawer there was a metal frame in which a small piece of card rested. There was writing on each card – presumably the name of the person whose body resided therein.

The man was standing in the centre of the room.

Sherlock couldn't see his face – he was wearing a scarf wrapped around the lower half, obscuring his chin, mouth and nose. He was staring at the drawers. He reached into his pocket and pulled out a piece of paper. After glancing at it for a few moments, he strode across to one of the drawers and checked the writing on the card that was attached to the front. He grunted, and moved to the next drawer. Again he looked at the piece of paper in his hand, checking the details. This must have been the right one, because he reached out with his right hand and opened the drawer.

Sherlock caught his breath. This was fascinating – it hadn't occurred to him before, but the thief was looking for particular bodies! He wasn't just taking a part from a body at random – he was specifically targeting them! Did that mean he was specifically targeting the parts as well? And if so – why?

While Sherlock was asking himself these questions, the thief was pulling the drawer fully open. The movement took a lot of effort, even though the drawer appeared to be sliding on greased runners. Eventually the drawer was completely open. Looking down on it from above, Sherlock could see a shape beneath a white sheet – presumably the dead body.

The thief reached out a hand. For a moment, with a shiver, Sherlock thought he was going to pull the sheet completely off, but instead he just pulled it up a little, revealing the corpse's feet. There was, Sherlock saw, a cardboard tag attached to the big toe of the left foot by a length of string. He supposed that was to make sure that the bodies didn't get mixed up.

Something moved beside Sherlock.

He jerked away, suddenly thinking that it might be the monkey, but when he whirled his head around to look it was only Matty. He must have found his own way up.

'What's goin' on?' Matty asked.

'Shh!' Sherlock said. He indicated the scene below.

Down in the mortuary storage room, the thief was checking the tag on the corpse's toe, double-checking that the name on the drawer matched and that he'd got the right one. He released the tag and reached into his pocket, taking something out and unfolding it with a click. It took Sherlock a moment to work out what it was, and then he realized – it was a knife!

The thief bent down and began to work on the corpse's right foot – the one without a tag.

''E's takin' its big toe off!' Matty breathed.

Indeed, that did appear to be what the thief was doing. He was working at cutting the corpse's right big toe off. It was hard work, and Sherlock heard some swearing coming from the room below, even through the glass. Eventually, however, he succeeded, and the big toe vanished into his pocket along with the knife. He quickly threw the sheet back over the corpse, pushed the drawer shut, and left.

Sherlock scrambled back across the tiled roof to the first skylight that he had looked through, trying to make as little noise as possible. He gazed down through the blurry glass as the man below entered the autopsy room again and began to make his way towards the door to the hall. His monkey was still sitting on the metal post-mortem table, alternately grooming its fur and looking around.

Sherlock felt a sudden cramp in his leg. He'd been crouched for too long in the cold. He tried to extend it surreptitiously, but he overbalanced and fell forward. He shifted his hands wider apart to take his weight, but there must have been a splinter of wood in the frame of the skylight, and he felt it jab into his palm. Without thinking he pulled his hand away, but his weight was too far forward and he fell into the glass and wood of the skylight.

Into, and through.

The skylight broke under his weight, and he fell head first into the room below. The metal autopsy table was directly beneath it. If he hit it he would probably break something – most likely his skull. He desperately twisted his body, trying to catch the edge of the skylight with his foot. He managed to hook the toe of his boot over the wood, and his body swung like a pendulum. His head rushed towards a set of chains and racks that were hanging from the ceiling, presumably for moving bodies around and holding them up, and he grabbed for it desperately with both hands. They caught hold just as his toe slipped off the frame of the skylight. He had a confused impression of the thief in the room below glancing upward in shock, and springing backwards the way he had come. Sherlock's body fell again, but this time swinging on the suspended racks like an acrobat on a trapeze. The metal was slippery beneath his fingers, and he lost his grip. He flew sideways, bouncing off the wall and landing on the tiled floor. His head hit the tiles and he saw a crimson galaxy of stars rotating in his field of view. He felt sick, and his hands were burning with pain.

Knowing that the thief was there, and desperate to get past him, Sherlock forced himself to his feet. His vision was blurry – he could see two thieves standing in two separate doorways – but he blinked hard until his head cleared.

The thief scowled at Sherlock. He was unshaven, with wild black hair and ears that looked as if they had been repeatedly hit by someone's fists. A boxer maybe, Sherlock thought muzzily. A boxer with a monkey – that probably meant he was from a funfair: a keeper for the animals and a participant in the boxing rings that were a central feature of most travelling fairs. Not the kind of person who would be stealing body parts, necessarily.

'A spy, eh?' he snarled. 'You workin' for the rozzers? That ain't goin' to stop me – I'll cut yer throat anyway!'

Desperately aware that he had ruined the whole plan, Sherlock held up his scratched and torn palms. 'Sorry – I was trying to get hold of –' he thought for a moment – 'some morphine. I've got a kind of . . . need for it!' He tried to sound as pathetic as possible. 'Look, I'll get out of your way. I won't try to stop you, and I won't come after you. I just want the morphine.'

'Students!' the thief growled, but as Sherlock edged one way around the metal table he went the other. He seemed to be accepting the possibility of Sherlock being a thief too, and despite his bluster he didn't seem to want any trouble. He just wanted to get out with his stolen toe.

His monkey, however, had other ideas.

It grabbed a scalpel from a metal tray and leaped at Sherlock's head, making a wild *chittering* sound. Sherlock saw the creature coming out of the corner of his eye and whirled around. He ducked just as the monkey got to him. It sailed over his head, slicing at Sherlock with the scalpel but missing.

'Barney! You stupid critter – come 'ere!' the thief yelled, moving fast towards the door, but the monkey wasn't listening. It landed on the metal table and whirled around, jumping straight back at Sherlock's chest. It grabbed hold of his shirt with its back paws and its front left paw, and jabbed the scalpel at Sherlock's left eye. Sherlock caught its arm in his left hand. It was thin, like a twig, but hairy and incredibly powerful. He could feel the muscles writhing beneath its skin as the monkey fought to force the scalpel closer to Sherlock's eye.

Sherlock forced his right hand between the monkey's

chest and his own and pushed. The monkey's back paws scratched the skin of his stomach as it scrabbled to get a grip. His shirt tore, but he managed to push the animal away. With one massive effort he threw it across the room. It hit the wall, screaming in anger, and dropped out of sight. The scalpel hit the wall and clattered to the floor. Sherlock could hear the monkey's claws clicking on the tiled floor as it moved, but he didn't know where it was. The thief didn't either – he was poised in the doorway, not sure whether to run or to rescue his creature.

Sherlock reached out his right hand for the metal tray where the monkey had got the scalpel. His hand was shaking from the unexpected fall and the shock of what was happening.

The monkey suddenly appeared around the edge of the metal table. Its wizened little face was contorted in rage. It grabbed hold of the table's edge with its left hand and swung itself up on to the surface, then jumped straight for Sherlock, screaming.

Sherlock brought the metal tray smartly around like a tennis racket and batted the creature across the room, towards the thief, who grabbed it out of the air, bundled it under his coat and ran.

Sherlock just stood there, breathing heavily. A noise from above made him glance upward. Matty's face was staring down at him.

'Are you all right?' he whispered.

'I'm . . . fine,' Sherlock said, although he didn't feel

fine at all. 'It was just a stupid fall. Now we'll never know where he goes!'

'Leave it to me,' Matty said. Before Sherlock could respond, the boy had vanished from sight. Sherlock had to stop himself from shouting after his friend. The thief had a knife, and a homicidal monkey. Matty was in incredible danger!

CHAPTER SEVEN

He left via the back door and sat outside for a while, in the cold breeze that blew across the hospital grounds, letting his body relax and his brain process what he had seen. On the one hand, things went pretty much as he had anticipated, apart from the fall through the skylight. On the other hand, the revelation that the thief was after a particular body this time, and presumably therefore every time, was entirely new. The important thing now, however, was whether Matty could follow him back to his base of operations.

A sudden thought made him laugh. What if the police had chosen that very night to mount an observation of their own? What if they had seen him there and decided to arrest him?

The thought provoked Sherlock into moving. After all, he couldn't stay there all night. He headed off towards the hole beneath the tree.

Initially Sherlock had intended to go back to Mrs McCrery's house, but he was worried about Matty, and so he went to the barge instead. Matty wouldn't risk heading for the boarding house and trying to wake Sherlock up. He would go back to the barge and wait – if he managed to get away from the thief, that was.

The barge was exactly where Sherlock remembered. Harold, the horse, was dozing in a field nearby. He slept standing up, with his head lowered, whickering gently as he dreamed of whatever things horses dreamed about. Hay, possibly, or maybe running free across fields and jumping hedges with his mane flowing in the wind.

Sherlock grabbed a blanket from inside the barge and settled down on the deck, wrapping himself up warmly and waiting for his friend to return.

He expected that the excitement of the evening and the worry over what was happening to Matty would mean that he wouldn't sleep, but he was wrong. He drifted gradually into a confused state where memories and dreams all mixed together into a strange landscape, like something Charles Dodgson – or his alter ego, Lewis Carroll – might write. It was only when the rising sun shone directly into his eyes as he lay there, with his cheek on the deck, that he woke up. His back ached and his feet and hands were chilled. The morning's dew had soaked into his clothes. He felt completely miserable.

There was no sign of Matty. Sherlock went inside the barge and found half a loaf of bread, which he ate hungrily, tearing it into pieces and wolfing it down without butter or jam or anything. All the time he ate he tormented himself with thoughts of Matty being discovered and beaten, maybe even killed. The boy was wily and quick, but he was neither invisible nor indestructible.

Sherlock was just about to go to the police and report

129

Matty missing when the boy arrived back at the barge. It was late in the morning, and the canal was busy with passing barges stacked up with coal or wood or crates. Matty looked, if possible, even worse than Sherlock felt. He threw himself on to the barge's deck in exhaustion.

'If I ever try that again,' he said, 'stop me.'

'What happened?' Sherlock asked.

'Nothin' actually happened. It's just that I've walked a long way, an' I've hidden in some uncomfortable places.' He sighed, turning over to stare upward. 'I s'pose you're not goin' to let me sleep until I tell you what 'appened.'

'I might let you sleep,' Sherlock conceded, 'but I'd check every ten minutes to see if you were awake yet. You wouldn't get much rest.'

'Yeah, that's what I figured.' He rubbed the back of his hand across his eyes. 'All right then. I followed that cove to a cart that he had outside the grounds. I knew if 'e'd just come on an 'orse then I'd never be able to keep up, but I managed to climb on the back of the cart an' 'ide under a tarpaulin without 'im seein' me. We drove for 'bout twenty minutes, an' every time we went over a bump in the road I felt it all the way from my head to my feet. Eventually, just as I was thinkin' I couldn't take it any more and I was about to jump off, we stopped. 'E got off, an' I waited a few minutes before followin'. Turns out that 'e's a local 'andyman – does some carpentry, some buildin', some gardenin'. 'E's got this barn place that 'e works out of, an' that's where we were.'

'And the monkey?'

''E got it off 'is dad, who used to take a barrel organ around the streets. The monkey used to collect the coins while 'e played the music. 'E retired a few years back.'

'And you know this how?'

Matty was indignant. 'Cos I asked around, didn't I?'

'So what did he do with the big toe?' Sherlock asked.

'I'm gettin' to that! I got inside the barn without 'im seein' me, and managed to get close to the office area where 'e was workin'. You'll never guess what 'e did!'

Sherlock thought for a moment. He actually had no idea, but he wasn't going to admit that to Matty. 'I never guess,' he said loftily. 'I make judgements based on evidence, and I haven't yet got enough evidence to make a judgement.'

'You mean you haven't got a clue.' Matty smiled. 'Actually, 'e put the toe in a wooden box. There was waxed canvas in the box, which I s'pose was there to stop the water leakin' out.'

'What water?' Sherlock asked.

'The water from the ice.'

Sherlock sighed patiently. The boy was tired, after all. 'What ice?'

'The ice that 'e filled the box with after 'e put the toe inside.' He frowned at Sherlock. 'Pay attention – I only got enough energy to tell this story once.' He closed his eyes and continued: ''E screwed the box down, wrapped

131

it in brown paper an' tied it up with string. Then 'e wrote an address on the front.'

'He's posting the body parts somewhere?' Sherlock was incredulous. He had never expected this. The ice he had expected – it was obviously necessary to stop the body parts from decomposing and becoming useless for whatever purpose they were intended – but he hadn't thought that the parts might be being stolen to order.

''E took the package outside, got in 'is cart an' drove off,' Matty went on. 'I could see what 'e was plannin', so I got there first an' 'id beneath the tarpaulin again. You'll never guess where 'e went next!'

'The post office,' Sherlock said.

''Ow did you know that?'

'He had a package. He was either going to give it to someone or send it to someone. The fact that he wrote an address on it strongly indicated the latter possibility.'

'Oh.' Matty's mouth twisted in disappointment. 'Well, you're right – 'e went straight to the post office an' waited for it to open. When it did 'e went in, went up to the counter, 'anded the package across an' passed some money over as well. Then 'e left.'

'I really wish we knew where he sent that package,' Sherlock said, feeling his heart sink. This looked like a dead end. The investigation was finished.

'Actually, we do.' Matty was grinning. 'I went in ten minutes later an' said that my employer 'ad brought a package in earlier but he thought 'e might've put the wrong address on, an' could I check? The bloke behind the counter went an' fetched the package an' let me take a look. Didn't let me touch it, but that was all right. I told 'im it was the correct address, an' I left.'

'Matty,' Sherlock said gently, 'you can't read.'

'No,' the boy replied obstinately, 'but I can draw. I memorized the shapes of the letters on the front an' wrote them down on a piece of paper before I left the post office. They've got lots of forms an' stuff, and pencils that people can use.' He reached into his trousers and pulled out a crumpled and dirty scrap of paper. 'This is it, best that I can recall.'

Sherlock took the scrap and looked at it in wonder. There, in careful, large capital letters, was an address:

MR THOMAS NATROUS
23 RYDAL CLOSE
EALING
LONDON

'Matty,' he said, 'you are amazing.'

'I know,' the boy said. He frowned, and glanced over at Sherlock. 'Is it okay? I mean, does that address make sense? Did I copy it down right'

'It does and you did.'

'Great. After that I walked back, an' it took me ages. I know where that cove lives now, in case you need 'im, but I'm guessing that you're more interested in the London end of things at the moment.' He yawned suddenly. 'I'm goin' to go to sleep now. Don't wake me up.'

'It's a bargain.'

'What are you goin' to do?'

'I,' Sherlock replied, 'am going to send a telegram to my brother. I did promise him that I would keep in touch.'

Sherlock left the barge and walked into Oxford. He debated going back to Mrs McCrery's house for a change of clothes, but he knew that he had to send that telegram as soon as possible. Letters and parcels were quick – the parcel might get to its intended address the next day, if not that very day, but telegrams were even quicker. He composed it in his mind as he walked – as short as possible, given that telegrams were paid for by the letter – and when he got to the central Oxford post office he was able to dictate it to the man at the counter straight away.

```
Dear brother. Am well. Vital that I know
what happens to package sent today to Thom.
Natrous, 23 Rydal Close, Ealing. Please answer
soonest. Regards, Sherlock.
```

Now there was nothing to do but wait.

The answer arrived two days later, delivered directly to Mrs McCrery's house. In the meantime Sherlock had checked out several lectures at Christ Church, as well as undertaken an expedition to the barn to which Matty had followed the thief. The lectures were more informative than the barn, which was, as Matty had observed, a workplace for someone who did a lot of different jobs for a lot of different people. Sherlock managed to get inside while the thief was out pruning someone's rose bushes, but there was no sign of any body parts there, or any reason why they might have been taken. This was just a way station, a point on their journey, not the final destination.

His next tutorial with Dodgson proved odder than Sherlock had been expecting, and he had been expecting *something* odd.

He turned up at ten o'clock precisely, outside Dodgson's rooms, to find a note pinned to the door. It said:

> Meet me down in the gardens between the college
>   and the river.
> Dodgson.

Sherlock walked back down the stairs again and found his way out through the college buildings to the gardens at the back, wondering all the time what Dodgson was up to. Was this some new lesson in logic that could only be undertaken outside, like the little exercises that Amyus Crowe used to carry out using animal tracks or the way that moss grew on the side of trees?

He found the tutor on a patch of grass near the river. He was setting up a complicated device that looked like a wooden box on stilts. It was tall and thin and ungainly, as was the man who was working on it. They made a perfect match. On the front of the box was a lens, like a small telescope. Nearby, a small tent had been set up, secured with guy ropes.

'Ah, Holmes,' Dodgson said, 'Just in t-t-time. Please go and stand in front of the c-c-camera.' He was, Sherlock noticed, still wearing the same white gloves as he had the first time Sherlock had met him.

'Which bit is the front?' Sherlock asked. 'Is that where the lens is?'

'Indeed.'

Sherlock moved to where Dodgson had indicated. On the way he passed close by the camera and saw that it also had a bellows-type arrangement of corrugated black material that allowed the distance between the lens and its back to be varied. The back was constructed so that a glass plate could be slipped into it. The variable distance must have something to do with the focal length of the lens, Sherlock assumed. A black cloth could be thrown over the whole device, presumably to keep any stray trace of light out of it.

Sherlock was going to have his photograph taken. He wasn't sure whether to be happy or apprehensive.

Dodgson bent over and threw the black cloth over himself and the camera. Sherlock could see his elbows moving as he fiddled with something. 'Strike a dramatic pose!' he called, his voice muffled by the cloth.

Sherlock tried various poses – hands on hips, hands behind his back, one hand in his pocket and the other slipped inside his jacket. Nothing felt natural. Eventually, and with some embarrassment, he folded his arms over his chest and scowled off into the distance, looking downriver.

'Raise your right hand and hold your chin!' Dodgson shouted. Sherlock complied, aware that people walking along the nearby path were staring at the two of them.

'Look thoughtful! At the moment you look like you are expecting a telegram telling you that your favourite dog has been eaten by a t-t-tiger!'

Sherlock tried his best to look thoughtful, even though he wasn't sure how. He tried to remember times in the recent past when he had been thoughtful, but that didn't help. In the end he recalled the sequence of numbers that Dodgson had tested him with a few days before – the sequence he hadn't been able to solve. He ran them through his mind now, trying to see if anything leaped out at him.

'Excellent!' Dodgson pulled his head out from underneath the cloth, moved to the front of the camera and glanced over at Sherlock. 'Yes, excellent.' Although Sherlock was staring away from the camera, he saw in the corner of his eye Dodgson reach out and take a cap off the lens. 'Now, don't move for another five m-m-minutes.'

'*What?*' he said through clenched teeth. He had to maintain this ridiculous pose for another five minutes?

'It's all to do with the amount of light that has to fall on the sensitized glass plate before an image will form. The Good Lord has blessed even the lowliest animal in his domain with eyes that can detect an image so q-q-quickly that it seems no time at all has passed, even in the darkest of conditions. C-c-chemistry, however, has a long way to come before it can match what God has made. Just be grateful that science has advanced at all. For the first known photograph that was taken, back in 1826, the exposure lasted for well over eight hours.' He paused. 'It wasn't a portrait, you will be pleased to hear,' he added. 'It was a l-l-landscape.'

Sherlock stood there for another five minutes, while people passed by. He could hear them talking, wondering what he and the tall, thin lecturer were doing. One or two of them had already heard of photography and made more informed comments. All of them ended up asking their companions who Sherlock was, and why he was so important that he was having his photograph taken. He asked himself the same question several times during those five minutes.

Dodgson eventually replaced the cap on the lens, stopping the light from falling on to the hidden glass plate. 'That's it!' he called. 'You can relax now.'

Sherlock walked over to join him, joints complaining at the sudden movement after the enforced stillness. Dodgson had dived beneath the black cloth again and was removing something from the camera. He emerged holding a thin wooden box.

'The plate is in here,' he announced, 'shielded from any more light that might fall upon it. The plate itself is coated with a mixture of collodion and silver nitrate. I now need to take it into the tent where I will "develop" the image with ferrous sulphate and then "fix" it using a solution of sodium th-th-thiosulphate so that light will not affect it any more. Both processes have to be done quickly otherwise the image will degrade. Please, stay here for a few minutes. We will talk later.'

He vanished into the tent. It was smaller than he was, and Sherlock imagined him kneeling inside, head bowed, pouring chemicals from glass bottles into a tray, opening the wooden box, taking the glass plate delicately from inside and then laying the plate in the tray so that the chemicals could wash across it. Even as he was picturing the scene he thought he could smell something pungent wafting from inside the tent. He didn't know how Dodgson could stand it, being so close to the chemicals.

Eventually Dodgson backed out of the tent and stood up. He was stiff from having been folded up for so long. He crossed over to where Sherlock was waiting.

'Please accept my apologies,' he said. He seemed embarrassed. 'My gloves grew wet in the sodium th-

th-thiosulphate solution, and I need to change them otherwise the chemical will make my skin peel. I have another pair.' Delicately he fished inside a jacket pocket and removed a folded pair of white gloves which he handed to Sherlock. 'Perhaps you could hold these for me for a moment.'

Sherlock took the gloves and watched as Dodgson peeled the wet gloves from his hands and dropped them on the grass.

His hands were mottled black and blue, as if badly bruised.

He saw the direction Sherlock was looking, and winced. 'Ah,' he said. 'Yes. Exciting though this new science of photography is, there is a d-d-downside. The light-sensitive silver nitrate solution that is used to coat the glass p-p-plates before they are put into the camera do tend to discolour the skin. It is a price we pay for experimentation, and for art.'

'I've seen something similar before,' Sherlock said quietly. 'I knew a man named Arrhenius who drank silver solution as a way to ward off disease. His skin was discoloured as well, but from the inside out, not the outside in.'

'And was he protected from d-d-disease?' Dodgson asked with interest, taking the pristine white gloves from Sherlock and slipping them on.

'He thought so.'

'Then let us hope that the silver nitrate has the same

effect on me.' He smiled. 'I must say, I don't recall having had a c-c-cold since taking up with photography.'

Sherlock glanced towards the tent. 'When will the plate be ready?' he asked.

'We need to let it dry. While it does, let us continue our t-t-tutorials in logic – ah, you thought I had forgotten! Come, walk this way.'

Dodgson led Sherlock away from the tent and the camera, over to a stone wall that projected from the wall of the college itself. 'This is the garden of the Master of Christ Church College. It is walled all around. If I told you that there was a p-p-pond inside, with fish swimming inside, could you t-t-tell me how large is the p-p-pond?'

Sherlock thought for a moment. 'Smaller than the area of the garden, obviously. Other than that, I couldn't say.' He looked around. There was a door in the wall, a little way away. 'If that door isn't locked then I could go inside and look. Otherwise, I suppose I could climb over the wall.' He checked the nearby buildings, looking for windows that overlooked the garden, but didn't find any. 'Apart from that, I'm not sure. Could I ask someone?'

'No. What if I told you that there was a way of estimating the size of the pond inside without moving from this spot or uttering a word to anyone else?'

Sherlock considered. 'I would believe you, but I wouldn't know how to begin.'

Dodgson bent and picked a stone up from the ground.

He handed it to Sherlock. 'Here, throw this st-st-stone over the wall.'

'Are you sure?'

'I am sure. Throw it.'

'But it's the Master's garden!'

'He won't mind. I'm always throwing st-st-stones into it.'

Sherlock looked dubiously at Dodgson. 'Well, if you're sure.'

'Trust me. Throw the stone.'

Not without some qualms, Sherlock threw the stone as hard as he could. It sailed over the wall and into the garden. Moments later he heard a clattering sound as it hit some paving, or a statue, or something else hard.

'Very good. Now throw another one. Aim at a different place in the garden.'

Sherlock picked up another stone and threw it, this time aiming more for the centre of the garden. A half-second after the stone vanished, he heard a *splash* as it hit water.

'Perfect! Now another.'

'Are you *absolutely* sure this is all right?'

'I am absolutely sure. Now, let us say that you throw one hundred st-st-stones, all aimed in slightly different directions but all landing inside the garden. Let us also say that thirty-three of the stones make a splashing sound when they l-l-land. The rest either hit stone, in which we hear an impact, or they hit earth or vegetation, in which case we hear n-n-nothing. What can we deduce from this information?'

It was as if a light had come on inside Sherlock's head, illuminating something that had been there all along but which he had never been aware of. 'It would indicate that the pond is one third the size of the garden. All we then have to do is to measure the size of the garden from outside, and we will know the size of the pond!'

'Precisely, and we don't have to move from this spot to do it. That is an example of logical deduction from a set of evidence.' He bent and picked up a third stone. 'Now, again! Let's complete the experiment.'

Sherlock chucked the stone, aiming this time for a point about two-thirds of the way along the garden's length. This time he heard a *clink* as the stone hit some pottery, followed by a bellowing shout of 'Dodgson – is that you again? Dash it all, man, I've warned you about this before!'

'Ah,' Dodgson said, 'he's in the garden. That's unfortunate.' He thought for a second. 'The lesson is over. You run, and I'll hide in the tent. Same time in t-t-two days?'

Without waiting for an answer, he dashed towards the tent and dived inside. His feet stuck out of the flap.

Sherlock heard someone throwing bolts inside the door that led to the garden. He ran as fast as he could, back towards the college, before the person coming out could see his face. He was laughing all the way.

Mycroft's telegram, when it arrived, was rather less terse than Sherlock's had been. Partly, Sherlock assumed, that was because Mycroft did not find it easy to be miserly with his words, and partly also because he was never miserly with his money. He would rather pay more to be completely understood than pay less and risk ambiguity.

Dear Sherlock. One of my agents waited at the address, which is a small house occupied by a former police constable, until the package arrived. My agent watched through a window as the ex-constable took the box inside and unwrapped it. Later he emerged, took a box - perhaps the same one - to a post office and sent it back to Oxford. Agent says that the wrapping looked quote different unquote, but cannot say how. The address is Gresham Lodge, Wolvercote, Oxon. 'Coals to Newcastle' is an appropriate phrase here. I would be fascinated to hear what is going on. Write soonest. Your loving brother, Mycroft.

Sherlock read the telegram in the dining room of Mrs McCrery's house. He had a plate of toast in front of him, and a glass of fresh apple juice. He read it again, just to make sure that he hadn't missed anything. The box had been sent back to Oxford? Why bother? Why did the thief not just take it to Gresham Lodge himself? It would save a lot of time, and the risk that the package might get lost in the post, as some of them did.

Mycroft's mention of the old phrase 'taking coals to Newcastle' was entirely appropriate. Newcastle was a major centre for coal production in England. Taking coals there would be pointless; just as pointless as sending a package from Oxford to London and then back to Oxford again. What was the point?

Of course! He almost hit himself in the centre of his forehead, but stopped himself just in time. It was obvious! The thief had been hired by someone in Oxford who wanted to remain anonymous. They got the thief to send the body parts to an address in London. That way, the only information the thief had was the London connection. The ex-police constable in London then rewrapped the box and sent it to the person in Oxford who was central to everything, but all the ex-constable knew was the address in Oxford – not what was in the box. The two critical bits of information – the address of the person in Oxford who was running all this and the fact that they were interested in fresh body parts – never existed together. It was very simple, and very clever!

What to do now? It was obvious – Sherlock had to investigate the address in Wolvercote. If he did it quickly, he might even be able to see the package being redelivered.

He headed down to the canal to meet Matty, and quickly updated his friend on what had happened. Matty grasped the logic immediately. 'This bloke is clever,' he said. ''E's very careful about coverin' 'is tracks. He's a real thinker, like you are.'

They set out after lunch. Wolvercote was a way away, and so they borrowed the same cart that Matty had used to help move Sherlock's luggage a week or so ago. There was something about the journey that Sherlock found familiar, and he realized after a while that they were travelling parallel to the path of the canal out of Oxford. He recognized some of the villages they went through, and even stretches of forest.

One of the larger villages near their goal had a small post office. Sherlock went inside and asked about how often the post was delivered around there. The postmistress was suspicious of him at first, but he got her talking and soon they were chatting like old friends. She told him that the area covered by her delivery boys was so large that there was only one delivery and collection a day, and that the boys hadn't left for that day's round yet because they were still waiting for the delivery to the post office to take place. That was exactly what Sherlock had wanted to hear.

As they neared their goal, Sherlock began to get the strangest feeling that he knew where they were going. As it turned out, he was right.

'Gresham Lodge' was a large house set in its own grounds. The wall around the grounds was too large to see over. Although the gates were padlocked, the house could be seen through its bars. Sherlock had seen it before. Once had been when he was on the barge, travelling towards Oxford with Matty. The second time had been when he was wandering around the local area, trying to get to grips with its geography. This was the house with the strange look to it, the house that gave the impression of being slightly twisted even though every line of its construction was straight and every angle square; the house that looked like it was being seen through the bottom of a glass bottle. Looking at it now gave Sherlock a slight headache.

'We've seen this place before,' Matty said. His voice was quiet. 'We was on the barge.'

'That's right,' Sherlock said. He didn't mention the massive, oddly shaped figure on the roof that time. Matty hadn't seen it, and Sherlock didn't want to worry him any more than he already was. Neither did he mention having come this way a few days later and having seen a man with a scarred hand going inside in a carriage.

'It still looks strange,' Matty observed. 'Even from this angle.' He looked around, making a quick mental calculation. 'The canal must be on the other side of it.'

'It is,' Sherlock confirmed.

'An' this is it? You sure?'

Sherlock reached up and pushed some ivy away from a pale stone set into the gatepost. Carved into the stone were the words 'Gresham Lodge'. 'Yes,' he said, 'this is it.'

'A boy can hope,' Matty murmured. 'Tell me we're not goin' inside.'

'Not right away,' Sherlock replied. 'We need to set watch – see when the post turns up. If the parcel isn't delivered this time around then we just come back tomorrow, and the next day, and the day after that, until it is.'

'This investigatin' lark – it's not the most fun thing in the world, is it?'

Sherlock smiled slightly. 'Depends on how seriously you take it.'

A few feet from the gates Sherlock noticed a large iron box attached to brackets in the wall. It was a post box. It had a slot in it, presumably for letters, and a door with a lock that must be for parcels. The postman would, presumably, have a key so that he could unlock the box and then lock it again. A small metal sign was attached to the box by means of a hinged rod. It took Sherlock only a few seconds to work out that it was a signal to the postman that there were letters in the box for him to take away. If the flag was up then the postman could unlock the door, regardless of whether he had any parcels or not, and take the letters. If the flag was down then, if he just had letters, he could post them through the slot and move on. Quite an elegant system.

He looked around. The edge of the forest was just across the road. There was plenty of cover there that he and Matty could exploit.

Together they drove the cart down the road and off into a space between trees where it would be hidden from the view of the road and from who wasn't specifically looking for it. They tied the horse to a tree within reach of sufficient grass and went back to the lodge. Finding a relatively comfortable position on the lowest branches of an old oak, they settled down to wait.

CHAPTER EIGHT

For Sherlock – and, he guessed, for Matty – it was a rerun of the watch they had made at the mortuary. It was just as dull, just as mentally numbing. Once another cart went down the road, and a boy went past on a bicycle, but that was it.

The sun wasn't visible from where the two of them sat. They were both on the thickest lower branches of the old oak tree, with their backs against the trunk, but they could plot the sun's progress by the way the shadows shifted on the road between the forest and the gates of the lodge. Minutes and then hours slowly marched past. Ants from a nearby nest investigated these newcomers to the forest. Sherlock felt them tickling his legs as they climbed on to him from the tree, and tracked their progress as the tickling sensation moved up his body. After a while the ants grew bored of him, presumably because he wasn't an obvious source of sugar, and moved on. To Matty, probably, judging by the muffled 'What the – get off me, you little vermin!' that Sherlock heard.

The breeze ruffled the leaves on the trees, making a soft *shushing* sound, like waves breaking against some faraway beach. Sherlock lost track of time entirely. There was just an ever-present moment stretching out in front of him as far as he could sense.

A sudden mechanical noise from the road shocked both the boys into full wakefulness. It was the sound of metal gears and chains – the sound of a bicycle. They stared towards the road, aware that it might just be someone going past, but also aware that it might be the postman, finally.

It *was* the postman. He slowed to a halt by the gates of Gresham Lodge, dismounting his bike smartly as he came to a standstill. He wasn't much older than Sherlock, but he was wearing a dark uniform and a peaked cap, and he had a bulging canvas sack strapped to the back of the bike. He unstrapped it, opened it up, delved inside and pulled out a small package. Turning to the post box attached to the wall he stared at it for a few moments, then stared at the package. Sherlock guessed he was trying to work out whether or not he could fit it through the slot. After a few moments he decided that it wasn't worth trying and dug into his pockets for a bunch of keys. Each key had a label attached. They must all fit different post boxes at different houses along his route – at least, those houses whose occupants locked their gates and had their post delivered to a box outside. In Sherlock's experience, most big houses preferred the postman to come to the front door to deliver and collect letters. Whoever lived in Gresham Lodge valued their privacy.

The postman opened the post box, put the package

inside, then locked it again. Within a few seconds he was cycling off, whistling a tune.

Matty's head appeared around the curve of the tree trunk. 'What do you want to do?' he hissed. 'Do you want to pick the lock an' take a look at the parcel?'

'There's no point,' Sherlock hissed back. 'We're pretty sure we know what's in it. You saw the box being packed. Let's wait and see who picks it up.'

The wait continued. The sun was lower in the sky now, and the weather was getting colder. Sherlock's stomach was rumbling, and he thought he could hear volcanic murmurings from Matty's direction as well. He tried to ignore the hunger as best he could.

It was late afternoon when he heard the noise of a key in a padlock. He snapped his gaze around from the squirrel it had been watching to the gates of Gresham Lodge. The sun was behind the house now, which meant that the walls around the grounds cast a long shadow over the road. The gates were almost invisible, but Sherlock thought he could just make out one of them swinging open. Nothing happened for a long moment. The woods seemed to quieten down – the birds and the insects suddenly hushing as if they were waiting for something bad to happen. Then, just as Sherlock thought that his eyes and his ears were tricking him, a darker shape slipped out from the gap between the open and the closed gates. As far as Sherlock was concerned it was just a patch of moving blackness, but somehow it gave the impression of being large, bulkier than a normal man, but hunched at the same time. It also gave the impression of wariness, as if it was watching its surroundings for anything that might threaten its safety. There was something feral, animal-like, about it.

The figure got to the post box, obscuring it in darkness, and Sherlock again heard a key being used. Moments later the shape headed back to the gates of the lodge. It paused there, and at that moment a ray of sunlight penetrated between two chimney pots on top of the house and illuminated the shape from behind. Whoever it was, they were bundled up in a thick leather coat and wearing a leather hat pulled down low over their face. Judging by the position of the top of their head, Sherlock reckoned they were somewhere near seven feet tall. It occurred to Sherlock that this had to be the same person he had seen on the roof of the house, when he was on the barge passing by, and then again in the carriage that had gone through the gates of the lodge a few days before. The man with the scars on his hands.

The man stayed there for a while, watching and waiting, and then he slipped back into the shadows. The gate closed with a *clank*, and then Sherlock heard the chain rattle and the padlock click close.

He counted to a hundred, in case the big man was still there, in the shadows, watching, and then he slipped down from the tree and ran across the road to the gates. They were, indeed, locked again.

Matty joined him. 'Well, it's been a fun afternoon,' he said, 'but I'm not sure how much more we know now than we did before.'

'We're just connecting dots,' Sherlock said thoughtfully. 'We've tracked the stolen items from the mortuary to here. We know that this place is connected to the thefts.'

'Great,' Matty said. 'So, back to Oxford for some nosh then?'

'I'm afraid not.'

Matty sighed. 'I thought you might say that. You want to go inside, don't you?'

'Only up to a window, just so I can see the package being opened. Any ideas?'

'Judgin' by how careful that bloke in the big coat was, 'e's not goin' to allow any gaps in the wall. 'E'll repair 'em as soon as 'e finds 'em. Out best chance is to find an overhangin' tree an' get over that way.'

'Won't he be regularly trimming back branches the way he'll be looking for gaps in the wall?'

Nah – cos 'e's such a big bloke, 'e'll only be lookin' for branches that could bear 'is own weight. 'E'll forget that there are smaller people around. Like me.'

'But I'm bigger than you,' Sherlock pointed out. 'A branch that would take your weight might break under mine.'

'Yeah,' Matty said, opening his jacket to reveal a rope wound around his waist, 'but I came prepared. I'll climb over, then throw this rope back so you can climb up it.'

'Can *you* take my weight?'

'If I can't find a tree trunk on the other side to secure the rope, then I'll 'ave to, won't I?'

It all worked out the way Matty had described. They walked around the walls of the lodge until they found a tree branch that projected over, then Matty scrambled up and along like a monkey. Once over he threw the rope back in Sherlock's direction. He must have found an anchor point of some kind, because when Sherlock tugged on it the rope went taut. He climbed the wall, feet against the bricks and hands holding tight to the rope. When he got to the top he paused, and looked around, but everything was quiet. The shadowed bulk of the house appeared to loom over him. Sherlock carefully slid into the grounds of Gresham Lodge. It felt like it was several degrees colder inside the grounds than it was outside, and even with his back to it Sherlock was aware that the house was there. He could feel it watching him. He shook himself, trying to get rid of the unwelcome sensation. Houses did not have eyes, and they did not have personalities. They did not watch people, or loom over them. He was just slightly disoriented from lack of food, that was all.

Looking sideways at Matty, Sherlock could see that the boy's face was pale and strained. He was feeling it too, whatever *it* was.

'Come on,' he said. 'Let's get this over with as quickly as possible.'

'Did I miss a sign?' Matty asked. 'Is this an asylum? Cos it certainly feels like one.'

'It's just a house.' He looked at its blank face again. 'Just an ordinary house.'

The two of them sprinted across the grounds, aiming for the corner of the house so that they were out of direct line of sight of any of the windows. When they got there they flattened themselves against the brickwork. The house felt strangely *warm* beneath Sherlock's palms. It must have been the heat of the sun still lingering in the bricks, he told himself.

He led the way along the side of the house to the nearest window and peered around the edge of the window frame. Inside looked like a dining room: a long dark table set with candles. The room was empty. He gestured to Matty, and they moved on to the next window.

This one gave on to a room that was lined with wooden display cabinets with glass fronts. From the angle he was looking at, Sherlock couldn't see what was in the cabinets. There were two doors out of the room – one directly across from the window, presumably leading out into a hall, and one to Sherlock's right, which he assumed led into another room.

He was about to shift position to get a better view when the door to the room opened and a man walked in.

The newcomer was the man who had collected the parcel from the post box. He had taken off his hat, but he was still wearing his bulky leather coat. He filled the doorway from side to side and top to bottom, but in the flickering gaslight that illuminated the room Sherlock could see that he had a leather mask over his face. He heard Matty beside him catch his breath as he saw it. The mask was made of fragments of leather of various shades, sizes and shapes, all sewn together in a patchwork. There were two holes for the eyes, but the gaslight didn't reach inside and they were just dark holes.

The figure was holding the box from the package. He walked across to one of the display cabinets and opened up the glass. He opened the box inside, took some object from within, then put it into the cabinet and closed the lid again. He stood, staring at it for a moment, then walked out of the room, taking the box with him. He shut the door behind him.

If that was the toe which had been stolen from the mortuary, then the mysterious man had placed it in a display. Logic told Sherlock that everything else in the display had to be a stolen body part as well, but why? What was the point?

He felt a burning wave of curiosity wash over him. He *had* to see inside the room! He *had* to know what was going on! 'Can we get in?' he whispered.

'I dunno – 'ave you got a monkey wiv you?'

Sherlock stared at his friend. 'Don't be facetious.'

'If I knew what that was, then I wouldn't be it.' Matty ran his hands around the window frame. 'This place is pretty old,' he whispered. 'I reckon I could prob'ly work some of this wood loose and pull the entire frame out, but I suppose you don't want to leave any traces.'

'That's right,' Sherlock hissed back. 'No noise and no evidence that we were here.'

'Hmm.' Matty's gaze flickered around the frame again. He pushed at the window experimentally. The bottom section was obviously designed to slide up, if someone in the house wanted to open the window, but there was a bolt connecting it to the upper section that stopped anyone outside opening it if it was closed. Sherlock heard it rattle. 'Right – I think I can do this.' Matty reached into his pocket and pulled out a spool of wire. Quickly he pulled a length of it straight and bent it to and fro a few times until it broke off. He then fashioned a loop at one end and lowered the hook through the gap between the two sections of the window. He fished around for a moment or two until the wire loop touched the bolt. He hooked the loop around the bolt and pulled. The bolt slid back.

'You've done that before,' Sherlock whispered accusingly.

'No, I haven't!'

'Then why do you keep a reel of wire in your pocket?'

'Cos it's useful for all sorts of things. Man's got a pocket knife an' a reel of wire an' he can pretty much do anything. An' repair anything.'

Sherlock glanced at the window. 'You seemed to know exactly what to do there.'

'Obvious, weren't it?' Matty protested.

Without replying, Sherlock carefully placed his hands against the glass of the lower section and pushed upward. There was a counterweighted sash somewhere inside, because it slid up noiselessly and without effort.

Sherlock glanced at Matty. 'Are you coming in?'

'You want me to, or you want me to stay out here an' stand guard?'

'I think there's a bigger risk of someone coming down the corridor and into the room than coming round the corner of the house and seeing the window open.'

'Fair enough.'

Sherlock climbed over the windowsill and into the room. He looked around at the glass cabinets and gasped.

They were full of bits of bodies.

Sherlock heard a thump on the carpet beside him as Matty entered the room. A few seconds later the boy gasped, and said, 'Oh my God!' What is this place?'

Sherlock didn't know. He was transfixed by the sight of arms, hands, legs, feet, eyes and ears, all carefully placed on purple velvet. All the hands were together in one case, all the ears in another . . . everything was clustered in groups of similar objects. Seeing them together, and divorced from their bodies, Sherlock was amazed at how different they were from one another. In the case of hands alone there were big hands, small hands, hairy hands with torn nails, delicate hands . . . all possible variations – and more than could have come from the Oxford mortuary, Sherlock realized. These thefts were much wider than he had thought.

The hands had been sliced neatly at the wrist, he noticed. There was no blood, no tearing or bruising of the flesh. They all looked as if they should still be attached to their owner.

There were labels beside each hand, he noticed. They were written in a neat copperplate script, and they appeared to relate to the occupation of the person whose hand it was. 'Manual labourer', one said. Another said: 'Typist'.

In Sherlock's mind, a theory began to form.

Matty was transfixed by a case of eyeballs. Sherlock moved across to join him. The eyes weren't as different from one another as the hands were, but each one was a different colour, and the labels this time read: 'Short-Sighted', 'Long-Sighted' and 'Blind'.

'They're lookin' at me,' Matty whispered hoarsely.

'It's your imagination.'

Matty took a step to one side. 'Nah, they're definitely lookin' at me. They're followin' me around the room.'

'It's an optical illusion. The same thing happens with well-painted portraits – they seem to be looking at you all the time.'

160

'Maybe they are as well.'

Actually, Sherlock had to admit that in the flickering gaslight it did look as if the eyes were shifting around slightly on their velvet.

'How come they're not, like, decayin'?' Matty asked. 'What's keepin' them fresh?'

'I was wondering that.'

'Are they, like, preserved in alcohol or somethin'?'

'They're not in bottles, floating in liquid.'

'Mummified then, like them blokes in Egypt?'

'Mummies are shrivelled and brown because of the preservation process. They don't look this fresh.'

'Well, what then? Magic?'

Sherlock indicated the hands in their case. 'Take a look at them. Do you notice anything?'

Matty bent over, not without a twitch of his shoulders. 'They look too good to be true. An' there should be some bruisin' or tearin' where they were cut away from the arm, but there's nothin'.'

'They're not real,' Sherlock announced firmly. 'Look at the skin – it's slightly shiny. These are wax models – not real hands at all.' He turned and indicated the eyes. 'If these were real they'd look more like poached eggs, all deflated and discoloured, but they're perfect. They're made out of wax as well, I think.'

Matty stared at Sherlock. 'So someone steals these things from the mortuary, sends 'em to London, where someone else sends 'em back, an' by the time they get back here they've turned from flesh to wax? That don't make any sense!'

'It does if the box that gets sent back isn't the one from the latest theft, it's the one from the theft before that.' Sherlock thought for a minute. 'Mycroft's agent didn't see what happened to the box while it was inside the house, and he can't be sure the one he sent was the same one as arrived. Somewhere in that time, the stolen toe was taken out and something else was put in the box or the box was swapped/exchanged for a similar one.' He looked around, trying to work out where the burly figure had been standing when he and Matty had been looking through the window. Yes, it was nearer the corner of the room. He crossed over and quickly scanned the cabinet. Eight fingers were lined up inside, on velvet. The ends appeared to have been neatly sliced through, showing bone and tissue and fat, but close up Sherlock could see that it was all too perfect. The flesh was the scarlet colour of fresh blood, not the rust of dried blood, and the shine of the wax made it look wet, not dried. One of the fake fingers was slightly twisted, as if it had been only recently put into the case, and in a hurry. 'This one – this is what we saw the man putting in just now. So – a real toe was stolen and a reproduction finger was returned. I guess that next time there's a theft, whatever is stolen will be sent to London and a wax toe will be returned. Someone in London is making wax reproductions of these stolen body parts.'

'What are they doing with the originals?' Matty wanted to know.

'Throwing them out,' Sherlock ventured. 'Or maybe burning them – if they've got any Christian feeling in them.'

Matty looked around again, but he was relaxing now that he knew the body parts weren't real. 'So this is – what? – some kind of exhibit? Like in a museum?'

'It must be. But why? What's it all for?'

Matty moved across to the door. 'Maybe there's other rooms with other stuff in that might tell us.' Before Sherlock could stop him he had eased the door open a crack and was looking out into the corridor. Quickly he pulled his head back again and shut the door.

'What happened?' Sherlock asked.

'It was a cat,' Matty said. 'It startled me.'

He opened the door again and glanced outside. 'Okay, it's gone now,' he said. 'Let's see what's next door.' Quickly he slipped outside. With a muffled curse, Sherlock followed.

The corridor had a door at one end and disappeared around a corner at the other. A cat sat at the far end, licking itself. There were three more doors leading off the corridor's length. Matty moved along to the next door and put his ear up against it. Sherlock joined him as quietly as he could. They both listened carefully, but could hear nothing from inside. Eventually Sherlock took hold of the doorknob and cautiously turned it.

There was no reaction from inside the room. He pushed the door open.

A wave of heat wafted out into the corridor, making Sherlock's eyes water. Matty winced. 'Someone certainly don't like the cold,' he murmured.

They both entered the room and closed the door behind them. This room was a lot darker than the previous one, lit not by gas lamps but by a coal fire that glowed balefully in the chimney place. There was a smell of something sharp, like vinegar.

Instead of glass cabinets, the room was lined with glass-fronted cases. They were, Sherlock thought, like the kinds of things you might keep fish in, but only a few of them were filled with water. The others had sand, or earth, or twigs from trees.

For a moment Sherlock's memory flashed back to the Passmore Edwards Museum in London, where he had once been attacked by a falcon. That had been filled with glass cases as well, and each case had been made to look like a particular environment – beach, or forest, or field. The inhabitants of those cases had been stuffed animals, made to look as lifelike as possible. Sherlock had a terrible feeling, based on the intense heat from the fire, that whatever was in these cases was not stuffed.

He moved closer to one of them, feeling a strange mixture of curiosity and repulsion.

This case was half-filled with gravel and pebbles. Sherlock couldn't see anything else inside. He bent closer, nose almost pressed against the glass.

One of the pebbles suddenly lashed out towards him.

Sherlock jerked backwards. What he had taken to be a large stone was actually some kind of spider. It had unfolded its legs and was poised, angled with its rear end raised. Its body extended at the back into a long tail which it was waving above its lowered head. A stinger at the end of the tail kept hitting the glass with a clicking noise, leaving viscous smears behind. A pair of sharp claws waved from the front of the spider, opening and closing with vicious intent. Sherlock had never seen anything like it before.

He moved away, towards the next case, and the spider paralleled his progress until it reached the glass at the far end of its tiny world.

The next case was filled with twigs, branches and leaves. Wary this time, Sherlock held back. He stared through the glass, trying to work out what kind of creature was inside. It took a few minutes, but he eventually realized that one of the twigs wasn't a twig at all – it was some kind of insect with a thin body and thinner legs, coloured to almost match the vegetation that it was hiding among. Its head was larger, its eyes larger still, but they were green, like a leaf.

Sherlock moved to the next case, feeling slightly sick.

This one was filled with water and had sand at the bottom. In the middle of it floated something that looked like a jelly with trailing tendrils that wafted gently in the currents. A handful of small striped fish were swimming in the tank as well, and Sherlock noticed that they kept well away from the jelly-like thing – all except for one of them, which was investigating the boundary between the glass and the sand when a tendril happened to brush across it. The fish jerked abruptly, then turned belly-up and began to float towards the surface of the water.

Poison, Sherlock thought. The jelly-like creature had poison in its tendrils. The spider had left trails of something on the glass that might well have been poison. Sherlock had a feeling that if he had reached inside the case with the twig-like insect and tried to touch it, then he would have discovered it to be poisonous as well.

'Look at this,' Matty breathed. Sherlock moved to join him.

The glass case that Matty was staring into with fascination was filled with bright green leaves. On some of the leaves, frogs were sitting, but these were different from the kinds of frogs that Sherlock was used to seeing in ponds. These were bright red, and no bigger than his thumb.

'What *is* this place? Some kind of *zoo*?' Matty asked in awed tones. 'I still get nightmares about them two big reptile things that attacked us in America! What are we going to find in the next room? A lion? A couple of crocodiles?'

'I don't think so.' Sherlock gazed around, trying to

take it all in. 'What's the first thing that occurs to you when you look around?'

'The first thing that occurs to me is – euch! The second thing is that I want to get out, quickly, an' have a long bath.'

'There's a reason for that,' Sherlock pointed out.

'Yeah – the reason is that these things are all horrible an' they make my skin crawl!'

'But *why* are they horrible?' Sherlock asked. '*Why* do they make your skin crawl? Look around – the fact is that they're all poisonous.' He pointed at the spider-thing, which had stopped stabbing at the glass with its tail and was now watching them with tiny, glittering black eyes. 'I think that's called a scorpion. It's got poison in its sting. They have them in Africa, and America, and other places.' He moved his finger to indicate the frogs. 'The bright colour of those amphibians is a warning to birds and other animals not to eat them, because they have poison in their skin. I remember reading somewhere that South American tribes use that poison on their arrows.' He moved in front of one of the water-filled tanks. Floating inside was a small fish. Sherlock rapped on the glass with a knuckle. Within a few seconds the fish had swollen to several times its previous size, and spines had emerged from its skin. 'This is a puffer fish. It swells up to deter predators, and its spines contain poison. I was told about it when I was in Japan.'

'I thought you were in China,' Matty asked.

167

Sherlock shrugged. 'On the way back we stopped in Japan for a few weeks.'

'You never mentioned that before.'

'There's a reason,' Sherlock said darkly. 'But anyway – this fish is a delicacy in Japan, but the chefs have to be careful to remove the poison sacs first, otherwise the diners might die.'

Matty indicated the tank with the jelly-like mass floating in it. 'That's a jellyfish, right? You get them at the seaside.'

'Not like that. If I've identified it correctly, that's a box jellyfish. It's got poison in its tendrils that's hundreds of times more toxic than snake venom.' He looked around again, taking in every tank. 'Yes, I think *everything* here is poisonous. What with that and the wax body parts, it all makes sense!'

'It does?' Matty didn't seem so sure.

'If you ask yourself, why would anybody have this kind of collection? What would they *use* it for?'

'I keep asking myself that.' Matty looked around dubiously. 'I can't think of an answer.'

Sherlock had just opened his mouth, ready to tell his friend what he had worked out, when the side door leading to the next room abruptly opened. A man stood in the doorway – not the big, scarred man that Sherlock had seen before, but a smaller man wearing a black suit and striped waistcoat. His head was shaved, and his tiny eyes were almost hidden in the flesh of his face. His gaze snapped instantly from Sherlock to Matty and back, and then he roared, 'Boss – we got burglars!'

'Quick,' Sherlock yelled to Matty, 'get to the—'

He was interrupted when the man rushed at him, fist raised.

Sherlock backed away, raising his own clenched fists in defence. The man threw a tight punch at Sherlock's head. Sherlock ducked to the right and brought his own fist up and crashing into the man's chin. It was like hitting brickwork. The man took a step back, scowling, while Sherlock nursed his aching knuckles.

The man stepped forward again. Blood dribbled from a split lip. He jabbed with his right fist again, but it was a feint. Sherlock didn't see his left hand swinging in from the side and it caught him on the ear. A spike of scarlet pain flashed through his head, and he fell sideways.

The man swung a foot at Sherlock's stomach. Sherlock rolled over, and the foot caught him in the back. Pain flared up and down his body, but through the haze of agony Sherlock knew that it was better than if the foot had hit its target. That would have disabled him for hours.

The shaven-headed man reached out to the fireplace and took a poker from a rack. It seemed to glow in the firelight. The man raised the poker above his head, intending to bring it down on to Sherlock's skull.

CHAPTER NINE

Sherlock scuttled backwards on elbows and knees, but the man followed him, preparing to strike.

From the shadows, Matty launched himself at the suited man, grabbing his upraised elbow and hanging on for dear life. The man fell backwards, with Matty's weight dragging him down. Matty tried to let go and fall away, but he was too late: the man's weight landed right on top of him. Sherlock heard the breath rush out of his friend's lungs with an audible *whoosh*!

To add injury to injury, the man jabbed backwards with his elbow, catching Matty in the stomach. As the man rolled away and climbed to his feet, Matty curled up into a ball, moaning.

The man looked from Sherlock to Matty and back again, trying to work out which of them to deal with first. Matty was out of the fight for the time being, so he advanced on Sherlock, still holding the poker.

Sherlock looked around desperately. He needed a weapon too!

The man swung the poker at Sherlock. Sherlock ducked, then converted the duck into a sideways dive that took him to the floor. He rolled, ending up near the fire. There weren't any more pokers in the rack, but there was a large pair of tongs for picking up lumps of coal. He grabbed them and briefly checked on Matty. 'Are you okay?'

'I will be,' the boy moaned. 'Just give me a minute. Or ten.'

Sherlock straightened up and turned just as the man rushed at him, his face was contorted into a diabolical scowl. 'I'm goin' to cripple you, you little –'

Before he finished the sentence, he swung the poker again. Sherlock blocked it with the tongs. A high metallic note rang through the room. The shock of the impact numbed Sherlock's arm right up to the shoulder. He stepped back, aware that the open door to the next room was just behind him. When the man rushed at him again, swinging the poker like a club this time, Sherlock took two steps back, grabbed the door handle and pulled the door half shut.

The man ran straight into the edge of the door. He bounced backwards, crying out in pain. He wiped a sleeve across his eye, smearing the blood across his face, and advanced into the next room, following Sherlock.

'Don't you *ever* stop?' Sherlock whispered, half to himself.

'Not ever,' the man replied. 'You can kill me, and I'll still keep on coming. My job is to protect this place from little thieves like you.'

Sherlock was about to say that he wasn't a thief, and neither was Matty, but he doubted the man would believe him. He was like some kind of unstoppable clockwork machine!

He suddenly lashed out at Sherlock with the poker. Sherlock blocked with the tongs again, then poked the tongs directly at the man's eyes. The man leaned backwards. Taken by surprise, Sherlock followed, suddenly overbalancing. The man abruptly changed his grip on the poker, holding it halfway up and jabbing the handle into Sherlock's ribs. It felt for a moment like he had broken one of them. Sherlock brought his left arm down to protect his side while he jabbed the tongs at the man's throat. He caught him just below the Adam's apple, and the man doubled up, choking. Sherlock hit him hard on the head with the tongs and he fell to his knees, gasping in pain.

Sherlock backed into the centre of the room, taking deep breaths while he could and looking around to see if there were any other weapons he could use. This room was lined with glass tanks too, but in the few seconds he had to make an analysis Sherlock saw that these tanks had snakes in: some the colour of sand and some brightly banded in red and yellow; some the size of Sherlock's little finger and one, in a triple-sized tank, as thick as Sherlock's arm. Attention attracted by the sudden movement, they followed Sherlock with eager eyes.

Sherlock realized that the man had climbed back to his feet again. Blood was streaming down his scalp but it still wasn't stopping him. In fact, it appeared to have made him even angrier.

'There ain't going to be enough of you left to fill a bucket when I've finished with you,' he growled. He swished the poker through the air in front of him. Sherlock could feel the breeze of its passage riffling his hair.

Behind him, Matty was still curled up on the floor.

The man charged, still waving the poker.

Sherlock took hold of his tongs with both hands and swiped sideways. The poker flew out of the man's hand and struck one of the tanks. The glass shattered.

The man grabbed hold of the other end of the tongs. For a moment the two of them stood there, each fighting for control, but the man was too strong. He tore the tongs from Sherlock's grasp and threw them away.

Directly into another tank. More glass shattered.

The man grabbed Sherlock by the throat and lifted. Sherlock suddenly couldn't breathe. His feet weren't touching the floor. A red mist came down over his vision, making everything foggy and distant. The man was saying something, his breath hot on Sherlock's face, but the words were muffled by the thudding of blood in Sherlock's ears. He tried to see over the man's shoulder in case Matty had got to his feet and was coming to help, but the boy was still curled into a ball.

This looked like the end. There was nothing Sherlock could do. Not all the puzzle solving in the world was

173

going to help him survive being strangled.

Something moved by his shoulder. He could hardly see now – his vision was restricted to a narrow tunnel surrounded by blackness – but there was definitely something there, waving slowly to and fro.

The man saw it as well. His face went pale. Before he could do anything more than ease his grip slightly, the thing lashed out, fastening itself on his cheek.

It was a snake: striped in vivid red, yellow and black. Sherlock grabbed at its body, which was whipping back and forth. He tried to pull it away, but its fangs were fastened in the man's flesh. The man himself was screaming now, face contorted in agony and terror.

Matty suddenly appeared at Sherlock's shoulder. He was hunched and pale, obviously still in pain, but at least he was moving. 'Let's get out,' he said urgently.

'Take hold of this thing!' Sherlock nodded towards the snake.

'Are you *mad*?'

'It's going to kill him!'

Matty scowled. 'So what? You were tryin' to kill 'im! 'E was tryin' to kill you! We need to escape!'

Sherlock could feel his lips tighten in stubborn anger. 'It doesn't matter. He's a human being, and he's in trouble because of us. Take hold of this thing now!'

Matty stared at Sherlock for a second, then at the window. Reluctantly he reached past Sherlock and grabbed the writhing reptile. 'I didn't sign up for this kind of thing,' he muttered.

Once Matty had a firm grip, Sherlock let go and moved past him, towards the bitten man. His eyes were closed and he was whimpering now. 'We're trying to help,' Sherlock said. 'Brace yourself.' He grabbed at the snake's jaws, careful to use the looser skin around the thing's mouth as protection against the teeth. It was dry and warm to the touch. Exerting pressure, he pulled the snake's mouth further open. The fangs in the top and bottom jaws slid out of the man's cheek, leaving four bloody holes behind.

Matty slid his hands up so that he was holding the snake just behind its head, preventing it from whipping around and biting him too. His arms flailed as the snake tried desperately to get out of his grip.

The man fell to his knees, still whimpering. Sherlock stared at the holes in his cheek. There would be poison in the wound now, and he hadn't got a clue what to do about it. Should he try to get hold of a doctor? Just how long did this snake's venom take to have an effect? Was it just disabling, or actually deadly?

'Sherlock . . .'

'Not now – trying to think!'

He had no idea what to do next. No idea at all.

'Sherlock,' Matty repeated, voice very quiet and controlled, 'look over there!'

Sherlock turned and looked to where Matty was

staring in horror. There, on the carpet, was another snake. It was larger than the one Matty was holding, and brown. It must have come out of the second shattered tank. As Sherlock watched, its head broadened out into a kind of hood that made it look more threatening. A sudden rattle made Sherlock look at its tail, which was raised above the carpet and shaking back and forth. There were little bony plates there that made the rattling noise when they vibrated – a warning perhaps? Not that either Sherlock or Matty needed a warning. They were scared enough already.

Sherlock froze. His gaze flickered around the room, searching for something he could use against the creature, but finding nothing. The tongs were in the shattered glass tank near the bitten man's head, while the poker was on the other side of the room, lying on the carpet amid shards of glass.

The snake opened its mouth wide, displaying the red flesh inside. Another warning.

The only thing that Sherlock could think of to do was to grab it when it struck. It was a risky option, and he didn't like it, but he wasn't sure he had a choice.

The snake's head drew back. It was going to launch itself at him. Sherlock braced himself.

Something moved in the doorway of the room they had come out of a few minutes earlier. The snake didn't react, but Sherlock glanced sideways.

The doorway was filled by a huge figure. It was the

man Sherlock had seen earlier, taking the parcel from the post box, and earlier than that, in a carriage entering the grounds of the house. He had taken off his bulky leather coat and hat, but he was still wearing the close-fitting jigsaw mask. In fact, Sherlock now saw that it was a hood that went entirely over his head. Bright blue eyes shone through the eyeholes. He held a gun in his hand, a hand so large that it made the weapon look like a toy. His eyes moved, taking in the scene. They ended up looking at Sherlock.

He raised the gun and fired.

Sherlock just stood there, frozen in place. He tried to work out where the bullet had hit. He couldn't feel any impact or pain – he must be in shock, he thought. Any second now the agony would start, and blood would begin to pulse from the wound.

After a few seconds in which nothing happened, apart from the smoke from the gun's barrel drifting through the room, Sherlock realized that there was no pain, no blood, and no wound. He looked down at himself to check, and saw nothing. Had the newcomer missed? Would he fire again?

He looked up again, but the man was looking over Sherlock's shoulder. Sherlock followed his gaze, to where the brown snake lay in two halves on the carpet, torn apart by the bullet from the gun.

The newcomer's gaze moved from the snake to Sherlock and then from Sherlock to Matty. 'I could shoot you both,' he said, voice muffled by the leather face mask, 'or you could help me save George's life, and then explain yourselves. You have five seconds to decide.' His voice sounded like rocks grinding together, it was so deep and hoarse.

'We help,' Sherlock said quickly, 'and then we explain.'

'Good choice.' The man lowered the gun and slipped it into the waistband of his trousers. 'You – smaller boy – give me that cobra.' He turned and quickly shut the snake in a box. 'You – bigger boy – get me that device and the knife from the mantelpiece.'

Sherlock followed where the man was pointing and saw an object the size of his fist on the mantelpiece. He scooped it up. It was a ball made out of a strange rubbery substance, connected to a metal valve and a nozzle which flared out to a conical opening, again made of that same rubbery substance. He handed it across to the man, who had moved to where the other man – George – was kneeling, moaning and holding his arms across his chest, and bent to kneel beside him.

'What's your name, boy?' the newcomer asked as he took the device.

'Sherlock. Sherlock Holmes.' He did think about lying, but decided that honesty was the best policy at the moment.

'And your little friend?'

'I ain't so little!' Matty muttered.

The newcomer squished the rubber ball in his hand,

squeezing the air out with a *hiss*.

He looked up at Sherlock. 'My name is Ferny Weston. I own this house. The man with the snake bite is George Squier. He acts as my manservant, cook and general handyman around the house. He's the only person I trust, and I don't intend losing him.' He handed the rubber and metal device to Sherlock. 'Keep that ball squeezed, for all that your life is worth,' he said, and took the knife from Sherlock's other hand. He turned to the bitten man, and before Sherlock could say anything he had put the knife against the skin of George's cheek and made two quick slashes in the shape of an X where the snake's teeth had pierced him.

'What are you doing?' Sherlock cried.

'Getting the poison out,' Weston said. He grabbed the device from Sherlock's grasp and placed the rubber funnel against the skin where he'd cut the X. He let the ball go, and it expanded slowly, the rubber seal making a sucking sound against the blood on George's skin. 'His blood will be pushing out from the wound, taking the poison with it, not going in, but we need to stop the poison diffusing through the tissue. The quicker we suck the poison out, the more chance we have of saving his life.' He squeezed the rubber ball hard, expelling the air. Sherlock heard something sticky gurgling inside. Again he placed it against the wound and sucked.

As the man worked, Sherlock couldn't help but notice the pattern of scars around his wrist and his fingers. He could see how anybody in the local area who saw him might have got the idea that he had been constructed from odd body parts. In fact, apart from the sheer implausibility of the idea, Sherlock wasn't entirely convinced that it wasn't true.

It took five goes before Weston was satisfied that he had either got all the poison out of George's cheek or the poison had diffused so far that it was pointless trying any more. As he pulled the rubber ball away for the last time Sherlock could hear liquid squishing inside. Blood and poison, he presumed.

George appeared to have lapsed into unconsciousness. His eyelids flickered. Weston laid him down gently on his back. 'We need to get him up to his room,' he said. 'I think he'll be all right, but I've got some drugs I can give him to help with the shock and the pain, and I need to dress the wound. You two will help.' It wasn't a question.

'Did you invent that device?' Sherlock asked, indicating the poison-sucking rubber ball.

Weston reached up to scratch his neck, pushing aside the hood so that he could get to the skin underneath. There were scars there too, extending around his neck. Was there *anywhere* on his body that didn't have scars? Sherlock wondered.

'It seemed to be a good idea if I was dealing with snakes,' Weston said.

'Why the snakes?' Sherlock asked. 'Why the –' he

pointed back to the other room – 'wax body parts? Why the *thefts*?'

'Long story, and I'm not sure I want to tell it to you. Not yet anyway, and I want to hear your story first. Let's get George here to bed and treat his wound, and then we'll talk about what happens to the two of you.'

The next hour or so was taken up with the three of them manoeuvring George's inert body out into the corridor, along the corridor and round the corner into the hall, then up two flights of stairs. George's room was at the top of the house, and when they laid him on his bed and placed a blanket over him they all breathed a sigh of relief.

Sherlock thought he heard a woman's voice, calling from downstairs, although he couldn't hear what she was saying. He turned to look at Weston questioningly. The big man had paused, listening.

'I need to go downstairs,' he said. The leather mask turned to face Sherlock. 'I need to get the first-aid kit and the drugs. You stay here with him. I'll only be a few minutes.'

Matty and Sherlock stayed there for a while. George slept, his breath whistling heavily through his mouth.

Sherlock crossed to the window and looked out. It was still dark. He thought he was probably looking down on to the canal, although he couldn't see it in the blackness. Looking down at the point where, little more than a week before, he had been looking up. How things had changed during that time.

Somewhere downstairs he thought he heard Weston's voice speaking, and then a woman's voice responding. There had to be someone else in the house that Weston was protecting, otherwise why not mention her?

After ten minutes or so Weston returned with the first-aid kit and a box of glass vials. He treated George's cheek with an ointment that left an orange stain, then placed a dressing on it and fastened the dressing in place with a bandage that went up across George's bald scalp, then down across his ear and under his chin. The last thing he did was to inject his servant in the arm with the contents of two different glass vials.

'He should be all right now. We'll let him sleep.' He stood up, his hooded head brushing against the low ceiling. 'He was lucky he was bitten by the coral snake. If it had been the black mamba then he would have been dead within minutes. And you two were lucky that the other snake was an ordinary cobra, not a spitting cobra. If venom had got into your eyes then you would have died screaming.'

'What is it with you and poisonous pets?' Matty asked. 'Can't you just keep dogs, or cats?'

The man laughed: a harsh, choking sound. 'They aren't pets, son – they're my work. At least, they were.' He glanced from Matty to Sherlock. 'Come on – let's get downstairs. I need a beer, and I've got some lemonade you two can have.'

'You don't strike me as a lemonade kind of person,' Sherlock said, trying to lead Weston on into saying something about the other person in the house. Weston just laughed. 'I like to have choices,' he said cryptically. 'I like to have examples of similar things that I can compare.'

He gestured to the two of them to go ahead down the stairs. When they got to the floor below Sherlock looked around to see if he could tell where the woman's voice had come from, but all the doors were closed. They kept on going, down to the ground floor and into a room on the other side of the house to where Sherlock and Matty had broken in.

The room was set up as a sitting room, with chairs and side tables. Weston left them there while he went into the kitchen to fetch the beer and the lemonade. Sherlock assumed that it was a test to see if the two of them would make a run for it – Weston had presumably locked the front door, as well as the doors into any side rooms where they could have got out through the windows, so there was no chance of escape. There was always the window in the sitting room, but when he opened the curtains Sherlock found that it was a French window leading out on to a stone veranda. He checked: it was locked.

After a few minutes Weston returned with a tray containing a bottle, a jug filled with a cloudy liquid, two glasses and a plate containing a pile of biscuits. He took the bottle and fell heavily back into a large armchair. Gesturing to the tray, he said, 'Help yourselves. You've had a busy night.'

Matty just stared at the cloudy liquid. 'How do we know,' he asked, 'that you haven't put some kind of poison in there? Maybe you dropped a frog in an' stirred it around with a spoon before scoopin' it out.'

Weston pulled the gun out of the waistband of his trousers and put it on the table next to him. 'Interesting though that would be, it would be quicker and more certain just to shoot you. In fact, I still may. Tell me why you're here, what you're looking for and who sent you. Don't lie to me – I will know if you are lying.'

Sherlock took a deep breath. He was taking a chance here that honesty was the best policy, but Weston didn't strike him as a villain. In fact, Sherlock was beginning to like him – or, at least, respect him. He was decisive, and he seemed to know what he was doing.

'I heard about the thefts of human body parts from the Oxford mortuary,' he said calmly. 'One of my friends was questioned over it, and the man who is tutoring me was also interviewed by the police. I talked to the pathologist, and he gave me enough information so that I could work out when the next theft was going to occur. Matty and I waited, saw the thief, and followed him back to where he lived—'

'That was me,' Matty muttered. '*I* followed him.'

Sherlock frowned at Matty. This was *his* story. 'We traced the thief to the post office, and then traced the package to London and then back here again, but it was a different package. I realize that now. We followed it here, and saw you pick it up. We broke into the house—'

'That was me too,' Matty murmured.

'. . . and we saw the collections of wax body parts and of poisonous creatures that you've put together. It's all very impressive – and "collection" is the right word, isn't it?'

Instead of answering, Weston stared at Sherlock through the eyeholes in his leather hood. 'You know something else,' he pointed out. 'Tell me.'

'How do you know that I know something else?'

'It's the direction you were looking when you were talking. You were looking straight ahead during most of your story, but your eyes weren't focused on anything in particular, which indicates that you were putting together a series of memories into a coherent order, but when you mentioned the pathologist at the Oxford mortuary you looked up and to the left. That indicates you were remembering something specific that he said, something important.'

'And you can tell all that just from the direction I was looking?' Sherlock asked, fascinated.

'To an extent. That's how I can tell when people are lying to me – their eyes drift to their right rather than their left. That means they're putting together stories, rather than remembering things. It's something I've observed over many years of having people tell me lies and tell me the truth. So – what is it that you were remembering?'

'The pathologist – Doctor Lukather – mentioned your name. He said that –' Sherlock tried to remember the exact words, and was suddenly very conscious that he was looking up and to the left – 'that you used to go and talk to him, keep him company, and then suddenly you stopped. He thought you'd got too bored of his stories.'

'Never bored,' Weston said, turning his head away and looking down. 'Never that. Something happened, that's all. Something that meant I couldn't go back.'

'An accident?' Sherlock guessed.

Weston reluctantly nodded. 'But we're getting the story out of order,' he said softly, the softness sounding strange in his grating tone of voice. 'It's important to remember that stories have to be told in the right order, and that you are sure of when they start.'

'What about when they stop?' Matty asked suddenly. 'Isn't that important?'

'Stories never stop,' Weston said. 'They go on forever.'

'And what about our stories?' Sherlock caught Weston's eye. 'Are *they* going to go on forever? Do you believe us?'

'What you said makes sense. All the facts hang together, and you didn't show any evidence of lying. I'm inclined to give you the benefit of the doubt. Besides – you neither look nor act like burglars.'

'So – tell us your story,' Sherlock challenged.

'What have you already worked out?' Weston countered.

Sherlock took a breath. 'You have a collection of poisonous creatures,' he pointed out. 'I suspect that it's the poison that interests you, not the creatures themselves. They are just a means to an end.'

'Go on.'

'You are researching the effects of poison – which ones are quick and which ones are slow, which ones leave obvious signs and which leave no trace at all.' Sherlock thought back to his conversation with Doctor Lukather. 'It's all to do with the evidence that substances leave behind, isn't it? Doctor Lukather was interested in that as well, but you've got further. You're testing the poisons so that you can observe their effects.'

Matty, who had taken a large gulp of lemonade, suddenly lowered the glass. 'I knew it,' he said bitterly.

CHAPTER TEN

Weston laughed. 'I don't test the poisons on humans,' he said, 'although I've come across some people in my time who might arguably deserve it. No, I catch rats and I use them. People poison rats all the time – I just vary the poison and I note the effects.' He paused for a moment. 'But what about the wax body parts? What am I doing with those?'

Remembering the handwritten labels that were beneath the body parts in the glass cases, Sherlock said, 'You're looking at the effects of people's lives on their bodies. You want to be able to look at a person and tell what they do for a living, where they've come from and how they live. You've been collecting body parts from a whole set of *different* people who have done different jobs, and you've been analysing them for characteristic traces.'

'You sound like you already know about this kind of thing.'

A sudden picture of Amyus Crowe's face flashed across Sherlock's memory. He caught his breath. He missed the big American. 'I had a friend who did something similar,' he said softly, 'although he wasn't as . . . organized . . . as you obviously are.'

'Very good.' The big, scarred man nodded. 'Yes, I have been developing a theory for a while now that the occupations people have leave traces on their bodies. Typists have flattened fingertips from the repeated hammering of their fingers against the keys, for instance. Violinists also have flattened fingertips, but only on one hand, from holding the strings down. Tattooists have *swollen* fingertips from where they have inadvertently pricked themselves while inking the tattoos, and picked up infections. Bookkeepers and clerks have a flattened area of hair running around their heads above their ears where the elastic that keeps their characteristic green eyeshades on has compressed the hair over many years. Whatever we do, whatever we are, leaves its traces on us.'

'Like photography,' Sherlock suddenly interrupted. 'The chemicals make your skin go black!'

'That's right.'

'What can you tell about me?' Matty challenged.

'You live on a barge, you have a horse and you steal food for a living. You also go through periods of extreme hunger and periods, like now, where you are eating very well.'

'How can you tell that?'

'Your hands have characteristic scratches from rough wood, which means you might be a carpenter's apprentice, but they are also rough on the inside of the fingers from pulling on thick ropes. Both signs together are a characteristic of sailors, but you haven't got a

189

sailor's tan and your eyes aren't lined from squinting into the sun. That strongly suggests a barge. A barge suggests a horse, and you have straw caught in your shoelaces. Your trousers and shirt are tight on you, but the creases and folds in them suggest that at times they have been looser. There are also indications that the trousers have been taken in at the waist on occasions, and let out on other occasions. This tells me that your weight varies, which means you sometimes eat well and sometimes not so well.'

'And the thieving of food?' Matty challenged. 'That's personal, that is.'

'You have scars on your right hand where someone, or several people, have lashed out at your hand with something. Some of the wounds indicate that a sharp object was used, while some suggest a heavy blunt object, implying that a range of weapons was called into play, almost certainly by different people at different times. So – you often reach out to take things with your right hand, which then gets attacked by the owners of the things you are trying to take. The leap to food was a guess on my part, but then what else is likely?'

'Oh.' Matty raised his right hand and inspected it. 'That's obvious then.'

'There's also the evidence of the biscuits.'

'The biscuits?'

Yes. There were ten biscuits on that plate when I brought it in. There are seven now, but I haven't seen you or your friend eat any. There is also a bulge inside your jacket that wasn't there when you came in. Obviously you're stocking up food for the future.'

Looking sheepish, Matty reached inside his jacket.

Weston waved a hand at him. 'Don't worry about it – they're only biscuits.'

Sherlock wanted to get back to the question of why Weston was doing all of this. 'You strike me as someone who is investigating crimes,' he said, 'but you're obviously very reluctant to leave your house and actually *do* any investigating. When you do leave you are big enough that people will notice you, even without the way you dress. So – what's going on?'

Weston took a sip of beer from the bottle. 'I used to be in the police,' he sighed. 'That was a few years back, mind. I was a detective inspector in South London before I moved here to Oxford. Lots of crimes there, many of them involving sailors who'd disembarked on shore leave, got drunk, lost their money and decided to get it back again with menaces. I became very interested in the traces that criminals leave behind – the evidence. Not a very popular position, I have to admit. The other inspectors I worked with were much more obvious in their approach – arrest the nearest person to the scene of the crime and then beat a confession out of them. I persevered in my approach, however, and became actually quite good at finding small bits of things that had been left behind and then using them to track down

191

the real criminals.' He shrugged. 'Let's take a real case that I was involved with. A witness saw a man rushing away from a house where a woman was found dead. The person running away had their face wrapped up in a scarf so they couldn't be recognized, but the witness noticed that the man had very pale hands. The usual approach would be to look at all the people who knew the victim and check whether any of them had very pale hands. I, on the other hand, went looking for a local baker. Their hands are pale because of the flour – it gets ingrained in their skin. It turned out that the victim owed the baker money, so I arrested him. He confessed while in custody, without the need to beat him up. I have to say that I was encouraged in my rather radical approach by a young man studying here at Oxford. His thoughts ran in similar channels to mine, and we used to talk a lot about the future of policing, where evidence would be everything in a case.'

'Mycroft Holmes,' Sherlock breathed. Matty stared at him, amazed.

Weston nodded. Although Sherlock couldn't see his face, he radiated an aura of satisfaction. 'When you said that your name was Sherlock Holmes, I thought that this was no accident. You are Mycroft's brother, aren't you?'

Sherlock could only nod his head. He was transfixed by two thoughts – the first that he remembered his brother talking of a policeman whom he knew here in Oxford, and the second that Mycroft had deliberately sent him here, hoping that the two of them would meet. He wasn't sure whether to be flattered, intrigued or furious. There were times when Mycroft's blatant and subtle interference in his life were very troubling. It was as if his brother didn't trust Sherlock to act on his own, and always sought to guide him through various means.

'Yes, I'm Mycroft's brother. You met him here, didn't you?'

'I did. We used to drink in the same tavern, and we got talking one night. I had married by that stage and transferred here to Oxford.'

'And then you had your accident,' Sherlock said.

There was silence for a while as Weston stared off into the shadows, remembering things that had happened in the past, things that had scarred him both mentally and physically. 'Yes,' he whispered eventually. 'Except that it wasn't an accident. It was a deliberate attempt on my life, by criminals here in Oxford who were worried that I was getting too close to catching them, and it almost succeeded. It caused me injuries that nearly cost me my life, and left me disfigured and in permanent pain, and also unable to work. The police threw me out like a used handkerchief. It also, more importantly, cost my wife the use of her legs, as she was with me at the time.' His hooded face turned towards Sherlock and Matty. 'Would you like to see the result?' he asked. Without waiting for an answer, he reached up and pulled the leather mask from his face.

Matty gasped, and Sherlock had to hold his breath so that he didn't do the same. Weston's face was a jigsaw puzzle of flesh and vivid scar tissue. The scars ran across his nose, his cheeks, his chin and his forehead. They also extended down his neck into his shirt. The scars themselves were dark and twisted lines, many of them criss-crossed by the signs of stitches. The flesh between the scars was of different colours – white, pale pink and maroon. The colours presumably depended on how badly the flesh had been damaged and how well the blood supply had reconnected, Sherlock assumed. Weston's scalp was partially bald and partially covered with hair. There was no rhyme or reason to which bits were which. One ear was intact while the other was half torn away.

He then slowly removed his gloves. His hands were in the same state – twisted and scarred. Most of the nails were missing. There were heavy scars around his left wrist, almost making it look as though the entire hand had come off and been replaced, although Sherlock knew that was an impossibility.

From the way the scars vanished into his sleeves and the neck of his shirt, it looked as if they continued over most of his body.

'This is how I was left,' he said evenly.

'What happened?' Sherlock asked.

'You can see the evidence – you tell me.'

Sherlock let his gaze travel over Weston's hands and face again, but this time looking analytically rather than emotionally. 'The damage is extensive,' he said eventually, 'but curiously random. If you had been attacked by a knife or a sword then the lines of the scars would be straighter. There are also no scars on the palms of your hands, I notice, although again, if you had been attacked by one man or several men with weapons then I would have expected you to hold your hands up defensively, and there would be significant cuts. The way the cuts *are* arranged, however, it looks as if a number of sharp things hit you at the same time from several directions.' He thought for a moment. 'I am thinking that you might have been in a carriage that crashed, falling apart so that the wood and metal of its construction left scars all over your body. He hesitated. 'No, I saw you a few days ago, in a carriage entering the grounds of this house, and you didn't seem at all perturbed or anxious by being inside, which you would have been had you already been in an accident involving a carriage.' Sherlock suddenly remembered plunging through the skylight at the Oxford mortuary – the way the glass and the wooden frame had come apart and clawed at him as he fell. He shivered. 'No, I think it's more likely that you were inside a building when it collapsed. That would explain everything I can see.'

Weston nodded slowly. 'You are right. I was sent an anonymous message telling me that the people I was chasing were inside a particular house in a slum area. I made my way there and went inside.' He hesitated, remembering. 'They had rigged the place with sticks of explosive. They lit the fuses as soon as they saw me go inside. One minute later, the explosives went off, bringing the house down around me. The last thing I remember is dust, fragments of brick, fragments of wood and shards of glass all seeming to float around me as if I was underwater, but at the same time watching as they cut me, sliced into me and stuck in me. Time itself appeared to slow down and stop.' He took another sip of the beer. 'I was dragged out of the wreckage covered in blood, with sharp objects projecting out of me all over like I was a hedgehog. I was in hospital for months, with stitches all over my body. The pain was . . . incredible. Unforgettable. I've always been a big man, with a healthy constitution, but the doctors say the only reason I survived was sheer willpower. I was determined to live. Nothing – not even the scale of my injuries – was going to stop that.'

'The criminals –' Sherlock asked – 'what was it they had been doing?' Partly he wanted to know, but partly he wanted to move Weston on from obsessing about the crash and its effects.

Weston frowned. 'I was beginning to suspect,' he said, 'that there were a group of thieves here in Oxford who specialized in robbing rich families of the worldly goods they had built up over time – the paintings, jewellery, statues and so on. They were intelligent, well-read men who would study old manuscripts and books in the hopes of finding out which families had these treasures and would then break into the houses secretly and steal everything. It would, of course, take them a long time to dispose of their haul – obviously gold can be melted down, but half the value of an antique ring is in the history associated with it, and stolen paintings have to be bought by someone who knows their value and is prepared to hide them away – but these art thieves were in it for the long haul, not the quick profit.'

'Did you ever catch them?' Matty asked.

'Oh no. The police let me go. I was no good to them like this. I can't walk properly, and on rainy days the pain makes me twist up in agony. People are scared of me, so I can't question them or interact with the public in any way, but neither can I sit straight at a desk for more than half an hour without cramps setting in, so a desk job is out of the question as well. They threw me out. I ended up here, in this house – a virtual recluse. So no – I never caught them. But I badly want to.'

'And that explains the collection of poisonous creatures,' Sherlock said, the words emerging from his mouth even as he thought them. 'You're still investigating, aren't you?'

'I am putting together the tools,' Weston admitted, 'although I am in no condition to use them. Other people will have to do that. And my knowledge is useful in other cases as well.'

'You're living here with your wife,' Sherlock

pointed out. 'You said she was caught in the same . . . accident . . . that you were, but she wasn't on the case with you, was she?'

Weston shook his head. 'No, but one of my colleagues sent a boy running to tell her what had happened. She came straight away to the wreckage of the house. The police were picking through it, still looking for me, but there were some areas they were scared to go because some of the upper floors were still hanging there, ready to fall at any moment. She was convinced I was in one of those areas, so she came in to get me. Not a thought for her own safety.' He smiled, scarred lips twisting as he remembered. A long pause. 'A section of the first-floor landing fell down while she was there. Just after she got to me, and shouted to the searchers that I was there, half a ton of brickwork fell on top of her. She'll never walk again.'

'And then the stories started,' Sherlock said quietly.

'Yes, the stories started. Not immediately, but as people gradually forgot about the accident, and as they moved away or moved into the area, they gradually forgot who I was and what had happened. I didn't help, of course, by staying out of sight, in the shadows. There's something about having a giant man covered in scars that makes people nervous. Stories started that I wasn't real, that I'd been constructed out of spare body parts, like that book – *Frankenstein*.'

'You didn't help the rumours either by stealing body

parts from the mortuary. That just made things worse.'

Weston sighed. 'I know, but I needed the parts to build up my collection – so that I could continue to teach myself how to identify a person's occupation from the small signs left on their bodies. I had no alternative.'

'And you had to steal them.'

'Yes. Oh, I could have approached Doctor Lukather, of course, and asked him to let me have the parts for free, but he would have said no. He's a very honourable man, and I knew that.'

'But you don't need the body parts themselves,' Sherlock pointed out. 'It's the wax copies that you need. The real body parts could be returned to the mortuary and buried along with the rest of the bodies.'

Weston shook his head. 'It takes a good few weeks to make the copies. I use a man named Oscar Meunier. He comes from Grenoble, but he is living in London at the moment and making a good living producing wax sculptures of the nobility. He also moonlights for me, making these copies. He finds the work fascinating, and he is a true artist. I need the copies, of course, because the real ones would decay. Even if I had them preserved they would undergo changes. The tissue would discolour, and they would be useless for my purposes. No, the copies have to be made, but it takes so long that the families have long since buried the rest of the bodies. Returning the parts that have been taken would be impossible, and distressing to boot. I make sure that my agents in London give them Christian burials in unmarked graves. It's the best I can do – and at least the bodies have been used for something important, something that will benefit the world.'

'Not if you stay in your house and keep all the information to yourself,' Sherlock pointed out. 'You can't solve cases sitting here, isolated. How are you going to see a *real* forearm, a *real* ear, and be able to tell the occupation of its owner, if you rarely leave and never see anybody else?'

There was a long silence as Weston digested Sherlock's words.

'I had hoped . . .' he said haltingly, and then stopped. He raised the bottle of beer to his lips, then lowered it again. 'What else can I do?' he asked plaintively. 'Detection is my life. It is what I do best. It is the *only* thing I can do. Am I supposed to sit around the house every day, having George cook and clean for me, and do *nothing*? Some people who have heard about me write to me with problems of their own – problems the police cannot or will not solve – and I give them the benefit of my experience. It's the best I can do.'

'You could pass on the stuff you know,' Matty said quietly. 'Take on a student. Sherlock 'ere, 'e's brilliant at spotting stuff, but 'e's been kind of learning on the job. You could teach 'im everythin' you know.'

'I suppose I could,' Weston said slowly. 'That at least

would mean that the information and skills that I have amassed would be of use.'

Sherlock leaned back in his chair, thinking. It looked as if moving to Oxford was going to be a lot more interesting than he had originally thought. What with Charles Dodgson teaching him about logic and Ferny Weston teaching him about the analysis of evidence, his days were going to be pretty full.

'Do I pay you?' he asked. 'Is there a fee for these lessons?'

'Only one,' Ferny said. 'I need you to investigate something for me. A case involving a man who wrote to me recently with an interesting problem.'

Sherlock and Matty looked at each other. 'What?' they both said at once.

'I will explain later. First I want to check on George, and I want you to meet my wife.'

He led the way out of the sitting room and up the stairs to the first floor. The doors were all still closed, and he knocked on the second one. 'Marie, my dear? We have guests. Can we come in?'

A voice from inside the room said: 'Yes, please do. I want to meet them.'

Ferny pushed the door open. 'Sherlock Holmes and Matty Arnatt – this is my wife, Marie Weston.'

Sherlock walked in, followed by Matty. Ferny, in the doorway, said, 'I need to go upstairs and check on George. I won't be more than five minutes. You can talk while I'm gone.'

The room was dark, with a single candle on a table beside a bed. In the bed, sitting up with a pillow behind her, was a woman with long dark hair and an angelic but pale face. She smiled at the two boys. 'Come in, please. It has been a long time since I saw anyone apart from Ferny and George.'

Sherlock moved to the side of the bed, while Matty stood at the end, shuffling from foot to foot.

'It's a pleasure to meet you,' Sherlock said. He gazed at her face, aware that he had seen it before somewhere, but uncertain where that could have been. She gazed at him as he wondered, a slight smile on her lips.

'You look as if you recognize me,' she said eventually, 'but I am sure that we have never met. I would remember a handsome boy like you.'

And then it came to him. 'You had your photograph taken,' he said. 'It was in a garden, about five years ago. Your husband was there, and so was my brother Mycroft.'

She clapped her hands together. 'I *remember*!' she exclaimed. 'It was a beautiful summer's day, and a friend of your brother had asked us if we would pose for him. Mortimer Maberley was there as well – he was Ferny's sergeant in the Oxford Police Force.'

'There was someone else there too,' Sherlock pointed out. 'A boy. He would be about my age now, I suppose.'

Marie Weston's face clouded over. She looked down at the bedspread. When she looked up, she said, 'That was a long time ago.' She paused, suppressing some deep emotion, then continued: 'Ferny tells me that you both broke in here. I presume, from the fact that he hasn't thrown you out, that you have explained yourselves to him adequately.'

'It was . . . something of a misunderstanding,' Sherlock said.

'We was lookin' for the bloke who was takin' all them bits of bodies,' Matty said. 'An' we found 'im.'

'Ah yes – Ferny's hobby. It is about the only thing that keeps him going from day to day.'

'He still seems to believe that he can be useful,' Sherlock said, 'that his knowledge can help other investigators in other cases.'

'He is fooling himself,' Marie said. 'I cannot tell him, and I beg you not to either, but his collection of poisons and of wax body parts is just . . . an obsession. He is unable to do anything with them. He sits there and looks at them, and analyses them, and writes lots of notes, but there is no *application* of his knowledge. He cannot investigate cases any more. Yes, people might write to him with problems, or he might read something in the newspaper, but if he cannot leave the house except under cover, then how can he actually *investigate*?'

'Your husband is very knowledgeable,' Sherlock said diplomatically. 'He must have been a very good police officer.'

'He was an *excellent* police officer,' she said, 'and that is why he and I are in the state we are in now. I would have preferred him to be a gardener or a baker, I think.' She shook her head violently. 'But then he wouldn't have been the man that I fell in love with and married. Life can be so very cruel sometimes. You can never plan what is going to happen to you – or, rather, you can plan your life, but it will never go the way you planned. We should have had children by now, and Ferny should be a superintendent of police. Instead . . .' She gestured at the bed. 'Instead this.'

'Man makes plans and God laughs,' Sherlock said. 'My Uncle Sherrinford used to say that. It's an old proverb apparently.'

'And a very true one,' Marie Weston said. 'Your uncle was a wise man.'

'Oh, I dunno,' Matty interjected. 'I always wanted to be on a barge on the canals, an' 'ere I am.'

Sherlock gazed at him sceptically. 'That's not really a plan,' he pointed out.

While Matty glowered, Sherlock's gaze was attracted by something on the wide table by Marie Weston's left arm. It took him a moment to work out what it was. 'That's the paper and string that the parcel was wrapped in, isn't it?' he asked. 'The one containing the . . .' He hesitated, not wanting to say the words 'body part' out loud in case it offended Mrs Weston. She was obviously of a delicate disposition.

'It is part of Ferny's work,' she said. 'For his collection. Every so often a parcel arrives in the post for him. He allows me to unwrap it, because I have so little else to occupy my time in this house, but he does not allow me to open the box inside in case the contents disturb me. I know they are only wax copies, but even so – he worries about the shock.'

'She insists on unwrapping the parcels,' Weston said, re-entering the room. 'I think it reminds her of Christmas.'

Sherlock smiled automatically, as Weston went across the room to his wife, but his gaze was still fixed on the brown paper and string. There was something odd about them, something that snagged his attention, but he wasn't sure what it was.

'George is resting,' Weston said as he kissed his wife on the forehead. 'The poison did not get into his system, thank the Lord. Given a good night's rest, he should be fine.'

'Dear George,' Mrs Weston murmured. 'What would we do without him?'

Weston perched himself on the edge of the bed. 'Now,' he said, glancing from Sherlock to Matty and back again, 'we have a discussion, you and I. Let us go downstairs and talk like gentlemen.'

'No, Ferny,' his wife said, placing her hand over his, 'please – stay here and talk. It is so rare that I get to hear a voice other than yours or George's, and these boys are delightful company.'

He nodded. 'Very well.'

'You mentioned a case,' Sherlock prompted. 'You said you wanted us to look into it for you.'

Weston nodded. 'Indeed. It is connected with the work I was doing as a policeman, but I am unable to complete the investigation now. The police force themselves are not interested – they have already decided that the man in question is hallucinating and that there is nothing to investigate. I, however, beg to differ. I think something very odd is going on, and I also think that a man's sanity, if not his life, is at stake. If I told anyone else this story then they would either think that I was making it up or they would blame supernatural elements – ghosts or some such – but from what I can see of you two boys, you are level-headed and intelligent, and you will not leap to conclusions.' He glanced from one to the other. 'Do you want me to go on?'

Sherlock looked at Matty, then back at Weston. He felt strangely excited. 'Tell us everything,' he said.

CHAPTER ELEVEN

'Where to begin?' Weston said. 'Well, let's start with Mortimer Maberley himself.'

'Dear Mortimer,' his wife said. As Weston's hand came down on to the bedspread she put her own hand on top of it. 'What a lovely man he was. What a good friend. Sherlock was saying just now that he had seen a photograph of the two of us with Mortimer, and with Sherlock's brother.'

Ferny frowned. 'That's the one with –' He stopped abruptly, then looked up at Sherlock and continued as if nothing had happened: 'Mortimer and I were in the Oxford Police Constabulary together. He was my sergeant. A very good officer, fair and even-handed. Older than me he was. His family was an old established family in the area, going back generations, right to the Civil War and before. They had once been rich, but a lot of the money vanished during the Interregnum, between the reigns of Charles I and Charles II, when Oliver Cromwell and his Roundheads controlled England with an iron fist. By the beginning of this century all the Maberleys had left was a large house twenty miles west of here and an adjoining orchard.' He smiled – a disquieting twist of his twisted lips. 'I recall that Maberley's father and grandfather had tried to make cider from the apples in the orchard, but the fruits were small and stunted, and the brew was like vinegar. It never sold, and they never became the cider millionaires they expected. Maberley joined the police force because it was a regular job that would at least provide some income to the family. Unfortunately his mother died of influenza when he was in his thirties, and his father of a heart attack a few years later, leaving him alone in the house. He never married.'

'Wasn't there some family legend of a treasure?' Marie Weston asked suddenly, straightening up in her bed. 'I recall he came to dinner one night and mentioned it.' She smiled. 'He brought two bottles of cider with him as a gift.' She giggled. 'We ended up emptying our glasses into a flowerpot while he wasn't looking.'

'Yes,' her husband said, his scarred forehead twisting in remembrance, 'there *was* something about a trove of gold and jewels that had been given to them by Prince Charles when he was on the run from the Roundheads back in 1651. Apparently, so the family legend went, they had hidden the Prince and his companions for several weeks when the Roundheads were scouring the countryside for them. In his gratitude, when he finally gained the throne, Charles II as he became gave them riches, but by Maberley's time nobody in the family knew what had happened to the gold and the jewels. I was always inclined to believe that there was little truth and much exaggeration in the story, but Maberley believed it. At least, he *wanted* to believe it, but no search of the house or the grounds ever turned anything up.' He shook his head, banishing the memories. 'Anyway, that is irrelevant. The point is that we worked together, and I owed him my life.'

'Because he pulled you from the collapsing building?' Sherlock ventured. 'The one that had been blown up with you inside?'

Weston nodded. 'Yes, he did – at great risk to himself – and then he went back in for Marie. That action is the bravest deed I have ever known anyone undertake.' He paused momentarily, eyes misting with emotion, then continued: 'He retired from the police shortly after I was invalided out, and retreated to his family home. He couldn't afford to take on any servants. He just potters along in that big house, all by himself, trying to do the cooking, the cleaning and the gardening. Once a week a boy from the village drops off a box of vegetables and meat, which the local tradesmen supply on a tab that keeps on growing and is never going to be paid off, but they don't care. They remember the Maberley family, and what they did for the village in times past. We correspond, intermittently. And then, less than a year ago, I got the strangest letter from him. He seemed . . . anxious and unsettled, if his handwriting and choice of words was anything to go by.'

Weston paused, almost seeming to be embarrassed by the story he was telling. Sherlock prompted him, asking, 'What was in the letter?'

'He wrote that he was under the impression that every night, while he was asleep, his house *moved*.'

Sherlock felt a chill run through him. A moving *house*? He suddenly remembered the words of Charles Dodgson, at their first meeting, talking about the Russian legend of Baba Yaga – the witch whose hut had legs, and could walk around by itself. Was that a coincidence, or did Dodgson know something about Maberley's problems and was trying to warn Sherlock in advance?

'What did he mean, his house *moved*?' Matty asked, leaning forward.

'You recall that I said all his family had was the house and an orchard?'

Matty nodded. 'Yeah.'

'The house was set by itself, in a small area of lawn,' Weston continued. 'On the south side of the lawn the orchard began, and ran for several acres. What Maberley told me was that sometimes, if he woke up in the small hours of the morning, he found that his house was not on the edge of the orchard at all – it was in the *middle* of the orchard!'

'In the *middle* of the orchard?' Sherlock repeated, wanting to be absolutely sure what Weston was saying.

'Indeed. He swore that if he looked out of his bedroom window then he could clearly see apple trees surrounding the house, rather than being all at the south end of the grounds. Somehow his house had *slipped* several hundred yards, as though it was trying to get somewhere. Maberley said that the shock of the sight normally sent him into a faint, and when he woke up the house was back where it was supposed to be, surrounded by lawn.'

'It was a dream,' Matty said firmly. 'I get dreams like that – ones that keep coming back. I always dream that—'

'And did this happen every night?' Sherlock interrupted.

'Not every night, no.' He turned his head to gaze at Matty. 'And he said that it couldn't be a dream, because every night that it happened he wrote down exactly what he saw, and in the morning the notes were still there, in his journal.'

'And did he ever try to force himself to stay awake to see what was actually happening?' Sherlock pressed.

'He said that he frequently tried to stay awake, using all kinds of methods to stave off sleep, but that whatever he tried, sleep managed to creep up on him, and if he woke up later on then it was to find himself in the middle of the orchard. And in addition—'

'Those evenings when he *tried* to keep himself awake,' Sherlock interrupted, 'did they *always* end up with him falling asleep?'

Weston frowned, and thought for a minute. He turned to his wife and said, 'You read the letters too, my dear – what exactly did he say?'

'As I recall,' Marie replied, closing her eyes and

frowning, 'he said that there were some evenings when he managed to stay awake all night, and nothing happened, but there were some evenings when he fell asleep and *then* awoke to find that the house had moved.' She gazed at Weston with sympathy in her expression. 'You must face it, Ferny – the balance of his mind was disturbed. It was obvious that he was hallucinating – probably after drinking too much of his family cider.'

Weston shook his head. 'Mortimer Maberley was the most stable of men. I do not see him as someone in the grip of mental imbalance – even now, given what he said in the letter.'

'It does look,' Matty said slowly, 'as if, on the evenings when he was awake, keeping watch, that he managed to somehow stop the movement of the house from happening, perhaps just by *being* awake.' He glanced at Marie Weston apologetically. '*If* he was in his right mind.'

'Or,' Sherlock pointed out slowly, 'the reverse is true – that he only went to sleep against his will when some force decided to move the house.' He shrugged. 'We have two alleged facts – Mr Maberley unwittingly falling asleep despite his precautions and the house apparently moving. We do not yet know which event caused the other – if indeed they are linked.' He smiled. 'If, of course, either event is true.' He turned to Weston. 'Did you write back?'

'I did.'

'What did you say?'

'I was sympathetic, and I asked many of the questions that you have asked. He wrote back with the answers that I have given you. His letters since then have become increasingly frantic. He fears to leave the house now, in case it isn't there when he returns. I fear that he may do something drastic if this situation is not resolved.'

Sherlock was about to ask what Weston thought he could do about it, but then a thought struck him. Actually, not so much a thought as a memory. The theatre, in London, a few weeks back, where he and his brother Mycroft had spent an evening listening to the violinist Pablo Sarasate. He remembered in particular the intermission between the halves of the performance, when he had left his brother sitting in a window seat in the theatre's bar. A man had come up to Mycroft and handed him a letter, and Mycroft had said – Sherlock had to ransack his brain to retrieve the errant memory – 'The Mortimer Maberley problem again – I don't know what he thinks I can do!'

The Mortimer Maberley problem. Mycroft knew about it!

'You told me,' he said to Weston, tightly controlling his tone of voice and his words, 'that you used to drink in a tavern with my brother Mycroft. Did Mortimer Maberley drink with you?'

'He did,' Weston replied. 'They got on very well. Why do you ask?'

'Because,' Sherlock said bitterly, 'I am beginning to realize that I am not here by accident.'

'Perhaps you are here as part of God's great design,' Weston said firmly. 'Mortimer Maberley needs my help, but I am unable to give it. I cannot travel more than a few miles from this house without provoking attention, and I cannot investigate Maberley's situation in a manner that might solve his problems. It may require discussion with local villagers, or liaison with the local police, and I am not able to do that.' He indicated his face with a wave of his hand. 'The minute people see my face they stop listening to what I say.'

'And you want Matty and me to investigate for you,' Sherlock said levelly.

'You have broken into my house, you have wreaked havoc among my specimens and you have invalided my servant George. I think you owe me.'

'You have broken the law by stealing body parts from the mortuaries at Oxford and elsewhere,' Sherlock pointed out. 'Whatever we might owe you is cancelled out by the fact that we were investigating your wrongdoings.'

The two of them stared at each other for a long moment, neither willing to back down. Eventually Marie Weston exclaimed, 'Oh, Ferny – this is foolish! You cannot involve these two *children* in a problem that isn't even yours! It would be wrong to send them to Mortimer's house.'

214

Weston opened his mouth to answer, but Sherlock beat him to it.

'Actually,' he said, 'I think it's an interesting problem. I wouldn't mind visiting Mr Maberley and having a look around. I can't promise anything, but—'

'Are you serious?' Matty asked.

'Perfectly.' Sherlock turned to look at his friend. 'Doesn't it strike you as interesting? I mean, a house that *moves*?'

'No,' Matty said honestly, 'it strikes me as being *mad*.'

'So you don't want to come with me?'

'That's a trick question, isn't it? Of course I'll come with you.' He glanced at Mrs Weston. 'Someone has to keep 'im out of trouble. 'E can be so single-minded 'e can see right what's in front of 'im in great detail but ignore all the dangerous stuff that's creepin' up on 'im.'

'In which case he sounds just like Ferny when he was on a case,' Marie replied with a wan smile.

'So,' Matty said brightly, 'what's the pay like?'

Sherlock and Weston both turned to stare at him. '*Pay?*' they both said in unison.

'Yeah, pay. You want Sherlock 'ere to do a job, so you gotta pay 'im for it. You don't expect a gardener to work for free, or a plumber.'

'I thought we had established,' Weston said patiently, 'that you two have trespassed in my house, assaulted my servant and have been responsible for the death of several of my animal specimens. I'll deduct your "pay" from the damages you owe me.'

'I thought we also established,' Matty said, equally patiently, 'that you've been engaged in illegal activities which we was investigatin', that your servant attacked *us*, not the other way around, an' that your precious specimens had to be destroyed to stop them from killin' people – like us an' your servant. I think *we're* the ones who are due damages – an' that's before we even discuss payment for services.'

'Matty, what are you doing?' Sherlock hissed.

'Establishin' your market worth,' his friend replied.

'Mr Weston and his wife don't have any money. Look around. They have no wages coming into the household.'

'They can afford a servant, and that bloke with the monkey,' Matty pointed out reasonably, 'an' presumably those wax body parts don't come free. I doubt you can just pick up a poisonous snake in Oxford market, so someone has to be paid to find the specimens, collect them and send 'em 'ere. All that takes money, but 'e's expectin' you to work for free?' He shook his head sadly. 'Sherlock, you need an agent.'

'It's true,' Ferny murmured, 'that I receive a generous pension from the police force, and my dear wife manages all our finances in such a way that we never seem to be short of money – I don't know how she does it. I cannot, however, say that we are *rich*.'

Sherlock went to say something, but Matty shushed him.

'We can discuss suitable remuneration when you return,' Weston continued after a long pause. 'When we see how much progress you have made towards a solution.'

'That sounds fair,' Sherlock said before Matty could argue further.

'I will write a letter to Mortimer Maberley,' Weston said, 'explaining who you are and what you hope to achieve. That way he will at least let you inside his house. I will also lend you two horses from the stables so you can ride there.'

''Orses, eh?' Matty said brightly. 'They don't come cheap neither.'

'When do you wish to set off?'

Sherlock glanced at Matty. 'I think tomorrow morning, after breakfast.'

Marie Weston beamed. 'Then you must stay here the night. We have spare beds. Ferny will cook a fine breakfast for you before you set off.'

They stayed awake for a while longer, talking not about the Mortimer Maberley case but instead discussing Weston's theories about the effects of occupation or career on the human body, and the symptoms caused by various poisons. While they talked, Weston took a sheet of paper from a desk in the bedroom and set about writing the letter of introduction to Mortimer Maberley that he had promised.

'You should read it,' he said, 'just in case you think I might be putting secret instructions in there.'

'Like in *Hamlet*,' Sherlock said, 'where Claudius sends Rosencrantz and Guildenstern to the English court carrying a letter that asks the King to kill their friend Hamlet, who is with them.'

'Except that Hamlet has rewritten the letter so that it is Rosencrantz and Guildenstern who are executed.' Weston grinned. 'I remember *Hamlet* being your brother's favourite Shakespeare play when he was here. You have obviously picked up his love of the Bard.'

'It's a family thing,' Sherlock said.

He scanned the letter, which just contained a set of initial salutations and then a paragraph where Weston told Maberley that he was sending two boys – Sherlock Holmes and Matthew Arnatt – to help sort out Maberley's problems. Forestalling any protests on Maberley's part, Weston added that although the boys might appear young, they were intelligent and tenacious.

'It looks fine,' Sherlock said, handing it back. Weston sealed it in an envelope with some wax and passed it back to Sherlock.

When Weston went to sort out the bedding in their rooms, his wife looked beseechingly at Sherlock. 'Please tell me that you won't go ahead with this,' she said piteously. 'Dear Ferny gets these obsessions in his head and cannot let them go. Supporting him merely

218

reinforces his obsessions. He needs to be able to let go of them.'

Sherlock was torn. On the one hand he wanted to aid Marie Weston in whatever way she needed, but on the other hand he was intrigued by the potential mystery. 'I promise,' he said eventually, 'that we will do our best to prove that Mr Maberley is imagining things, and that there is a simple explanation.'

The next morning they ate a huge breakfast of bacon, eggs and fried bread, they were introduced to the horses and they set out before the sun had climbed very far in the sky. Sherlock had the letter to Mortimer Maberley tucked inside his jacket, while Matty had a hand-drawn map tucked inside his. Strangely, the house looked nowhere near as threatening in the warm morning light. Its lines and angles appeared charmingly eccentric rather than sinister. Or perhaps it was just the knowledge of what was really inside that made it less malevolent.

'How are you feeling?' Sherlock called as they rode.

'Could've done wiv a better night's sleep,' Matty called back. 'I kept thinkin' I could hear somethin' slitherin' under the bed. An' then, at breakfast, I was fine until I started wonderin' if that was really bacon or if that Weston bloke had just fried up the meat from one of 'is snakes, so as not to waste it.'

'You really do have an active imagination, don't you?' Sherlock said.

'I say that, but if it *was* snake then we're missing a

trick 'ere in England. It was very tasty.'

The ride took nearly an hour. Eventually Matty announced that they were approaching Mortimer Maberley's house. The countryside there was lush and green and relatively flat, with fields interspersed with copses of beeches and the occasional orchard of apple or pear trees. There were low hills on the horizon.

The Maberley house was set back from the road, nowhere near any other properties. A fringe of bushes in the overgrown grounds hid the building from sight until Sherlock and Matty had tied their horses up, made their way through the rusty gate and pushed through the shrubbery.

'This must be the place,' Matty said, looking at it aghast.

'Do you think so?' Sherlock responded.

The house was small – two storeys, with rooms either side of a central front door. It was also badly maintained – the thatched roof was mossy, and some of the bricks were crumbling at the edges. What made it unique, however, was the wooden beams that had been set up at one end of the house, bracing it diagonally from roof to ground.

''E's serious about this house-moving lark then?'

'Serious enough to do something to stop it,' Sherlock agreed.

'Can't be workin', or we wouldn't be 'ere.'

'Let's take a look around before we knock on the front door.'

Matty followed Sherlock as he headed towards the corner of the house where the wooden bracing beams were fixed. Standing there, Sherlock gazed out across the wild lawn to where the apple orchard began – hundreds of trees about twice his height, spaced ten feet or so apart in a regular pattern. The lawn continued out under the trees and through the orchard without a break. There were no apples on the trees – it was too early in the year for that.

He let his gaze fall to the grass between the house and the first row of trees. If the house had moved – *if* it had, he emphasized in his mind, rather than the whole thing being an invention of the overheated mind of Mortimer Maberley – then there should be traces on the lawn. He could see nothing – no drag marks, no scuffing, nothing to indicate that anything heavy had been pulled or pushed across there. In fact, looking back at the house, it was obvious that it didn't just rest on the surface. No house ever did. There would be foundations dug into the ground, if not a coal cellar as well. If the house did move, then what happened to all those underground parts – did they stay where they were, or did they move too? No, the whole thing was just too stupid.

He glanced back at the lawn. Kneeling down, he looked straight at the apple trees, trying to establish if there was any slope to the ground. He supposed it might just be possible, if the house *was* flat on the surface of the ground, and *if* the ground was muddy enough and sloped enough, that the house could *slide* towards the orchard, but that would require some kind of triggering event, like an earthquake, that would be more suited to a foreign country than to England. It would leave traces as well – gouge marks in the earth. The trouble was that even if all of those things were true, the house might well slide in one direction, but how could it possibly slide back again? And do so repeatedly?

He stood up, sighing. The whole theory was improbable, if only because the ground did not slope in the slightest.

'Get out!' a voice shouted from behind him. 'I said, get out!'

With a deafening *bang!* a patch of overgrown lawn beside Sherlock suddenly exploded in a spray of earth and bits of leaf. He felt moisture from the grass splatter his cheek. He turned – slowly, so that he didn't spook the man who had shouted. 'I'm sorry,' he called, 'but we're here to help. Ferny Weston sent us! We have a letter from him!'

As he turned, he saw a man leaning out of an upstairs window. He was pointing a gun at Sherlock – a massive fowling piece with a long barrel. It would shoot lots of small lead balls, Sherlock knew – making a mess of whatever they hit.

The man with the gun was unshaven. His wild white hair stuck out in all directions, and his small, round glasses were askew on his nose. His eyes, behind the glasses, glared wildly at Sherlock and Matty.

'You, boy!' the man cried, waving the gun in Matty's direction. 'Go and stand beside your friend. I want you close enough that I can hit you both with a single shot! You say you have a letter?'

'Yes.' Sherlock pulled it from his jacket and waved it. 'Are you Mortimer Maberley?'

'I might be. Wait there.' He vanished from the window. Sherlock and Matty just stood there as he made his way through the house, eventually appearing at the front door. 'Come over here and let me see.'

Sherlock and Matty made their way to the front door, painfully aware that the gun was pointed at them again, and equally aware that Mortimer Maberley was not the most stable of men. Sherlock handed the letter across and they waited while Maberley opened it, squinted at it, adjusted his glasses so they were nearly straight and then read it again. Eventually he put it down and stared at them.

'So, Weston sent you to help, eh?'

'Sherlock 'ere is very good with puzzles an' stuff,' Matty boasted, 'an' I'm good with scams an' confidence tricks. Whatever's goin' on, we can solve it!'

'Neither of you has any expertise in the field of evil spirits then?'

The boys looked at each other.

'No,' Matty said. 'Why?'

'Isn't it obvious? Demons are trying to drag this house

223

to hell, but the angels keep stopping them and moving it back again.'

'Why would demons want to drag your house to hell?' Sherlock asked reasonably.

'If I knew that,' Maberley snapped, 'then I wouldn't need the services of an expert, would I?' He realized that he was still pointing the gun at them and swung it away. 'You'd better come in. I can make some tea, or there's cider if you prefer. A lot of cider.'

'Tea would be wonderful,' Sherlock said.

Maberley led them into a living room that was cluttered with bric-a-brac, old furniture and books in piles. There was a smell to the house that Sherlock found familiar – a medicinal smell that made his flesh creep for some reason. He filed that information away for later consideration.

Once Maberley had vanished off into what Sherlock presumed was the kitchen, Matty glanced at Sherlock. ''E's crackers,' he muttered. 'I think we know what the story is 'ere.'

'I'm not so sure,' Sherlock replied. 'Let's keep our minds open until we know more.'

Maberley came back with a pot of tea and three mismatched cups, and they all sat down wherever they could find a space. Maberley read Weston's letter again, and then gazed at them over the top of his glasses.

'You must think I'm mad,' he said directly.

'Yes,' Matty responded.

'No,' Sherlock said.

Maberley gazed at the two of them through eyes that were bloodshot and watery. 'You're just kids,' he said softly. 'What can you do to help?'

Matty bristled, preparing to make a strong retort, but Sherlock gestured him to silence. 'We can be witnesses,' he said softly. 'We can see what happens, and if what you say is right then we can tell people. We can corroborate your story.'

Maberley nodded. 'That is good enough for me,' he said soberly.

'Now,' Sherlock continued in a deliberately businesslike tone, 'tell us everything.'

'Did Ferny Weston not tell you himself?'

'He did, but I want to hear it from your lips. There may be things that you forgot to mention to Ferny, things that seemed so simple or so obvious that you left them out, but which could prove the key to the whole affair. Or there might have been things that he skipped over in your letter because they were trivial details, but which might help unravel the mystery. It's always better to go to the original source for a story, rather than rely on it being told second-hand.'

Maberley nodded. 'You know that I used to be in the Oxford police?

Sherlock nodded.

'Well,' he continued, 'that attitude of yours was one that Ferny and I tried to get our constables to follow, but they rarely did. They would far prefer to believe a story if it was colourful and it backed up their prejudices than if they had tracked it back to an original, and probably more boring, source.'

'Not,' Sherlock said, 'that I think your story will be boring.'

'I hope not. Very well – I will tell you everything as if I have never told it before and you have never heard it before.'

CHAPTER TWELVE

The story was, to be fair, pretty much the same as the one that Ferny had told them, with some changes in emphasis, but in Mortimer Maberley's voice it took on an added immediacy. He had lived through these events, and it was obvious from his tone, and his expression, that he completely believed that they had happened. When he came to talk about the sight of the tops of the apple trees waving outside his bedroom window, in a place that they should not have been, his voice was filled with a kind of uncomprehending horror. The natural order of things had gone awry – nature was not as it should be, and he was scared.

'You say that you tried to keep yourself awake, to see these things start,' Sherlock asked. 'How exactly did you do that?'

'One night I tried making a pot of strong coffee,' Maberley answered, 'and drinking one cup every half hour, regularly. Another night I held a bell in my hand, so that if I became sleepy and my hand dropped then the bell would ring, or if it hit the floor then the same thing would happen. A third night I stood up all the time.' He laughed suddenly. 'A fourth night I tried balancing a tumbler of water on my head, but that was a failure from the start. But no, it didn't matter what I tried – on the nights when the house moved into the orchard I would invariably fall asleep, only to wake up for a little bit, then fall back asleep again.'

'Or,' Sherlock pointed out, as he had done earlier to Ferny Weston, 'the nights when you fell asleep despite your best efforts were the nights when the house seemed to move. We do not know, as yet, which one caused the other – if they are linked at all.'

'You think they are,' Matty said excitedly. 'I know that expression. You know what's going on.'

'I know some of it,' Sherlock said. 'The rest I am beginning to work out. I just need to ask two questions, and then my friend and I need to look around.'

'Very well,' Maberley said.

'Firstly, on those nights when the house does appear to move, and you sleep heavily, do you feel rested when you wake up?'

Maberley thought for a moment. 'No,' he said slowly. 'When I wake I actually feel as if my head is filled with a heavy weight and I find it difficult to move.'

'Ah – very interesting. And can I ask about the windows in the house – do they open easily?'

'They used to, but I think the wood of the frames has warped. It must be something to do with moisture in the atmosphere. I cannot get them open now, no matter how hard I pull. If I need to air the house, then I open the front and back doors and let the breeze do the job.'

'Just as I thought,' Sherlock said. 'He glanced at Matty. 'Right – can you check all around the outside of the house while I check inside? Give it an hour and then we can swap. If one of us has missed something then the other one will find it.'

'What am I looking for?' Matty asked.

'Anything out of the ordinary.'

'Do you want to narrow that down?'

'Absolutely not.'

'And I,' Maberley announced, 'will make some sandwiches. Will fish paste do?'

'Over the next sixty minutes, Sherlock visited every room in the house. Some were as filled with stuff as the sitting room, while others were virtually empty. All of them had that faint medicinal smell to them.

Remembering the story that Ferny Weston had told him and Matty about Cavalier refugees hiding in the house from Oliver Cromwell's Roundhead forces during the English Civil War, Sherlock checked all the walls and floors, looking for secret passages or hidden rooms. He carefully paced out the length of each room, and then checked those dimensions against the lengths of the corridors outside, but there were no discrepancies. As far as he could tell – and he'd had a lot of experience – there was nowhere in the house that even one person could have been hidden, let alone several. No priest's hole, nothing. Either he was missing something, or the family legend just wasn't true.

Sherlock also checked all of the windows in the house as he was going around. He found, as he had expected, that the windows had been nailed so that they could not be opened, with the nails passing through the bottom of each frame and into the wood of the sill. The heads of the nails had been dabbed with a brown paint so that they could not be seen unless you knew to look for them. Working on the assumption that Maberley hadn't done it himself and then forgotten about it, someone had been inside the house without his knowledge, and for some time as well.

Sherlock also found holes in the wooden skirting board of every room. They looked, at first glance, like mouse holes, but they were strangely regular – as if they had been drilled, rather than nibbled or scratched. There were no signs of mouse droppings either.

He passed Maberley on the stairs at one point – him going down, Maberley going up. 'Did you ever think,' he asked, 'that any of your possessions had been moved around, or made more untidy?'

'Quite the reverse,' Maberley said, running a hand through his wild white hair. 'Before all this bizarre stuff started happening with the house moving at night, there were a few days when I thought that the place was tidier than usual. Very strange it was.'

A little later, when Sherlock was searching through the kitchen, Maberley entered to make another cup of tea.

'Do you have much of a problem with mice, or cockroaches, or any other kind of vermin?' Sherlock said over his shoulder.

'I used to.' Maberley shrugged. 'They seem to have all vanished now. I think the moving of the house has scared them off.'

'That's one explanation,' Sherlock muttered.

'Pardon?'

'I'll explain later.'

At the end of the hour he met Matty in the hall. 'Anything?' he inquired.

''Oles in the walls,' Matty said. 'They ain't natural either.'

'Yes, I found the other ends inside the house. Anything else?'

Matty nodded. 'A couple of things. Come and look at this.'

He led the way outside the front door, to the scruffy mass of grass and weeds that counted as a lawn. He gestured at a particular patch that appeared no different from the rest.

'What do you make of that?' he asked.

Sherlock looked closer, but he could see nothing. 'Make of what?' he asked.

Matty glanced around, frustrated. 'Come over here,' he said, pulling Sherlock's arm. 'It's easier to see if the light from the sun is behind you.'

Sherlock looked again, and suddenly he could see

what Matty was talking about. There was a circular patch of grass that was slightly different from the rest. Sherlock wasn't sure if it was slightly greener, or slightly taller, or what. 'Some kind of fungus?' he guessed.

'Or a fairy ring,' Matty countered. 'I dunno what it is, but there's a few of them.'

Sherlock estimated the size of the ring. It was about as wide as he could stretch his arms. He looked around. Matty was right – there were other rings around, and some of them overlapped.

'All right – that's a puzzle,' he said. 'It might not have anything to do with the house supposedly moving, however.'

'Then what about this?' Matty asked. He led Sherlock to near the point where the orchard began, where he stopped. 'Look.' He pointed at the ground.

Sherlock bent down. 'What am I looking at?' he asked.

'Look sideways,' Matty urged.

Sherlock turned his head and moved down until he could feel blades of grass tickling his ear. He stared back towards the house. For a minute all he saw was grass, weeds and the occasional ant, but then, like an optical illusion suddenly resolving itself, he suddenly saw what it was that Matty had noticed. The grass seemed to be *bent*. Close to the ground it grew straight up, but after a few inches it suddenly but unmistakably veered sideways, pointing towards the orchard. It was almost impossible to see from above, there being so many blades of grass being ruffled in different directions by the breeze, but at ground level there was an obvious kink in the way the grass was growing.

'It looks like it's been flattened by something heavy,' he murmured.

'Flattened by something heavy moving towards the orchard,' Matty said pointedly. He stared at Sherlock and raised an eyebrow. 'Like, oh, I don't know, a *house* perhaps?'

Sherlock scuttled across the lawn on hands and knees, keeping his head close to the ground. 'No!' he exclaimed. 'Look – the grass *here* is *straight*!'

Matty crouched down to join him. Together they gazed through the grass.

'You're right,' Matty breathed. 'So there's a line of bent grass, running from the house to the orchard, but then it stops – an' it's not wide enough to be the house makin' it. Not *nearly* wide enough.'

Sherlock turned his head and looked the other way. The line of bent grass pointed straight towards one of the aisles that had been left between the apple trees so that the pickers could get to the apples easily.

He moved on a little bit. Within about six feet he found another line of bent grass, also pointing away from the house towards the orchard. He showed Matty.

'You know what these look like?' Matty said.

'Wheel tracks,' Sherlock answered. 'From some kind of cart.'

'Yeah, but they ain't deep enough, an' they're too wide.'

Sherlock nodded. 'But imagine that the cart's wheels have been wrapped in something really soft.' He thought for a second. 'Pillows! Imagine that pillows had been strapped to the wheels of the cart. No – imagine that the edges of the wheels had been built out with wooden extensions, so that they were wider, and *then* strapped up with pillows. That width would mean that less force would be applied per square inch to the ground, spreading the weight out so that ruts didn't form. The pillows would help with that. All the weight did was to bend the grass over. The grass sprang back when the cart had gone past, but a mark was left behind. An almost invisible mark.'

'Why would you strap pillows to the wheels of a cart?' Matty scratched his head. 'It don't make any sense.'

'It does if you want to keep the cart quiet,' Sherlock said, standing. 'And it also makes sense if the cart is carrying something heavy and you want to spread the load out so that the cart's wheels don't leave ruts in the ground.'

'So which is it – quietness or weight?' Matty stood up too.

'It's both,' Sherlock said.

Matty turned to stare at the house in amazement. 'So it's true then – the house *is* being moved, but it's being moved on some kind of *cart*!'

'That,' Sherlock said quietly, 'is certainly one explanation. Now – let's go and have some fish-paste sandwiches, and then you can search inside the house while I search outside in the garden and the orchard.'

Despite Mortimer Maberley's crazy appearance and the untidy state of the house, he made some excellent sandwiches – small, neat and with the crusts cut off. While he and the boys ate, he told them stories about his time in the Oxford police force – some funny, some tragic, but all of them entertaining. Sherlock asked about his brother, and Maberley – after an initial amazement that Sherlock and Mycroft were related – told him several stories of tricks that had been played on Mycroft while he was in Oxford. There was tea with the sandwiches as well, and biscuits to follow.

After lunch, Sherlock spent the next few hours searching outside the house. He quickly found the other ends of the holes that he had already discovered in the various rooms inside. Matty had previously drawn his attention to the rows of bent grass, but Sherlock also found other rows, this time leading towards the house rather than away from it. That would make sense if the house was somehow being moved on a cart, or several carts, towards the orchard – it would have to be brought back, after all – but that wasn't what Sherlock thought was happening. No, something very different, but equally strange, was going on.

To check his developing theory, he went deep inside

the orchard. The trees were taller than him, with spindly branches that clawed at the sky, but Sherlock had seen orchards before and this one looked stunted, as if the soil had lost its nutrients.

He knelt down and dug in the dirt around one of the trees. It was loose, as if it had been previously dug over and then left to lie. It certainly wasn't as dense as he would have expected. He felt around in the soil for a while, looking for something in particular, but he didn't find it. He would probably need a spade for that, and quite a bit of time.

Before going back to the house, Sherlock wandered through the trees to the edge of the orchard. There was a stone wall there, and beyond it the ground fell gradually away to a patchwork of fields in the distance. He could see horses grazing, and a herd of cows as well. The road that passed by Mortimer Maberley's house went down the gentle hillside, winding back and forth to minimize the slope for any carts that used it. It was as bucolic and perfect an English landscape as anyone could want.

And yet somewhere here there was a great crime being committed, and committed very slowly. He shivered. There was an unseen force here, a guiding hand that he could detect but could not identify. Perhaps tonight would bring answers.

There would be somewhere nearby for the criminals to base themselves, Sherlock knew. They would need a barn, or several barns, to contain their equipment. They certainly wouldn't want to bring it all the way from the nearest town or village every time they decided to trespass on Mortimer Maberley's property. He couldn't see anything suitable down the slope, but that made sense. They wouldn't want to bring it uphill each time they used it. No, it would all be stored somewhere back along the road, just off in a shielded area.

He turned and headed back towards the house, but as he walked along the aisle between the trees his attention was caught. Some of the trees were thinner or thicker than the others, and their bark was slightly different shades. Now that he came to look at the trees specifically, Sherlock could see that they were of several different species. This orchard wasn't for just one kind of apple – it was growing several. Why would the original planters have done that? If you were going to plant several different types of apple tree, then why not keep them separate, so that you didn't get them mixed up?

He shrugged. There were a lot of mysteries here, and he had to concentrate on the important ones or he would get distracted.

Back at the house, he and Matty compared notes. Matty hadn't discovered anything that Sherlock hadn't already seen during his search – apart from a surprising number of dried-up cockroaches beneath the floorboards, along with a few dead mice.

'Mr Maberley – would we be able to stay the night so that we can see what happens?' Sherlock asked.

'Of course,' he replied.

'And could we perhaps get some sleep now, so that we can be fresh later?'

'I ain't tired,' Matty protested, but Sherlock shushed him.

'I have two spare rooms,' said Maberley. 'Move the stuff off the beds and you'll be all right.'

Sherlock turned to Matty. 'Do you still have that knife you used to carry around?'

'Course I do.'

'I'll need to borrow it.' He turned to Mortimer Maberley. 'And I'll need a fork, if you would be so kind.'

'A fork?' Maberley was confused.

'Yes, please.'

Before settling down to sleep, Sherlock went through all three bedrooms – Maberley's and the two spare rooms – and carefully prised the nails he'd spotted earlier out of the window frames by sliding the blade of Matty's knife underneath them, levering them partially out and then getting them the rest of the way using Maberley's fork. He then slid the windows up, opening them a crack so that fresh air could get in and out. He didn't want them to be open so far that anyone outside would notice, but he did need that fresh air for his idea to work. He closed the curtains so that nobody outside could see in – specifically so that nobody could see him and Matty. After that, he went to sleep.

It was almost midnight when he awoke. There was

no light from outside trickling around the edges of the curtains in his room. The house was quiet.

He moved to the next room and woke Matty, and then the two of them went to Maberley's bedroom, where a flickering candle flame was visible through the partially open door. Mortimer Maberley was in the chair, reading a book by the light of a single candle. He glanced up as the two boys entered the room.

'Are you ready for an adventure?' he asked.

'As ready as we will ever be,' Sherlock responded.

Matty asked, 'What do we do now?'

'We sit and we wait.'

'What for?'

'For the house to move.'

Sherlock and Matty took seats near to Maberley. They arranged themselves in comfortable positions, and waited. Sherlock didn't know what Matty was thinking about, but in his own mind he was going over the chain of evidence and deduction that he had constructed, checking that every link held.

It turned out that Matty had been doing something similar.

'It's some kind of gas, innit?' he whispered after a long while. 'Somethin' that makes people go to sleep. I've 'eard that they use it for operations now, in 'ospitals, to knock people out so they don't feel the pain if their leg's bein' cut off, or if there's some surgeon muckin' around inside their chest.'

'They're called "anaesthetics",' Sherlock whispered back. 'There's a couple of different ones that have been known about for a while, but chloroform is the newest, and the safest.' He paused, and smiled bitterly, although he knew that nobody could see. 'The Paradol Chamber have something that they use which is based on morphine, but I think that it's complicated to get hold of, and difficult to use. These criminals will be using something simpler, and chloroform is surprisingly easy to make.'

'An' you think these blokes are pumpin' it in through those holes in the walls, don't you?'

'It's the only thing that makes sense. That's why Mr Maberley keeps falling asleep just when they're beginning their work. It's not tiredness – they're drugging him to stop him from interfering.'

'Why don't they just kill 'im an' 'ave done wiv it?' Matty asked.

'Because Ferny Weston and my brother and various other people would realize that he had stopped writing to them, and they would come to investigate. That would completely wreck the crooks' plans. They need Maberley here, but incapacitated, so they pump the gas in until they've finished.'

'An' you opened the windows so that the gas would be blown out an' fresh air would get in, so we don't go to sleep like he did. Very clever.'

'Thank you.' Sherlock paused. 'Do you understand

that, Mr Maberley? The falling asleep – it's all part of their plan. They're doing it to you!'

The only answer from Malcolm Maberley was a deep snore.

'Sherlock . . .' Matty said, but his voice sounded slow and distant.

Sherlock tried to get up, but his hands fumbled on the arms of his chair and he fell backwards. He could smell something medicinal, like the smell of a hospital. He realized it had been there for a while, getting stronger without his noticing. His head was heavy, and his eyes kept closing even though he was trying to force them to stay open. He got one hand on to the arm of the chair and levered himself partially upright, then used his other hand to push himself to completely standing. He could feel himself swaying. His stomach felt nauseous, as if he'd drunk some spoilt milk by mistake.

With a soft *thump*, Matty's head fell back against his headrest.

Sherlock staggered across to the window and reached out to grasp the curtain, but the cloth slipped through his fingers and he couldn't get a grip. He forced himself to concentrate, despite his blurry vision, and to close his fingers on the edge. Finally he got a grip, and pulled the curtain open.

The window had been pulled shut.

Through the foggy mess of Sherlock's brain, a single thought glowed. He'd been outwitted! Someone had

241

noticed the partially open windows, despite his best efforts to hide them, and they had simply closed them one by one when nobody was in the rooms. Then they had gone about their normal business, pumping anaesthetic gas into the house through the holes they had drilled previously.

He staggered back into the room and quenched the candle with his fingertips, then went back to the window. Now that it was dark inside the room, nobody would see what he was doing. He took hold of the window with fingers that felt rubbery and huge, and he pulled upward with all his strength.

Nothing happened. Surely they hadn't nailed the windows shut again?

He pulled again, and heard a *squeal* of wood rubbing against wood. The window eased up an inch, and then stuck. Sherlock bent down and put his mouth to the gap. Fresh night air coursed into his lungs, and it was like pure water to a man who had spent days in the desert. He breathed it in, gulping it down, and he could actually feel his thoughts becoming clearer and the heaviness trickling away from his muscles.

Something moved outside the window.

He ducked further down, still keeping his mouth as close to the crack as possible, and looked over the top of the window's bottom edge.

A tree was passing by outside.

Sherlock could see the tops of the branches clearly.

They looked like skeletal hands clawing at the stars. As he watched, they moved slowly past the window. With his fingers resting on the sill, Sherlock could feel a dull rumbling from outside.

He dropped to the floor and scuttled across to where Matty was slumped in his chair. He pulled the boy out and dragged him across the room to the window, then held his face up to the fresh air until he began to move.

'Wha . . .'

'*Sssshh!*'

'Okay.' Matty took a few deep breaths. '"S'all right, mate,' he slurred. 'I'm okay.' He shrugged off Sherlock's arm and stood up shakily.

'Take a look outside,' Sherlock said.

Together the two boys gazed out of the window. For a moment all they could see was the star-spattered sky and the dark bulk of the land below, but then another set of branches slid past the window.

Matty gasped. 'So it's true then?'

'It depends what you mean,' Sherlock said. 'Let's go down and take a look.'

'What about Maberley?' Matty asked. 'Shouldn't we open some more windows or something?'

'He's been okay every night so far,' Sherlock pointed out. 'I think these people know what they're doing. The chances are, if we wake him up then he'll charge out of the house with his fowling piece, and then all hell might break loose.'

'Good point.'

The two of them headed downstairs and made their way towards the front door. Sherlock opened it a crack and looked outside. The front door faced away from the orchard, and there was nobody between them and the low wall that separated the grounds of the house from the road.

Sherlock nudged Matty, and indicated the wall and the road. 'Same distance as it was this afternoon,' he pointed out in a whisper. 'The house hasn't moved.'

'But if the house hasn't moved then what did we see from the window just now?' Matty asked.

'Well,' Sherlock said, 'if the house isn't moving, then it must be the orchard, mustn't it? The house moving is physically impossible. The orchard moving is just . . . improbable.'

They slipped out of the house and into the night. Sherlock led the way along the wall of the house, past the window to the sitting room. That had been closed from the outside as well. Someone was obviously checking carefully before making any move. The brains behind this criminal activity was very clever, and very cautious.

A little way along the wall was a window into one of the inside rooms – the dining room, Sherlock thought. That window had been closed as well, but more importantly there was a device sitting on the ground nearby. It was like a large milk churn, with a rubber hose leading from the top of it into one of the holes that Matty and Sherlock had observed earlier – the holes drilled from the outside of the house to the inside. There must be some reservoir of liquid chloroform inside that container, Sherlock theorized, and the evaporated vapour was creeping into the house. All of the other holes were presumably being used as well. He cursed himself for his stupidity in thinking that simply opening a few windows was going to stop something so fiendishly clever.

When they got to the corner of the house, Sherlock stopped and peered around the edge. Matty knelt down and did the same.

The untidy lawn had been transformed. That afternoon there had been nothing there over knee height, but now it was filled with trees. They were the trees from the orchard, but they appeared taller. It took a moment for Sherlock to see why, but when he did he smiled. It was, of course, the most logical solution.

The roots of the trees weren't buried in the soil, as they had been in the orchard. That would, of course, have made it impossible for them to be moved unless they had been dug up one by one, which would have taken too much time and left traces. It was apparent now that when the trees had been planted a couple of hundred years before, they had been planted in large wooden barrels which had been sunk into the earth. Their roots had grown inside the barrels as the years went on. If the roots had ever got to the edge of the barrels then they would have been forced back on themselves, which might explain why the trees were stunted. Now whoever was moving the trees had just pulled the barrels up out of the ground, taking the trees with them. Looking at the tops of the barrels now, Sherlock could see loops of thick rope that had been attached to them. They must have been buried loosely in the soil as well. The people moving the trees would just have to dig around until they found the rope loops, and then it would have been relatively easy to pull the barrels up.

Relatively easy. It still would have taken a fair amount of time, and a fair number of people, which is why Maberley had to be drugged every time they did it.

The apple trees weren't arranged in nice rows, the way they had been in the orchard. They were just set down higgledy-piggledy, wherever the movers could find a space.

Sherlock had been aware for some time of a rumbling noise, but now it was getting louder. He moved back a fraction, and pulled Matty back as well.

Around the distant next corner of the house came a cart. Not the normal kind of cart that you could see on any road on any day, but a big, heavy cart with wheels as wide as Sherlock's forearm. As he had suspected, the wheels were padded with big pillow-like objects that squashed under the weight of the cart and its contents as they moved. The cart was pulled by three enormous shire horses, and the horses were being guided by a team of men dressed in black, with black masks over their faces.

On the cart, of course, were two apple trees in barrels that must have been removed from the ground only a few moments before.

From down near his waist, Sherlock heard Matty make a hissing noise. 'It's obvious, ain't it?' he whispered. 'If the house ain't movin', then it must be the orchard that moves!'

'Oh, yes, *now* it's obvious,' Sherlock muttered. 'It wasn't so obvious earlier on, was it?'

Another man, tall but thinner than the others, walked behind the cart, checking where it was going. He communicated with the others through hand gestures. It looked as if he was the one in charge.

As Sherlock and Matty watched, the cart slowed to a halt and the masked men scrambled up on top of it. Each one took hold of a rope loop, and together they lifted the first tree, moved it to the edge of the cart and lowered it down to the ground.

'The fairy rings!' Matty whispered.

'No fairies,' Sherlock pointed out. 'Just thieves.'

'But I still don't understand – what are they stealin'? Not the trees – they always put them back again when they've finished.' Matty hesitated, then hit his forehead with his palm. 'Of course – they think there's somethin' *under* the trees!'

'Let's go and check,' Sherlock said.

CHAPTER THIRTEEN

The men had finished dropping the trees off the cart now, and were leading the shire horses around in a wide half-circle so they could take them back to the orchard again and, presumably, pick up another couple of trees. The thinner man who was supervising them took a last look around, glanced at the house, then followed them back.

Sherlock and Matty moved cautiously along the side of the house, keeping low so that their bodies would just be dark shapes against the blackness of the house itself. When they got to the end they peered around the edge. They were looking towards the orchard now, and past more of the relocated trees. The empty cart was rumbling slowly down a gap that had been left between the trees.

Sherlock spotted a large bush over near the waist-high wall that bounded the house's grounds. He glanced around to check that they weren't being watched, then dragged Matty across the open ground and dived behind the bush. They were looking diagonally across at the orchard now, and it was obvious what was happening.

The apple trees nearest the house had been removed and relocated to the lawn. The trees further into the orchard had been moved as well, some of them to the lawn and some of them put into the holes left by trees that had already been moved. There was now a gap in the middle of the orchard where there had previously been apple trees, but now there were only dark holes, like pockmarks in the earth. The thinner man and a couple of his companions were bent down at the edge of one of the holes, staring in. As Sherlock watched, one of them jumped in. His head ducked out of sight as he crouched and began to hunt around inside. The thinner man, on the lip of the hole, looked as if he was whispering instructions.

'They're lookin' for somethin' that's been buried,' Matty observed. 'The problem is, they don't know *where* it's been buried, just that it's under one of them apple trees.'

'That's right. They're working their way across the orchard in a logical sequence, from the easiest trees to the most difficult to reach.' Sherlock felt a warm glow of satisfaction. He had been right in his deductions. 'Do you remember the story that Ferny Weston told us, the one about the orchard having been planted around the same time as the English Civil War? He said that there was a rumour that Prince Charles had been hidden here from Oliver Cromwell's Roundhead forces, and that in return he had given the Maberley family a great treasure when he was finally crowned king. I'd been wondering where exactly the Cavalier sympathizers and the Prince could have been hidden – there's nowhere in the house they could have been secreted. I think it's obvious now that there are hiding places beneath the trees of the orchard. The holes must go deeper than the barrels, leaving space for refugees to curl up and wait until the searchers had gone away, when the trees could be pulled up again and they could be rescued. They must have taken food down with them, and maybe even oil lamps so they could read, and keep warm.' He gestured to the searching men. 'I think that *they* think that the treasure is hidden in one of the holes as well, and that would make perfect sense. We know they searched Maberley's house first off, because he said that there was a time when he woke up to find the house *tidier* than it had been. They didn't find the treasure in the house anywhere, so they started on the orchard. Very clever of them to work that out.'

'An' they've been workin' all this time to find the treasure? That's dedication for you.'

'It's probably something incredibly valuable – jewels and gold certainly, but the historical connections would make it much more important.'

Matty sounded grudgingly impressed. 'All that time, night after night, an' they keep on goin'.'

'I don't know why,' Sherlock murmured. 'It's obvious where the treasure *actually* is.'

'Is that right?' a voice said loudly behind them. 'In that case, you can save us all a lot of effort.'

Sherlock and Matty turned around. Behind them three masked men stood. Two of them held knives – wickedly curved and serrated. The other held a gun, which was pointed mid-way between the two boys.

'We should've woken Maberley up,' Matty pointed out. 'Or at least taken 'is gun.'

'Don't tell me that *now*,' Sherlock muttered. 'Tell me that half an hour ago.'

'Hey, you're supposed to be the intelligent one.'

'No talking,' the man with the gun said. 'At least, not for a few minutes. Then you can talk all you want. In fact, you won't be able to talk fast enough.' He gestured with the gun. 'Go on – into the orchard.'

The group moved off, with Sherlock and Matty in the lead and their captors bringing up the rear. The two men with knives spread out to either side, in case Sherlock or Matty made a run for it. They walked across the lawn, between the massive barrels that held the apple trees, and into the orchard itself.

In the centre of the orchard there were twelve holes where trees had been removed. In the light of the stars and the three-quarter moon, and the shielded lamps that he now saw the men were using, the sides of the holes looked smooth, lined with tiny roots and soil. He glanced into one, and saw that the bottom was circular, but that there was a smaller square hole dug into the earth in its centre. That hole was lined with wood – it looked like a crate had been dropped in and the top taken off. That, he guessed, was where the Cavalier refugees would have hidden from the Roundhead searchers.

'Who's this?' a voice said. Sherlock looked up, and

saw the thinner masked man that he had seen directing the others earlier. The boss. The one in charge.

'We found them over by the house, boss. They were watching you.'

'Oh, really?' The man walked over to look at Sherlock. 'What is it that you want?'

Sherlock shrugged. 'Just to know what's going on. Mr Maberley told us his story – about the house moving. I wanted to see what the truth was.'

The man – in fact, by the tone of his voice he was closer to a boy – laughed. 'Yes, he's been telling that story for a while now. At first I thought someone might listen to him, check what was going on, but they didn't, so I stopped worrying. What's your name?'

'Does it matter?' Sherlock stared at the boy's eyes, which were clear and blue beneath the mask. 'I don't think you're going to let us go, are you?'

'No, I'm not. Maybe, like you, I just wanted to know.'

The man with the gun stepped forward. 'He said he knows where the treasure is.'

The boyish leader moved to face Sherlock and stared into his eyes for a long moment. 'He doesn't,' he said eventually, with complete confidence. 'He thinks he does, but it's just a guess. He isn't sure.'

'But if he does, he could save us all a lot of time.'

The boy shook his head again. 'He doesn't. He's just inflating the importance of some small deduction he has made, trying to keep himself and his friend alive.'

'But—'

The boy made a chopping motion with his hand. 'Enough. The subject is closed.' He turned back to Sherlock, and pulled his mask abruptly off. He was about the same age as Sherlock, and about the same height, although his brown hair was longer. He stared at Sherlock challengingly. 'I thought you might want to see my face, before you die,' he said. 'A last courtesy.'

'Very kind.' Sherlock smiled. 'Or is it more that you're tired of nobody knowing who you are, and you want at least one person to see your face, to know your name and to tell you how clever you are before this is all over?'

The boy shrugged. 'Fame has its benefits, and its problems. That being said, I've been unknown for a good while now. Maybe that should change.'

'What is your name?'

'Jude,' the boy said.

'Jude what?'

He smiled. 'That's all you're getting for the moment. And you are . . . ?'

'Sherlock Holmes. And this is Matthew Arnatt. I must admit, I'm impressed at how you manage to keep all these men in line – you being so young and inexperienced, and them being so much bigger and stronger than you. I'm surprised it hasn't occurred to them to get rid of you and take over. That way they'd get a bigger share of the treasure, and they wouldn't have to take orders from a kid.'

The boy laughed. 'You're trying to drive a wedge between us,' he said. 'It won't work. They know I'm going to give them what they want.'

'They want money,' Sherlock pointed out. 'It's not that hard to work out.'

Jude shook his head. 'That's not it. Everyone wants something different – but they almost always think that money will get it for them.' He indicated one of the men, who was trying to get an apple tree out of the ground. 'Take Sutton there. He *says* he wants money, but what he actually wants is good health, and an end to the terrible pain he gets from his rotten teeth. I know that. I can talk to him about it, and take him seriously.' He pointed to another man, this one patrolling the edge of the orchard. 'Dillman, over there, also says he wants money, but he really wants a family who love him – a wife and three kids. I understand that, and he knows that I understand. That's why they all follow me – I know their deepest desires.'

'How can you do that?' Sherlock asked, intrigued.

'I can see what people want. I can tell from the way they look off to one side when they speak, or the way they play with their fingers, even the specific words they use. It's a talent I've always had.'

'What do I want then?' Matty asked pugnaciously.

Jude glanced at him. 'You want a good kicking,' he snapped.

Matty scowled at him. 'You know what – I don't like you.'

'Imagine the pain that gives me,' Jude said, looking away. 'Regardless – your own particular desires and wishes are irrelevant. As of now, what happens to you is what *I* want.'

'You were a student at the University,' Sherlock guessed. 'Allowed in early because of your academic brilliance.'

'Well deduced. I was a scholarship pupil – I got in on my merits, not because my parents paid. They weren't rich enough, or of the right social circle.'

'And you were thrown out.'

Jude nodded. 'Things went missing. Money was stolen. I was younger then, and I was inexperienced. I hadn't thought through the implications of what I was doing. I acted impulsively, rather than thinking things through. So – they got rid of me. The University authorities didn't have enough evidence to go to the police with, but that didn't stop them. I stayed in the area, and I started specializing in high-end robberies – artworks, statues, that kind of thing. There are a lot of rich people with nice rare stuff around Oxford, and there are a lot of even richer people further away from Oxford who don't have this nice rare stuff but want it. I decided to act as a middle-man, taking from the rich and giving – well, selling – to the even richer. It's funded a very comfortable lifestyle for me, and it has bought the loyalty of these excellent fellows, each of whom is earning the kind of money that an Oxford lecturer might expect, as well as satisfying their own deepest desires.'

Sherlock remembered something that Ferny Weston had told him, about a gang of art thieves that couldn't be caught. 'You kept evading the police,' he said. 'You must have had inside information – not only about the big houses and their art collections, but also about the progress of the police investigation.'

The boy smiled. 'Inside information is my speciality. It's what gives me my edge.'

'Who was it? Who gave you the information about the big houses and the police?'

'Now that,' Jude said, laughing, 'is a step too far. I don't mind gloating about how clever *I* am, but I'm not going to risk telling you how clever other people are, especially if they work for me.'

'Or you work for them.' Sherlock caught the telltale twitch of Jude's lip. 'Yes, you're not the top dog, are you? You're not quite as clever as you want us to think.'

Jude turned to the man with the gun. 'I've had my fun,' he said curtly. 'Throw them into a hole, put a tree on top of them, and leave them to starve or suffocate.'

The man looked at his gun. 'Why not just shoot them?' he asked, puzzled.

'I don't like them,' the boy said, staring at Sherlock. 'This one's too clever by half. I want them to suffer, and as they lie there, dying, I want them to remember who it was that bested them.'

He stalked off. Matty looked up at Sherlock and said:

''E's not as bright as 'e thinks 'e is, is 'e?'

'Like a lot of people,' Sherlock replied, 'he's clever in one direction, but not in others.'

'Enough talking.' The man with the gun stepped forward, pointing the gun at Sherlock. 'Get in the hole.'

'Or what?' Sherlock challenged. 'You're going to shoot me? Your boss specifically told you not to.'

The man didn't say anything in reply. He just stepped forward and lashed out at Sherlock with his gun. The barrel caught Sherlock on his forehead. Through the haze of pain, Sherlock felt himself being pushed by someone's foot closer and closer to the edge of the nearest hole. He tried desperately to dig his fingers into the soil to stop himself moving, but it was no good. If he did manage to get a grip, the person moving him just kicked him in the stomach until he let go.

'There ain't room for both of them in the same hole!' someone called.

The man pushing Sherlock responded: 'It's not like they're going to be there forever. The air'll run out before they get too uncomfortable! Let them squash up – the other one's a tiddler anyway!'

'No, I mean with two of them in the same hole we won't be able to get the tree back in properly. It'll stick up, and someone'll notice.'

A hesitation, then: 'All right – put the small one in that hole over there. I've just about got this one in here.'

Sherlock glanced around desperately, tying to see where Matty was. He got one fragmentary glimpse of the boy over to his right, fighting with his captors, and then Sherlock felt his shoulders tip over the edge of the hole and into empty space. He tried to roll back, but a firm boot between his shoulderblades dissuaded him. The boot pushed hard, and he was falling, dropping through the air with a circle of sky getting ever-smaller above him. His shoulders and back smashed into the soil lip around the top of the crate that was buried inside the hole, while his legs fell inside. A spike of raw agony flared through him. He thought he might have broken his back. The weight of his legs falling into the crate pulled the rest of him over the edge. He tried to get his legs working beneath him so that he could push himself up and climb back out – although what he intended to do then wasn't exactly obvious. One step at a time. He could feel his legs, thank heavens, but they refused to obey his orders, and just gave way like rubber when he tried to put any weight on them.

He glanced up frantically, trying to work out if he'd been left there alone while they dealt with Matty or whether they were all clustered around the edge of the hole, looking at him and laughing, but all he could see was the rapidly descending lid of the crate as it was thrown in after him. He ducked so that he was completely inside the crate, and the lid banged down on top. It was partially rotated so that it was caught by the corners but there were gaps all around, through which light still trickled in.

Until they put the barrel containing the apple tree back in the hole.

Light vanished, and soil fell inside the crate from the roots of the tree as it slammed down into the hole, sealing Sherlock in.

All he could smell was damp earth. All he could hear was the rasp of his own breathing. He tried again to stand up, and found that his legs were working better now. The paralysis had only been temporary, which meant that his back was all right. That was scant comfort, because the rest of him wasn't.

Something alive dropped in through one of the gaps from the tree's roots. He felt it hit his shoulder and run across his neck, hard little legs catching against his skin as it moved. It was a beetle, he thought. Harmless. More frightened of him than he was of it.

He turned his attention back to standing up. His shoulders and the back of his head hit the lid of the crate – and stopped. There was no movement there at all, no leverage. The weight of the entire apple tree above him effectively sealed the crate shut.

He was alone, and he was trapped. Those thoughts kept rotating around in his head. There was no way out. Matty was trapped as well, and Maberley was drugged. Nobody else knew where they were, and the criminals weren't going to have a last-minute fit of guilt and let them out. This was it. This was the end.

No, this *wasn't* it. The thought surfaced in the confusion of his mind like something vast and certain breaking the surface of a choppy sea. This was *not* it. He would get out. Logic would get him out.

He rested on his haunches as he tried to work through everything he had heard about Royalist hiding places, and everything he had thought about when Ferny Weston had been telling the story. He tried to imagine what the Royalists or the Maberley family would have thought as they were digging the holes and constructing the hiding places. There were so many holes – twenty, thirty, maybe more. Even if only half of them were occupied, then there would be a lot of people trapped underground waiting for the searchers to go away, and that might take hours. Perhaps even days. Some of the people hiding might be claustrophobic and would panic. Some would have problems breathing. Others would get hungry. It would make sense to build some kind of escape route for them, perhaps a set of tunnels *underneath* the crates, so that if there was an emergency then the hiders could get out, even if it was difficult and took time. Yes, that made perfect sense.

Sherlock started feeling around the edges of the crate, looking for signs of hinges or a catch of some kind. In the back of his mind was the unwelcome thought that he was inventing something that might not – in fact, probably *didn't* – exist, but he refused to let that thought get more than a small amount of purchase. He had to stay calm, he had to stay sane and he had to get out. Logic told him that the builders would have put in an escape route, and therefore he would find it. Job done.

Except that he couldn't feel any hinges or any catch. He had tried the panel in front of him, so he shuffled around to his right and repeated the procedure. Still nothing. He shuffled again, so that he was facing backwards. Still nothing. One more rotation – he *had* to find the hinges on this side. They *had* to be there.

But they weren't.

He felt his breath rasping in his throat. His fingers were raw with the effort of scrabbling at the wood of the crate. He could hear a distant moaning sound, and for a second he thought someone was taking the apple tree away and calling to him, but then he realized that the sound was coming from his own throat. Despite his logic, a part of him was succumbing to panic and despair.

He had tried all four sides, and he knew that the lid above him wouldn't move.

That still left one direction.

Sherlock's fingers felt around the bottom of the crate. It was awkward, and he had to keep moving his feet and rotating his body slightly, but he knew that this was his last chance and he had to do it properly.

His fingertips brushed against something metallic, and then moved on. He scrambled back, trying to find it again. Yes, there it was! He tried to work out in the absolute blackness what it was. Rectangular, yes, and metallic. It could be a hinge. If it was, then there would be another one, round about . . . there! Yes, there it was. He felt his heart beginning to calm down now, and before continuing he took several calming breaths. All right, if there was a hinge *there* and a hinge *there*, then there would be a catch on the other side, surely. He flattened his right hand and brushed it along the base of the crate. Something squirmed beneath his hand – a worm maybe? He swallowed his sudden nausea and kept going.

Yes! There was a metal fixture in the junction between the bottom and the side of the crate. It seemed to Sherlock that the entire bottom of the crate was hinged so that it would open downward, into another space.

Except that he couldn't get the fixture to move. It was holding the bottom of the crate shut, but his weight on the wood was jamming it, preventing it from moving. He had a sudden frustrated flash of imagining the initial designers of the hiding places, two hundred or more years ago, looking at their handiwork and congratulating themselves on its impeccable design without actually having tried it to see if it worked in practice.

He had to make it work. He had two hinges, a catch and a base that worked like a trapdoor – that was significantly better than he'd had five minutes before.

Sherlock braced his legs against the sides of the crate, taking his weight off the base, and tried again to move the catch with his fingers. This time there was movement, and he put all of his energy into sliding that bolt sideways. The muscles of his legs felt like they were bathed in acid, and splinters were digging into him all over, but he was going to move that bolt. Despite two centuries of neglect, despite rust and rot and whatever else nature might have thrown at it, that bolt was between him and freedom, and it was going to move!

The bolt slid calmly sideways as if that had been its plan all along. The bottom of the crate dropped away and Sherlock fell into a narrow and damp space.

Feeling around, he appeared to be at a crossroads. Tunnels led off ahead of him, to either side and behind him. The sides of the tunnels were made of earth, with roots and other organic debris growing into them. Every foot or so, wooden planks stopped the tunnels collapsing.

Which way to go? One option was to head for the nearest edge of the orchard, which was likely to have a way to the surface, but that would leave Matty trapped and panicking. No, he had to go and get his friend first.

Which direction? Matty had been off to Sherlock's right when Sherlock had been thrown into the hole, but Sherlock had made a three-quarters turn inside the crate when he was trying to find a way out. That meant . . . that meant Matty was behind him.

He turned around in the narrow tunnel, soil cascading over him as his shoulders brushed the tunnel sides and his head brushed its top. He tried to estimate how far away the next hole had been. Ten feet maybe? He started to crawl, fingers digging into the earth of the tunnel's floor. Small beetles and other invertebrates scattered from beneath his fingers as he moved, but he ignored them. His back ached from being crouched over, but he ignored that as well. Everything else was a distraction – he had to get to Matty, and then get them both out of there.

Something made a snorting noise ahead of him.

He stopped dead in the tunnel, listening.

A grunting noise, and a shuffling.

There was something in the tunnel with him.

CHAPTER FOURTEEN

His mind flashed through the possibilities. It sounded too large to be an insect or a beetle. Far too large. Snakes and beetles didn't grunt or snort either. A fox, maybe? Perhaps over the years foxes had taken over the tunnels, using them as their dens rather than dig new ones.

Or maybe it was a badger. A sudden chill washed over him like freezing water. Badgers were notoriously dangerous. They had sharp digging claws, sharp teeth and bad tempers. They had no natural predators – nothing was going to risk going up against a badger. They were vicious.

And he was trapped in a tunnel with one.

He began to edge backwards, very quietly and very calmly.

'Sherlock – is that you?' a voice whispered.

'Matty!' Relief filled him, making him giddy. 'What are you doing?'

'Escapin'. What are *you* doin'?'

'The same thing. You found the hatch in the bottom of the crate then?'

'Actually,' Matty said, 'I fell through. The wood was rotten. Knocked myself out for a minute or two. When I came round I thought I'd explore a bit. These are escape tunnels then?'

'Looks like it.'

'Which way's out?'

Sherlock considered for a moment. His initial thought was that there would be exits at the end of each tunnel, but he could see now that he'd been wrong about that. Tunnel exits all around the orchard would be easy to spot, and would make the whole cleverness about the apple trees, the barrels and the holes pointless. No, there would be one way out, cleverly disguised; probably only accessible from the inside, and not visible from the outside until it was opened. If there was only one exit, however, but there was a grid of tunnels, then how to find the way? Yes, perhaps the original hiders would have had oil lamps, but maybe they wouldn't. There had to be some way of indicating to them which way was out in the event of an emergency.

'Sherlock?'

'Thinking.'

'Okay. Don't take too long.'

Sherlock backed up slightly until he was beneath the crate he had started off in. He was at the crossroads of four tunnels now. He carefully checked each corner where two tunnels met. Somewhere there, he felt sure, there would be a sign, an indication. Yes! Set just inside one tunnel he felt a round, smooth stone, completely different from anything else he could feel on the tunnel walls. It was a marker – or at least, it was the closest thing to a marker he was going to get.

'I think I've got it. Follow me.'

Sherlock made his way along the tunnel to the next junction, with Matty following. It took him a few moments to locate the smooth stone there, but it was to the left. He went that way, making sure that Matty knew which direction he had gone.

Right at the next, then straight on for the next three. The next few turns were strange – left, then right, then right again, and then left, as if they were detouring around something. After that it was straight on again for five junctions. That brought him up against a hard barrier.

Matty crashed into him from behind. 'Sorry!'

'I think we're there.'

He pushed, first tentatively, then harder. Nothing shifted. He examined the barrier with his fingers. It felt like it was constructed of similarly sized rough rocks arranged into a wall. Sherlock settled back and thought for a moment. There would be no point in allowing hidden Cavalier sympathizers to get this far and then frustrating their efforts to escape at the last minute. There had to be an answer to this conundrum, as there had been to the others.

Some kind of tool, perhaps? He gingerly felt around in the soil to his left and to his right, hoping that if there was a tool that it hadn't been removed by some foraging animal looking for material to build a den with.

Just as he was about to ask Matty to check around

where he was crouching, his questing fingers brushed across a hard metal object. It was cold to the touch. He dug it out of the earth and checked it from one end to the other. It felt like a crowbar – a metal shaft with carved metal spikes at one end. Just the kind of thing one might use to lever stones out of a wall.

It took him five minutes, and he was damp with sweat when he had finished, but he made a gap in the stone wall large enough to wriggle through. Beyond the wall was soft earth, which he scooped away until he could feel fresh air on his face. He threw his head back and breathed gratefully, then pushed the last remnants of soil out of the way and crawled through a barrier of moss and leaves out into the open.

The moon was shining down, and it seemed like the brightest light he had ever seen. He blinked, dazzled, as Matty scrambled out beside him.

They were on the far side of the orchard, where he had been earlier in the day. The ground sloped away in front of them to a distant landscape of dark fields and black copses of trees.

Looking back, he could see that the exit would have been completely invisible from the outside – until it was broken through. He quickly spread some moss and branches back across the hole to help disguise it from anyone who happened to look over the orchard wall.

'That,' he whispered, 'was too close.'

'I knew you'd get us out,' Matty said quietly. His hand

closed on Sherlock's shoulder. 'Thanks, mate.'

'No problem.'

'What now?' he asked.

'Now we go and alert the police. I'm not risking a fight with those guys. I'm exhausted, and there are too many of them and they're armed.'

'Amen to that,' Matty murmured.

Sherlock calculated which way to go. The road that led past Maberley's house was a black ribbon off to his right. If they went over there then they could make their way back to where their horses were tied up – assuming they were still there.

'Come on,' he said.

His legs were wobbly and weak, but standing up was a blessing, and the breeze on his face was a delight. As the two of them walked sideways along the slope he listened out for any sound from the criminals in the orchard, but he could hear nothing. They were, when all was said and done, very professional in their approach.

Sherlock, however, had an advantage. He had already worked out where the treasure was. He had no doubt that if he went back later, in daylight, he could find it.

They made it on to the smoother surface of the road and headed on up the slope to where it crested the ridge. The orchard was visible away to their right, and they kept low and quiet as they moved. They reached the gateway into the grounds of Maberley's house and halted, looking for any signs of activity.

The lawn was almost completely clear of trees now. The muffled cart that had been used to move them was sitting, abandoned, just outside the house, with the shire horses contentedly munching grass. Sherlock assumed that the criminals were in the orchard, busy putting all the trees back. They obviously hadn't found the treasure yet, and they were preparing to leave, only to come back again on another night. He was going to lose them unless he did something.

His brain whirled, thinking through all the options.

He had speculated earlier that the gang had access to some kind of empty barn nearby, where they could store the huge modified cart when they weren't using it. They certainly wouldn't want to be driving it around the roads during daylight hours. They would be heading off there soon, while it was still dark, and presumably resting there for a little while, getting some sleep maybe, or having a rough meal, before dispersing to their various homes until the next time they were required. Sherlock had to somehow find out where their base was and keep them all there so that the police could apprehend the entire gang.

Something was nagging at his brain. The solution was there, in front of him, if he could only see it.

While nobody was about, he dashed across to the muffled cart and looked inside. It was empty apart from a lot of soil left behind by the trees, some coils of rope and a few tarpaulins. He assumed that the men would just pile into it and be pulled back to their base, so even if he managed to get inside the cart and cover himself with a tarpaulin or something he would be discovered fairly quickly when someone kicked him, or fell across him, or just decided they were cold and pulled the tarpaulin off him. No, there had to be another way.

Follow them on horseback? They would be watching out for anyone who showed too much interest in them, and if he was riding close enough to keep tabs on the cart then the people inside would undoubtedly see him.

He crouched down and glanced underneath the cart. The axles were reinforced, to take the weight of the trees. Each axle ran through several thick iron hoops, which were riveted to the cart's wooden underside. The hoops were larger than the axles, which meant there was a space between the bottom of the rotating axle and the inside of the hoop. That gave Sherlock an idea.

He stood up, reached into the back of the cart and grabbed a coil of rope.

'Quickly,' he said to Matty, 'help me string this rope between the axle hoops underneath this thing. I need to build a kind of hammock for myself.'

The expression on Matty's face indicated that he didn't understand why Sherlock wanted to do that, but he complied. Quickly, before any of the gang came back – and working on the side of the cart facing away from the orchard so that they wouldn't be seen by anyone returning – they cut lengths of rope with Matty's knife and tied them into a rough web that hung beneath the cart, fastened at each axle hoop.

When they had finished, Sherlock patted Matty on the shoulder. 'Good work. Your job now is to go inside and wake Maberley when the gang have left. They'll obviously take the chloroform with them, in the cart, rather than leave it behind to be discovered. When Maberley's awake, explain to him what's been going on, then the two of you head into the nearest village and rouse as many police and interested citizens as you can. Our horses are here, tied up, and I assume Maberley has a horse. If not, use mine. Get the police back here.'

'Where will you be?' Matty asked.

'I don't know yet, but I'll send a signal telling you. Somehow.'

Matty stared at him for a moment. 'I hate it when you don't have a plan,' he said finally. 'You don't do well when you're improvisin'.'

'Hey, I got you out of the orchard in one piece, didn't I?'

Matty nodded. 'You did at that. All right then – take care of yourself. Don't die.'

'I'll try not to.'

Matty ran off towards the house, and Sherlock crawled into the web of rope beneath the cart. His weight pulled it further down towards the ground than he had intended, and he had a sudden horrible thought that he might end up being dragged along the road rather than hanging above it, but suddenly it was too late to do anything about it. He heard the sounds of men returning from the orchard and muffled conversations.

'Get the chloroform canisters,' Jude's voice said – higher and smoother than the others, but his tone conveyed unmistakably that he was in charge.

The rope was cutting into Sherlock as he lay there, face down. He could feel it pressing his chest and forcing his arms back in an uncomfortable way. He tried to worm his hands through the strands, but then they just hung down almost to the ground, and he knew that when the cart started moving his knuckles or his fingertips would be dragged in the dirt, so he pulled them in again. One strand of rope crossed his throat, and he felt like gagging every time he moved his head and it pressed on his windpipe.

This was maybe not the smartest move ever.

He felt the cart rock as objects were loaded on and people climbed aboard. The wooden underneath bowed closer and closer as people weighed it down. Eventually, at some silent signal, the horses took up the slack on their harnesses and the cart began to move.

The padding on the wheels made it a smooth ride, but even so Sherlock found himself moving around, swinging from side to side. The road rolled past just a few inches beneath him, and he found himself fixating on particular stones set into the earth as they entered his field of view. He felt sick. It was like being on a ship, with the exception that he couldn't see the horizon or feel the breeze. On a ship below decks, maybe.

Under better circumstances, rocking back and forth like that might have sent him to sleep, but he was concerned about the knots holding the web of rope on to the iron axle loops. If just one of those knots slipped, then the best thing that could happen was that he would be dropped into the road and left behind. The worst outcome would be that his foot might get caught in the ropes and he would be dragged along underneath the cart, his skin shredded by every rock, until he looked like a side of beef hanging in a butcher's window.

The dust rising from the road made his throat dry. He would give a hundred pounds for a glass of water, just at that moment.

The journey seemed to last forever, but in reality they couldn't have gone more than half a mile down the road before the cart slowed down and began a ponderous turn into a gated field. It was still dark, but when the moon's light was eclipsed by some dark bulk Sherlock knew that his deduction about a barn had been correct. The cart rolled inside and stopped. Sherlock waited as the men on board disembarked and the horses were untied.

'There's beer, bread and meat on the trestle tables,' the boy, Jude, yelled. 'Get a few hours' sleep once you've eaten and drunk your fill. If you're going to smoke, do it outside – this hay is dry, and one dropped cigarette could set light to the whole place. When the sun's up you can leave, but don't all set off at once. Make sure you go only one or two at a time so you don't raise suspicions, and take different routes back to your homes. Back here tomorrow night at sundown – I think we're close now, and I want to keep up the pace.' His voice got louder. 'Trust me, lads – we'll be in the money soon!'

There was a ragged cheer, and then half an hour or so of conversation and the sounds of people satisfying their hunger and their thirst, but the men must have been tired after their endeavours because they pretty soon quietened down and started to snore.

Sherlock gave them ten more minutes before he wriggled free of the ropes down on to the dirt floor of the barn.

He cautiously crawled out into the open, ready to run for it if anyone was still awake and saw him, but the men were all sprawled out on piles of hay, mouths open and eyes closed. Sherlock cast an envious eye at the jug of beer on the trestle table, but he'd have to step over half a dozen men to get to it. Not worth the risk, he thought.

He looked around. The barn looked like it was newly constructed – he could still smell the fresh timber and the creosote that had been used to protect it against the weather. The boy, Jude, had probably had it built just for this enterprise. Sherlock found himself admiring the boy more and more – all the planning he was doing, plus the way he managed to give orders to men three or four times his age without them arguing, meant that he had a strong personality and a convincing manner. In another life he would have made a good soldier, or maybe a detective, but he had chosen an apparently easier but less moral path.

Thinking of Jude, Sherlock looked around the barn to see where he was, but the boy wasn't visible. Maybe he had curled up beneath a pile of hay.

What to do now? Jude had mentioned the dryness of the hay. Sherlock could easily start a fire in the barn, but what then? That might disrupt Jude's plans, but the gang would scatter and they would never be brought to justice. And besides – people might die. They might be bad, but they didn't deserve execution, and Sherlock didn't want their deaths on his conscience.

He was going to have to follow the plan that had come into his head back at Mortimer Maberley's house and hope that it all worked out.

Taking a last look around, he climbed on to the cart. As he had expected, the milk churns full of chloroform were still there. No point in unloading them and then loading them back up again.

It took him barely five minutes to unscrew all of the lids.

The characteristic smell began to drift across the barn, and Sherlock felt his eyes getting prickly and his limbs heavy. Quickly he jumped off the cart and ran towards the door. Before leaving he took a couple of handfuls of hay. The large doors had been closed, all but for a small gap; he squeezed through and pushed them completely closed, then went along the lower edges and stuffed the hay in there to stop the chloroform from leaking out. There were probably all kinds of holes in the barn, but if he was lucky then the chloroform would evaporate from the cans faster than it would leak out of the building. The thugs inside would sleep sweetly until the police got there.

Which reminded him . . . he still had to set some kind of sign for Matty and the police to find when they got there.

He was outside the barn now, in an open yard. Discarded farm equipment lay around. He quickly made a mental inventory of what he saw: hoes, ploughs, wooden beams, tins of creosote . . . Creosote! That was flammable!

Even as he hurried over towards the tins, he was refining his plans. For a few seconds he considered making a pile of wood and setting fire to it, but if any of the men woke up and realized what was happening, then they could put it out pretty easily. Instead he carried the tins towards the road. It only took him a minute or so to pour the sticky liquid out. Some of the creosote sank into the dirt, but it was thick, like treacle, and after a few seconds of pouring it began to pool on the surface: a glittering brown stain in the shape of a giant arrow, pointing towards the barn.

All he needed now was a flame.

Sherlock had taken to carrying a flint and stone inside

a small metal case in his pocket. Life, he had found, was full of times when you wished you could start a fire. He had some scraps of paper in his pocket as well, so he tore them up, piled them on the creosote, took the flint out and struck it a few times. Within moments the paper took light, and then so did the creosote. He backed away rapidly as the flames began to spread: a fiery sign that nobody could miss, right in the centre of the road. He felt the warmth of the fire on his cheeks and forehead as he backed away.

'I have to give you credit,' a voice said behind him, 'you're inventive. I could tell you were going to be trouble just from your face. How did you escape from beneath the tree?'

Sherlock turned around. Jude was standing a few feet away. He had some kind of farm tool in his hands: a long wooden pole with a sharp curved blade at the end, like a crescent moon. A scythe, Sherlock thought; something for slicing through hay at harvest time. Not that he was an expert on farm implements, but during the past few years he'd managed to amass quite a working knowledge of sharp weapons.

'You read people,' he said; 'I read situations. I look for evidence where you look for twitches of the mouth or flickers of the eyelids. There had to be a way out, for the people who hid there. An emergency exit.'

'Very clever, spotting that.' Jude nodded. 'Maybe you did manage to work out where the treasure was hidden.

I should have given you more credit.'

'To be fair,' Sherlock admitted, 'when we last spoke I only knew how to work it out, not where it actually was. Since then, though, I actually have worked it out.'

'Do you fancy telling me?'

Sherlock shook his head. 'Not a chance.'

Jude hefted the scythe. 'Can I convince you?'

'You can try.'

'I'd offer you a weapon as well, but –' he shrugged – 'that would even the odds, and I like to have the odds in my favour whenever I –'

Without finishing the sentence, he swung the scythe at Sherlock's head. It was only a twitch in the muscles of his right hand that gave him away. Sherlock ducked, and the scythe swished through the air above his head. He could feel the coldness of its swift passage.

Sherlock straightened up to see Jude swinging the scythe upward, ready to bring it down on to Sherlock's skull. He kicked out with his right foot, sending one of the pots of creosote flying towards the boy. It caught Jude on the knee, splashing oily liquid everywhere. Jude's leg gave way and he crumpled sideways, the scythe unbalancing him as it completed its swing downward and its blade embedded itself in the dirt.

Sherlock launched himself at Jude before the boy could recover. His head hit Jude's chest, pushing him backwards, as he tried to get a grip on the boy's clothes. They rolled together on the ground, Sherlock uppermost first and then Jude. They ended up with Jude kneeling above Sherlock, having twisted out of Sherlock's grip. He glanced quickly around, looking for the scythe, but it was too far away for him to grab. Instead he started punching Sherlock in the face – right fist, left fist, left fist again.

Sherlock could taste blood. He was blocking with his forearms as much as he could, but Jude's fists were like hammers flying at him from all sides.

He brought his right leg up sharply. His knee struck Jude in the small of his back and the boy lurched forward, toppling towards Sherlock, arms automatically flung out to break his fall. Taking advantage of his momentary distraction, Sherlock shoved a hand up beneath the boy's chin and pushed hard. He felt a sharp click as Jude's teeth snapped shut. Or maybe it was his neck breaking as his head went backwards.

Sherlock twisted out from beneath the falling boy and scrabbled sideways, towards where the scythe was sticking out of the ground. If Jude was still alive, still mobile, then the scythe seemed like his only chance to even up the fight.

As his fingers touched the wooden shaft he saw a dark object hurtling towards him from the side. He only had time to move his head slightly to see what it was when something hard and sharp caught him above his left eye. He fell sideways, fireworks of pain exploding in his head.

CHAPTER FIFTEEN

Sherlock felt his face smash into the ground as he fell. There was something sticky all over his forehead, his cheek and his chin. Was it blood? How badly was he injured?

He rolled sideways, in case Jude was following up the attack by running at him. The stuff on his hands was brown, not red. It was creosote. Jude must have thrown one of the cans at him, and it had caught him in the head.

Relieved that he wasn't bleeding – well, not too much anyway – he stood up. The scythe was a few feet away, and he reached out to pull it from the ground. Turning, tasting the tarry creosote in his mouth now, Sherlock saw that Jude was crouching over near the barn. He had something in his hand, retrieved from on top of a pile of logs, and when he turned around Sherlock saw that it was a sickle – a curved blade like the one on top of the scythe, but with a short handle instead of a long shaft.

'Blade against blade,' Jude muttered. His voice was slurred. 'How very historical. And how apt, considering that this is all about a Cavalier treasure hoard.'

'It doesn't have to be this way,' Sherlock pointed out, panting. 'We're pretty evenly matched. We'll just keep on hurting each other, and the police are on their way. You've seen the sign I left them.'

Jude glanced over towards the road, and then back to Sherlock. His expression, beneath the blood, the dirt and the creosote that now covered both boys, was thoughtful.

'I know what you're thinking,' Sherlock said. 'You're trying to work out whether you can get to the flames and put them out before I can stop you, but you can't. You can either fight me or put out the flames, but you can't do both things at once.'

'And I know what *you're* thinking,' Jude responded. Somewhere along the way his lip had been split. It was beginning to swell up, and was making it difficult for him to speak. 'You don't want to kill me, and you're only willing to injure me as much as it takes to stop me. You have scruples, and I have none, which means I will win in the end, all other things being equal.' He gestured at himself, and then at Sherlock. 'And they are equal, aren't they? We're both about the same size, the same strength and the same ability and we now have a similar weapon. The only thing that differentiates us is: how much damage are we willing to cause to the other? I think I can win on that one.'

Sherlock shook his head. 'I don't think so.' He knew that the conversation wasn't going anywhere, but he needed to catch his breath, and he suspected that Jude did too.

'I really need to put that signal out,' Jude said. His

body hunched, as if he was going to make some sudden and explosive movement and was preparing himself for it. 'In fact, I want it so badly that I'm willing to kill you to do it. Are you willing to kill me to stop me, because you're going to have to.' He smiled – lopsidedly, because of the split lip. 'I can read your character from your expression. I don't think you have it in you to be a killer.'

Sherlock knew what Jude was doing. He was trying to affect Sherlock's confidence, his ability to fight, trying to undermine Sherlock's belief in himself, and it wasn't going to work.

'I've killed before,' Sherlock said flatly. He wasn't proud of it, but it was a fact.

The boy put his head to one side. 'Not through choice, I think. In the heat of the moment maybe. By accident perhaps. But I don't think you can make the decision to kill me in –'

Without finishing the sentence, he started to sprint towards the flaming sign out on the road, limping badly on his right leg but still covering the ground with amazing speed.

Sherlock threw the scythe like a spear.

The wooden shaft passed between Jude's legs, tripping him up. The boy cartwheeled, head over heels, across the ground. Sherlock ran past him, ignoring the scythe but determined to get between Jude and the flaming arrow.

When he got out into the road and turned, Jude was already standing in the gateway, and still holding the sickle. What with the sticky creosote, the dirt and the blood, he looked like something out of a nightmare. Sherlock suspected that he didn't look that much better.

'What *is* it with you?' Jude snarled. 'What drives you on? I just can't –'

Again, he left the sentence hanging and suddenly ran towards Sherlock, but Sherlock knew the trick by now and was ready. He backed up a few paces until he could see the burning creosote on the road out of the corner of his eye, then he bent down, scooped some of the creosote up in his hand and flung it at the running boy.

The flames burned his hand, and he quickly rubbed it in the dirt of the road to scrub the sticky liquid off, but the effect on Jude was more dramatic. The flames caught the creosote on his clothes, setting them alight. He threw the sickle away and dived to the ground, rolling in the dirt until the flames were extinguished. Standing slowly, he checked his arms and legs for any more burning areas. The bits of his clothes that weren't covered in creosote were now burned black, and his skin was blistered.

'What is so important that you keep on going?' he shouted. 'Why can't you just *stop*? You should have *stopped* by now!'

'I've got a job to do,' Sherlock said simply, and the simplicity of the words caught him by surprise as much as they did Jude. 'I promised someone that I'd help their friend solve a mystery, and I intend to do that.'

'Who is that important that you care so much about

'keeping a promise?' Jude wanted to know.

'Nobody important. His name is Ferny Weston. He's a policeman. He *was* a policeman.'

The name seemed to strike Jude like a bucket of cold water. He straightened up, his face immobile. For a long moment he stood there, staring at Sherlock, then he turned away and ran back towards the barn.

Sherlock put his hands on his knees and rested for a moment or two. He was almost finished. He had nothing left. All he could do was to wait for the police and Matty to arrive, and hope that Jude wasn't about to launch another attack.

Thoughts flew around his brain – jagged jigsaw pieces that revolved around each other, sometimes hitting each other with a jangle of pain before ricocheting away again. Jude. His face when Sherlock had mentioned Ferny Weston. His admission that he had been given inside information about the art robberies he and his men had committed. The photograph Sherlock had seen in Charles Dodgson's study showing Ferny Weston, his wife Marie and a boy, together with Mortimer Maberley and Mycroft Holmes.

And he suddenly knew where Jude had run to, and what he was going to do.

This wasn't over yet.

Leaving the burning sign and the barn full of comatose criminals, Sherlock staggered back along the road to where he and Matty had left their horses outside Mortimer

Maberley's house. He remembered dimly suggesting to Matty that Maberley use his horse if he didn't have one of his own. He now hoped desperately that Maberley did actually have a horse, because otherwise he'd have to go *back* to the barn and hope that the criminals had left some of their own horses there – apart from the shire horses, of course, which were great at pulling things but not so good at galloping fast.

His thoughts were wandering, and he tried to force them into some kind of order. He realized that he was staggering sideways, so he concentrated on particular features of the road ahead and tried to walk straight for them. Somehow he found himself at the back of Maberley's house, saddling up his horse, with only a foggy memory of how he had got from the road to there. His fingers were clumsy, but he managed in the end. Pulling himself up into the saddle of the patiently waiting horse, he urged it onward, back to the Westons' house – where, he suspected, a rather uncomfortable family reunion was about to take place.

In later years, Sherlock could remember nothing of that wild ride but nightmare images, like a set of pictures snatched by some insane photographer – churches flashing past, clouds scudding against the moon, the relentless pounding of the horse's hoofs on the road. The horse itself seemed to intuit, through some supernatural means, where he wanted it to go. Certainly he was no use in guiding it.

The ride took forever, or only a few moments. It felt like both.

Ferny Weston's house was as twisted as Sherlock remembered from the first time he saw it. The front gate was open, and the horse galloped up the drive to the front door and then stopped, letting Sherlock half slide, half fall to the ground. He staggered in through the open front door. He didn't bother checking the ground-floor rooms – he knew where this was going to end. Where it had to end.

When he pushed open the door of Marie Weston's bedroom, there were three people inside.

Marie was, as before, in bed. Her face was pale, but she looked self-possessed as she pulled the bedsheet up to protect her. Ferny was by her side, half sitting on the bed with an arm around her. He was wearing his leather mask.

Jude – Jude Weston – was standing at the foot of the bed, pointing Ferny Weston's gun at the two of them. He was burned, blistered, dirty and smeared with creosote, but his whole body burned with a terrible rage.

He swung the gun to cover Sherlock. 'Yes, of course it's you. How could it be anyone else? Please, come in and join the family.'

Sherlock walked past Jude to get to the head of the bed. For a mad second he wondered if he could grab the gun from the boy's hand, but he could see from Jude's wide eyes and fevered expression that he was on a knife edge. One twitch, one slight move, and the gun would fire.

Sherlock went to stand by Ferny Weston.

'I solved Mr Maberley's problem,' he said brightly, wanting to break the heavy silence somehow. 'It turns out that the house never moved, but the orchard did. It was all about the Cavalier treasure in the end.'

'And that's a conversation that you and I need to have,' Jude said. 'But first, I think my father has an apology to make.'

'An apology?' Ferny's voice was low and guttural, full of anger. 'You whelp! *You* are the one who left home. *You* are the one who dishonoured the family name.'

'You knew he was behind the art thefts?' Sherlock guessed.

'I suspected – more and more as time went on – but I never had any proof. The boy was always very clever, but he never had any morals, any scruples. Anything he wanted, he would take. I tried disciplining him, sending him to harsh schools, but nothing had any effect. Worse – he seemed to take them over, by sheer force of personality, turning the pupils against the masters and fomenting rebellion. People would follow him, always, anywhere. He had that kind of personality. He got a scholarship to Oxford, although I suspect he cheated to get it, but when they threw him out he vanished. We never heard from him after that.'

'Let me see your face, Father, if you are going to talk

about me like that,' Jude said in a mock-sweet voice. 'Take off your mask, why don't you? Look me in the eye.'

'Jude – no!' his mother cried, but Jude jerked the gun towards her and she was quiet.

Ferny Weston reached up and undid the catches on his mask. He slipped it off, revealing his scarred, broken face, his jigsaw scalp, his burning eyes.

'You did this to me,' he said. 'You set that trap, in the house that we thought was your hideout.'

'I did – and now I intend finishing what I started. You interfered with my work then, and you're still interfering now, by sending this . . . *child detective* . . . to stop me.'

He swung the gun to point directly at Ferny's face. 'Say goodnight, Father,' he snarled.

'One question,' Ferny said quietly. 'You owe me that.'

'I owe you nothing, but ask anyway. It might amuse me to answer.'

'Who in the police force was providing you with the information about our investigation? I could never work it out. Just tell me that, then kill us both, if that's what you have to do. God knows it would be a blessing for us both.'

'Oh, I'm not going to kill you both,' Jude said. He glanced at Sherlock. 'Tell him why. I know from your eyes, and the way you have tightened your lips, that you already know.'

'Know what?' Ferny demanded.

Sherlock sighed. 'It wasn't that hard to figure out,' he said. 'It's the same person who told Jude about Mortimer Maberley, and his Cavalier treasure. It's the person from whom he inherited his criminal tendencies. It's your wife, Ferny.'

The words hung in the air like the vibration of a heavy bell.

'But –' Ferny said, then stopped. His face went through many different emotions, one after another – disbelief, understanding, anger and reluctant acceptance.

'She masterminded the whole thing, as far as I can tell,' Sherlock went on.

'But – the house? The trap? She was caught in it!'

'An accident, I expect.' Sherlock glanced past Ferny to Marie, who was watching proceedings with an expression of alert interest. 'She went in to check that you were actually dead, but she was caught when a beam fell on her. She's needed you ever since, and with you invalided out of the police force, you weren't a threat to them any more. She has been in communication with Jude ever since, giving him the praise he needs and giving him his orders, while he has been keeping her informed as to the progress of his crimes.'

'But – how?' Ferny spluttered. Sherlock noticed that his hand had come off that of his wife and was clenching on the bedspread.

Sherlock nodded towards the brown paper and string that were still on the bedside table, left over from the package containing the wax body part that he and Matty had tracked, it seemed weeks ago now. 'It's the string, isn't it?' he asked Marie. 'There are too many knots, and they're spaced oddly. I noticed that the first time I saw it. There's a code there, isn't there, in the way the knots are arranged?' He glanced back at Ferny. 'One of their agents got to the packages before they got here and rewrapped them, encoding their messages into the string. I presume that there was a similar system going out – did your wife get you to post a lot of packages that she had wrapped herself?'

'Embroidery,' Ferny murmured, still screwing the bedspread up with his clumsy, broken fingers. 'She sent embroidery to her friends – all over the world, it seemed. I never understood how she knew so many people.'

'Ah,' Sherlock said, 'embroidery is really just a series of knots, all together, isn't it?'

'Enough,' Marie Weston interrupted in her bright, friendly voice. She sounded like a schoolmistress talking to a class of unruly children. 'This could go on all day if we don't put a stop to it. Jude – I don't want any blood in here. Take the two of them out and shoot them in the garden, then bury the bodies. You may as well move back in. Things are going to change.'

'What about George?' Jude asked.

'He's still ill upstairs after he stupidly let one of the snakes bite him, otherwise I would tell him to help.'

With his eye Sherlock measured the distance between

himself and the boy, but it was too far. Jude would shoot him before he moved. He sensed Ferny tensing beside him, and put his hand on the man's shoulder, holding him back. They might get a chance as they were going downstairs, or when they got to the ground floor. Might. He wasn't confident, though. Jude Weston was dangerously intelligent, and he could likely read what Sherlock was going to do even before he did it just from a twist in his shoulders.

'Up,' Jude said, gesturing with the gun. 'Out.' He backed into the hall so that they could get to the door, but so that they were still far enough away that they couldn't attack him before he could pull the trigger.

'Marie . . . ?' Ferny said plaintively. He reached out to take his wife's hand. She patted his with her other hand, smiled at him and said, 'Don't worry, dear. Jude will be quick. This is just business to him, and to me. Just business.'

Ferny stood up, and he seemed to Sherlock to have shrunk into himself. He was a broken man now, emotionally as well as physically.

Sherlock walked out into the hall, with Ferny following. Jude had backed along the hallway, away from the stairs. He kept the gun pointed at Sherlock's forehead. 'Now downstairs,' he said, 'and slowly. If you move suddenly, or even turn around, I will put a bullet through your head.'

Sherlock turned to face the stairs. He couldn't think of

a single thing to do. Jude had worked out all the angles, all the moves. He could predict Sherlock's every likely move, and counter it.

Despair filled him as he took his first step towards the stairs and towards his own death.

Something rose up from where it had been hidden in the first few treads of the stairs.

It was Matty. He had something in his hand. Something bright red.

'Duck,' he said.

Sherlock dived to the ground. As he did so he saw Matty pull back his arm and throw the red object as hard as he could. From behind, Sherlock heard Jude shout, 'What the—' The words were cut off by a wet *thud!* and a choking noise.

Turning, even as he dived, Sherlock saw Jude Weston standing there, at the back of the hall. There was something red sticking out of his mouth. He was still holding the gun, but he didn't seem to know what to do with it. His hand was dropping to his side, taking the gun with it. His eyes were wide open, frenzied, and he was gurgling.

He fell forward like a tree that had been chopped through at the base and hit the carpet hard. His father watched, incredulous.

Sherlock turned to Matty, climbing to his feet. 'What did you do?' he asked.

His friend's face was pale and sweating. 'Got to the

barn,' he said, raw pain in his voice. 'Saw the sign. Followed you here, cos people had seen you ride past like a bat out of hell. Got here an' couldn't work out what to do. Didn't 'ave a weapon, so I scooped up one of Ferny's poison frogs from a tank downstairs. Thought it might not be poisonous to the touch, just if you got the poison inside you. That's why I threw it at 'im.'

He held up a blistered and weeping right hand.

'Think I was wrong,' he said, and collapsed into Sherlock's arms.

EPILOGUE

The sun was shining out of a perfect blue sky, reflecting off the shiny brass instruments of the military band as they sat on the bandstand. The musicians all faced the uniformed conductor in the centre, watching as he raised his baton. He brought it down dramatically, and they all started playing a rousing march.

The park was filled with people – couples walking together, parents with children, and the occasional older man in black suit, top hat and cane strolling in the sunshine. Most of the deckchairs surrounding the bandstand were occupied, but Sherlock and Mycroft had managed to find two chairs together that were in the shade and were also separated from everyone else by an empty row.

'This is the life,' Mycroft said. He was holding an ice-cream cone in his hand, occasionally licking the drops of melting ice cream as they trickled down the cornet. 'Family, sunshine, ice cream and a brass band. I do think that England has the best martial music in the world. The Italians have Verdi and Rossini, the Austrians have Mozart and the Germans have several generations of Bach, but we have brass bands and rousing marches. I think we have the better part of the deal.'

'You kept me in the dark,' Sherlock said quietly. He desperately wanted to be angry with his brother, but he was holding an ice-cream cone too, and that made it difficult.

'I suspect that the United States of America will overtake us with regard to marching music,' Mycroft went on as if Sherlock had said nothing. 'I am already hearing good reports of a young composer there named John Philip Sousa. However, at the moment we are still pre-eminent in the field. You cannot beat a good military march.'

'Mycroft—'

'How is your little friend Matthew?' Mycroft interrupted.

'He's recovering.' Sherlock winced, thinking about how close Matty had come to dying. Only the quick reaction of Ferny Weston in scrubbing Matty's hands with charcoal and injecting him with a drug that counteracted the poison in the frog's skin had saved him. Once he was stable, Sherlock had moved him to Mrs McCrery's house, where there was a spare bed. Mrs McCrery seemed to have taken a shine to Matty, and so he was tucked up warmly there and being fed on an almost hourly basis. Sherlock expected that Matty would have put on a lot of weight by the time he returned from London.

'Good. He is a brave and resourceful boy. A world without him in it would be a poorer world.'

'He wouldn't have been in danger in the first place if you had been honest with me!' Sherlock snapped. Annoyed with himself for the emotional reaction, he licked at his ice cream.

Mycroft sighed heavily – which was, Sherlock reflected, about the only way his brother *could* sigh these days. 'It is not as if I was deliberately withholding information. I merely did not wish you to be overburdened by it when you first arrived in Oxford. My intention was to send you a letter after a few weeks mentioning in passing the Mortimer Maberley situation and suggesting that you take a look as you were in the vicinity. I would have told you about Ferny Weston as well, in the fullness of time. I just—'

'You just wanted me to think I was a free agent, rather than one of *your* agents, for as long as possible,' Sherlock said.

'Indeed.' Mycroft's face was unreadable. 'The best agent is the one who does not even realize he is an agent.'

'Was Mortimer Maberley the whole reason you sent me to Oxford in the first place?' Sherlock asked.

'Absolutely not. Oxford is the best place for you to be at this point in your life. The fact that my attention had been drawn to Mr Maberley's predicament by an anonymous letter from Ferny Weston was purely coincidental. What I had not anticipated was that you would be so quick to discover the problem and to solve it. Or that young Matthew would be so badly hurt in the process.' He paused for a moment. 'Sherlock, be assured that if I had sent you to Cambridge instead, there are matters there that beg some investigation as well. In fact, wherever you might go in England there are questions and mysteries to be solved that the local police force seem incapable of addressing.'

Sherlock shrugged. 'Then it looks as if the whole of England needs some form of detective who is better informed and more tenacious than the police.'

'A thought you might do well to bear in mind for the future.' Mycroft licked his ice cream. 'Ferny Weston thought he might be that detective, but much as I respect the man, he does have a policeman's brain. His thoughts travel in straight lines. It does not handle corners easily, whereas yours does.'

'What about his wife? What will happen to her?'

'The more we investigate, the more we find,' Mycroft said enigmatically.

'We?' Sherlock challenged. 'I thought you were with the Foreign Office, not the police?'

'Last year an American railway entrepreneur died while eating soup in a very expensive restaurant, the day before he could sign an important business deal. Initially a heart attack was suspected, but further investigation revealed the presence of a fast-acting poison in his lobster bisque – a poison derived from the box jellyfish. Two days later a Russian company signed the business deal instead of him. Three months after that a judge in Italy died while drinking a glass of wine, just before he was about to begin presiding over the trial of a Vatican official for bank fraud. Again, a heart attack was suspected; again it proved to be poison – this time derived from a rattlesnake. The trial subsequently collapsed, as no judge would step into the breach. I could draw your attention to twenty, perhaps thirty, similar cases around the world in the time since Ferny Weston and his wife suffered their "accident".'

'She was supplying poisons to criminals around the world?' Sherlock was aghast.

'She was,' his brother confirmed. 'Poison is a woman's weapon. The spread of cases around the world, and the destabilizing effects on politics and on governments, make it a Foreign Office matter.'

'She was so nice.' Sherlock remembered the conversation he'd had with Marie Weston, in her bedroom. 'And she was pretty.'

'"One may smile, and smile, and be a villain",' Mycroft said softly. 'Or so William Shakespeare said in *Hamlet*. I have said it before and I will say it again: the solution to any political problem can be found somewhere in *Hamlet*.'

'But she couldn't have been providing the poisons on her own – someone must have been helping her, and I refuse to believe that it was Ferny.'

'I suspect the servant – George. He is under investigation too. And, to answer your earlier question,

I anticipate that nothing at all will happen to Mrs Weston. She is paralysed, and bedridden and, as you have pointed out, beautiful. Taking such a woman to trial would cause consternation and anger among the general populace. No, she will be sternly warned, and she will be watched. All post to and from the house will be opened and inspected. Her life will be under constant scrutiny. Worse – her husband will know everything. He will not leave the house, but he will abandon her in all but geographical terms. A sad end to things.' Abruptly changing the subject, he went on: 'But what of this Cavalier treasure? After the boy and his mother spent so long searching for it, please do not tell me that you have just stumbled across it?'

'Hardly "stumbled",' Sherlock said. 'I had noticed that the apple trees in the orchard were of different varieties, and it occurred to me that whoever planted them might have left a clue as to where the treasure was buried – if, for instance, there was only one apple tree of the King Variety, or the Garden Royal. Later on, though, when Matty and I were going through that maze of tunnels, I realized that there was one tree whose barrelled roots we diverted completely around. The only reason for there to be no tunnels going to or from that tree would be if nobody had ever hidden there, which meant that it was the perfect location for the treasure.'

'Ah,' Mycroft said, 'of course. How simple.'

'Simple if you were there,' Sherlock muttered.

'What do you think of Charles Dodgson?' Mycroft continued as if Sherlock had said nothing.

'His brain works like a corkscrew,' Sherlock said, smiling. 'His love of wordplay and of mathematical puzzles is quite amazing. I feel as if I have to run just to stay in one place with him, mentally at least. It's a very refreshing feeling.'

'He thinks a great deal of you,' Mycroft said. 'He has written to tell me so. He finds you an excellent student.' He smiled. 'I am pleased.'

The military band finished their tune, and the crowd clapped. Sherlock and Mycroft did their best to join in, given that they were both holding ice-cream cones.

'If you do not like Oxford,' Mycroft went on, 'then you can return to London. I would not wish to force you into any course of action you dislike.'

Sherlock thought for a while. 'No,' he said eventually, 'I think I will stay. I'm having fun. And, of course, Matty is in no condition to move at the moment.'

'Indeed.' Mycroft was silent for a while. 'Perhaps I could send him a hamper of food,' he added. 'As an apology.'

'I think he's getting more than enough food where he is,' Sherlock answered. He laughed suddenly.

'What is it?'

'You could always have his barge repaired and repainted while he's confined to bed. I think he would appreciate that.'

'Then I shall do that.' Mycroft settled back into his deckchair and closed his eyes as the band struck up another tune. 'Ah,' he murmured, 'this is just perfect. I wish I could capture this moment in time forever. I wish I could capture a portrait of you, as you are now, before you get any older and become a man rather than a boy.'

Sherlock thought back to the time a little while ago, on the banks of the River Isis, with Charles Dodgson taking his photograph. 'One day,' he said quietly, 'we will *all* have little devices the size of a matchbox, with levers on the side, and when we press the levers a glass plate inside the box will record exactly what we have seen and preserve it for posterity.'

'How fanciful,' Mycroft replied, eyes still closed. 'You might just as well claim that we will have other little boxes that will, at the press of a lever, somehow magically record this wonderful music that we are listening to for us to replay later, in the convenience of our own homes.'

Sherlock smiled. 'New things are being developed all the time,' he replied. 'Perhaps it will even be the same box.'

Mycroft snorted. 'Enjoy the moment,' he said. 'Enjoy it while you can. It can never be recreated.'

Sherlock shut his eyes and lay back in the deckchair. He knew that his brother was wrong in this respect, and Mycroft's insistence that the world would always be pretty much the way it was now worried him. There were changes ahead – big changes – and the world needed to be ready for them.

AUTHOR'S NOTE

This book, the seventh in the Young Sherlock Holmes series, is an odd hybrid. At least, that's the way it's turned out in my mind. On the one hand it marks a break with the past: moving Sherlock away from the comforts of having his aunt and uncle's house as a base (even though he hadn't actually been there for the past two books) and towards a future that involves starting a course at university, and also away from his comforting support network of friends like Rufus Stone, Virginia Crowe and Amyus Crowe, and towards a future when he is on his own. On the other hand it's a return to the kind of stripped-down, pure version of the books that I managed to hit in *Death Cloud* – Sherlock and Matty working alone together to solve a crime. What the future holds is anyone's guess – although I do have a file of notes.

As usual I've done a fair amount of research to make sure that the history and the people are more or less accurate. I managed to pull descriptions of the Oxford town and Oxford University of the time from *Victorian Oxford* by W. R. Ward (Frank Cass and Co. Ltd, 1965), while Charles Dodgson's eccentric character and history I took from three books: *Lewis Carroll in Numberland: His Fantastical Mathematical Logical Life* by Robin Wilson (Allen Lane, 2008), *Lewis Carroll and Alice* by Stephanie Lovett Stoffel (Thames and Hudson, 1997) and *In the Shadow of the Dreamchild: A New Understanding of Lewis Carroll* by Karoline Leach (Peter Owen Ltd, 1999). The Victorian attitude towards death and dead bodies was taken from the excellent *Necropolis: London and Its Dead* by Catharine Arnold (Simon and Schuster, 2006), which I have used before in *Fire Storm*. Wikipedia has, of course, been used to fill in the gaps and answer sudden questions, such as, 'When were ice-cream cones invented?' (The answer is that they were first mentioned in the year 1825, where they were said to have been made from 'little waffles', so, when Sherlock and Mycroft have their ice creams in the park in the epilogue, it's all historically accurate.)

The bit when Sherlock has just met his landlady, Mrs McCrery, for the first time, and is introduced to her stuffed cat, Macallistair, really happened to me, by the way. I was in Wigtown, which is a small town out in Dumfries and Galloway, in Scotland. I was there for a literary festival and I arrived late one night after a long journey up by plane, by train and by car. It was dark, I was tired and I was hungry. The festival organizers had, very nicely, put me up in a local farmhouse that also did a good line in bed and breakfast. The lovely lady who ran the place ushered me into her small sitting room and said she'd go and make me a pot of tea and some warm scones. I settled down to relax. There was a cat, curled up by the fire. I went over to stroke it, because I love cats and I wanted to make friends with it. You can guess the rest. It was, and still is, one of the more bizarre events that has ever happened to me. Perhaps I just lead a sheltered life.

With luck, and a good headwind, I will be starting work on the next book in the series soon. It might be called *Wind Chill*, or it might be called *Night Break* – I'm not yet sure. I'm pretty sure, however, that Charles Dodgson will play a part, and that it might involve Sherlock returning to his family home to see his mother and his sister. It might also involve the case of Mr James Phillimore, who, stepping back into his own house to get his umbrella, was never more seen in this world.

Until then, take care.

ABOUT THE AUTHOR

Andrew Lane is the author of the bestselling Young Sherlock Holmes series and of Lost Worlds. Young Sherlock Holmes has been published around the world and is available in thirty-seven different languages. Not only is Andrew a lifelong fan of Arthur Conan Doyle's great detective, he is also an expert on the books and is the only children's writer endorsed by the Sherlock Holmes Conan Doyle estate. Andrew writes other things too, including adult thrillers (under a pseudonym), TV adaptations (including *Doctor Who*) and non-fiction books (about things as wide-ranging as James Bond and Wallace & Gromit). He lives in Dorset with his wife and son and a vast collection of Sherlock Holmes books, the first of which he found in a jumble sale over forty years ago.

LOST WORLDS

ANDREW LANE

**IN THE BLINK OF AN EYE, CALUM'S LIFE
CHANGED. IN THE CLICK OF A MOUSE,
IT WILL CHANGE AGAIN . . .**

Partially paralysed in the crash that killed his parents,
teenager Calum Challenger lives alone, searching the net
for proof that 'extinct' creatures exist. He believes that,
if they do, their DNA could cure him.

When something that looks like a yeti is spotted in the
Georgian mountains, Calum springs into action – but so
does a corporation called Nemor. Calum wants to harvest
the creature's DNA and then protect it. Nemor wants to
harvest its DNA and then kill it.

From his high-tech apartment, Calum uses cutting-edge
technology to direct a group of misfit friends on a deadly
chase in the harshest of environments. As danger mounts,
fear starts to spread: can the team really trust the boy on
whom they are dependent for survival? And how can they
save a creature already on the brink of extinction?

READ THEM ALL!

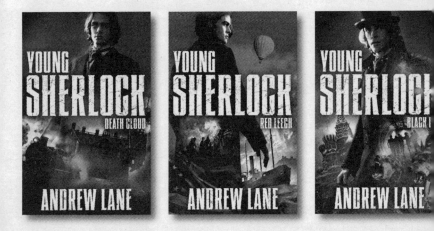
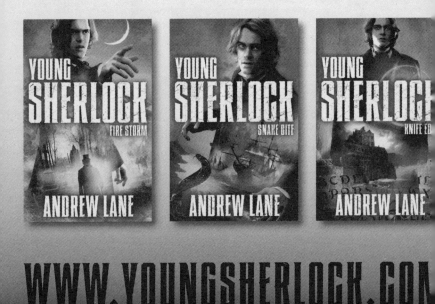